ROME NOIR

ROME NOIR

EDITED BY
CHIARA STANGALINO
& MAXIM JAKUBOWSKI

Translated by Anne Milano Appel,
Ann Goldstein, and Kathrine Jason

AKASHIC BOOKS
NEW YORK

Published by Akashic Books
©2009 Akashic Books

©2009 Carlo Lucarelli for the story "Beret" (titled "Mephisto" in its original Italian form), published by arrangement with Roberto Santachiara at Agenzia Letteraria.

Series concept by Tim McLoughlin and Johnny Temple
Rome map by Sohrab Habibion

ISBN-13: 978-1-933354-64-4
Library of Congress Control Number: 2008925936
All rights reserved

First printing

Akashic Books
PO Box 1456
New York, NY 10009
info@akashicbooks.com
www.akashicbooks.com

Also in the Akashic Noir Series:

Forthcoming:

Calcata

Via Marco
Aurelio

Villa
Borghese

Tiburtina
Station

Via
Veneto

Quartiere
Pigneto

VATICAN

Piazza dei
Cinquecento

Stazione
Termini

Montecitorio

Vicolo del
Bologna

Via Ascoli
Piceno

Colosseum

FORUM

Via Appia
Antica

CIRCUS MAXIMUS

Fiumicino

Ostia

Tangenziale

ROME

TABLE OF CONTENTS

INTRODUCTION
CRADLE OR GRAVE?

R ome: The cradle of civilization or just another city with a dark side, a secret life?

Well, something of both.

The flocks of tourists who visit the city today see the obvious monuments to a lost age, the innumerable churches, the fashionable shops, the Colosseum, the Via Veneto, the Piazza Navona, the Spanish Steps, and the quietly coursing Tiber River that bisects the city. They line up single file for hours on end to enter the Vatican, and it must all feel—at least to the more cinematically literate of them—like stepping into a Federico Fellini movie. They walk around, awed by the timeless majesty of the old stones, walls, and busy streets; they enjoy wonderful food, take countless photographs, and retreat with tired souls and feet to their hotel rooms or pensiones, and then all too quickly it's time to go home and leave the splendor of Rome behind.

But how much have they really seen of the city, the dimension in which actual contemporary Romans live? Unless they have a solid acquaintance with resident Italians and are invited into their homes and shown what lies beyond the shiny façade of postcard Rome, they have in fact barely skimmed the surface of this complex city.

The same applies, of course, to many cities, and it's often only through living in their midst for a substantial period of time that one begins to really "know" a place, to understand its often shocking intimacies.

According to the legend, Rome owes its origins to a murder—when one brother killed another in order to grab the crown. Since then, there has been a dark tapestry of misdeeds, plots, and assassinations alongside some of the cruelest crimes in the history of mankind, beginning with Nero and Caligula, all through myriad bloody Vatican intrigues, wars by the handful, urban terrorism, and the arcane modern collusions between politics and the Mafia.

For some of us walking through the city today, despite the incessant roar of traffic (echoed by so many of the stories in this collection), our imaginations evoke the old Roman Empire (helped in one way or another by images and memories of films and TV shows recreating the glory, the togas, and the slum-level sordidness of antiquity); we dream of the legions marching up the Via Appia back from so many wars, Romulus and Remus and the surrounding hills (which are not always so visible these days if you are staying in the heart of town), the ruthless cruelty of Caesar and Caligula and so many other fabled emperors and dignitaries. Or, if your mind is set to different eras, you may think of the Borgias, or the decadent as well as earnest popes in situations so full of pomp and circumstance, or then again the more recent shadow of Mussolini's fascists and their relentless program of monument building which still leaves its mark on the city. The possibilities are endless.

But for Romans it's just another city, the one they live in, where the past is often of little consequence. A city for today, affected by globalization, the ever-shifting Italian rigmarole of politics, a harbor of coffee bars, trattorias, golden youth on motorbikes, a city both old and young. A capital strongly marked by the shadow of today's waves of illegal immigration and social injustice which color so many of our writers' sometimes bleak and shocking stories.

The contrast in the stories we have collected is between the glories of the past and a mainly dark and often pessimistic view of the present, in which the frailties of human nature are pronounced. Many of these writers are struck by the poverty that afflicts the lower classes in Rome, gypsies and unwelcome immigrants from poorer countries who congregate here, and this is expressed through the eyes of both visitors to the city and Romans themselves. Through it all looms the crumbling majesty of the Colosseum, the very heartbeat of Rome, which acts as a leitmotif from story to story, alongside the tales of tender and fierce love that this unforgettable capital acts as a background for.

Our writers' inspiration comes from the walls and streets of Rome, representing the crème de la crème of Italian mystery and mainstream writing, and many of them are permanent residents of the Italian best-seller lists. Umberto Eco recently wrote that "noir literature is a mirror for the state of literature in any given country." This anthology is, we believe, a strong reflection of the health of Italian writing.

Italian crime writing has always bathed in a sea of social realism, but curiously enough, few major writers in the genre have actually been Roman or written about this place. Turin, Milan, and Bologna, as well as the inevitable Mafia-drenched atmospheres of Sardinia, Naples, and Sicily, have long proven fertile ground for the pens of local crime and mystery writers. There have, naturally, been worthy exceptions, such as the recent success (as both a book and later a powerful movie) of Giancarlo De Cataldo's *Romanzo Criminale*, a saga of Roman misfits and criminals that spans several decades. But Italian crime writing has often found its poles of attraction elsewhere, what with Giorgio Scerbanenco's doughty Milan cops, the Turin and Bologna schools of mystery writing, respectively exemplified by Andrea G. Pinketts and Carlo Lucarelli, and Andrea Camilleri's strongly ironic view of Sicilian mores.

Which is why several writers were puzzled when we approached them for new stories set in Italy's capital city.

Should they move one of their characters there? some asked.

Should they write about the Rome a few of them did not know intimately, or should they just write their dream of Rome?

We gave them carte blanche and we think the results speak for themselves. The tales you are about to read are varied, both harsh and funny, poignant and gripping. There is an undeniable renaissance of crime and mystery writing in Italy right now, and we could have invited yet a further fifteen or so additional authors to contribute to this collection if we had enough space; we are confident the ensuing stories would have been as strong as the ones in the following pages.

A handful of the writers who embarked on this adventure have had books already translated into English, while others have not. We hope more of them will find a home in America and Britain as a result of their appearance here.

And next time you are visiting Italy, enjoy your tourist pursuits but on occasion pause for a moment and try and see what lies beyond the corner of the alley or street you are walking down, or attempt to imagine what might be happening beyond those closed curtains you are passing. But until then, let your imagination take a dip into *Rome Noir*, and travel the city from its trunk roads to its highways, past the notorious Stazione Termini and the shadow of the iconic Colosseum, and through both the fashionable and sometimes undesirable areas that have inspired our writers.

Grazie mille and *ciao*.

Chiara Stangalino & Maxim Jakubowski
Rome, Italy
November 2008

PART I

WALLS & STONES

PASOLINI'S SHADOW

Nicoletta Vallorani

Piazza dei Cinquecento

Translated by Anne Milano Appel

*Once life is finished it acquires a sense; up to that point it has not
got a sense; its sense is suspended and therefore ambiguous.*
—P. P. Pasolini

We all drift silently in a world of shadows.
The right night, a place I know. The station hunkers in the heart of this city.
Without a history.

We are all without a history, because we are overwhelmed by it. By the lack of reason, in a civil society that is breaking up, forgetting everything.

The Romans were builders of roads. I, who am a foreigner, travel them. I seek a familiarity that I will not find, I already know that, but it is enough for me to seek it: It is an uncodified move, a journey with eyes wide open. Rome is a body whose strong legs and dirty feet are known to me, hands quick to steal money from your pockets, hired sex, soft, dark hair, muscles that slither, breath that stinks of cigarette smoke and cheap liquor.

Roads. The houses like people: They have a worn, dusty

nobility, in this Rome, that yields to time unsparingly. And time, silently, crumbles bricks, molds pavement, brushes bodies with the same gentle, profound caress that I would like to have or experience.

Roads. A troublesome object that I do not see on the asphalt, and the car jerks. A tire absorbs the jolt, smashing what lies beneath it and continuing on its way: maybe a small life has ended, perhaps only a shattered object. At the end of life, the two are equivalent.

Roads. Where I ran as a child there was dirt and grass. I splashed about up to my knees, happy. That time is gone.

Roads. The Romans were builders of roads, but that time is gone as well.

Piazza dei Cinquecento, legs spread, lies there waiting. The fools, those who can't see, think they can rape her, possess her. But in this dark, nocturnal cavity they are lost, devoured, chewed up and spit out as small white bones. I, on the other hand, know. I know the secret, and will not get lost.

The station is a door: From there you go or return.

The station is a lady covered in rags, with garbage for jewels. She laughs, deceptively indulgent and defenseless, hiding the gnashing of her teeth behind the trains' clatter. She whispers promises she will not keep, but she is always a mystery because men believe in lies and let themselves be lulled by them. Rome knows all secrets, protects all sins. It is a museum of sorrow and shame, where the executioner laughs at the victim whose head he is preparing to lop off, with no remorse whatsoever and with unbounded craving.

The little garden is a place of bones. It is a city of secrets, catacombs, buried memories replaced by artfully constructed recollections. But here, in the little bone garden, it is impossible to lie. There are places where the city reveals itself. It can do so because nobody really looks, no one sees anything except what he wants to see.

But I know.

I am aware of the fraud. I revealed the secret. Still, I am not a danger, since no one will believe me. Rome can do this: display the truth, make it her whore, and sell it to the highest bidder.

Ghosts crouch in the little bone garden.

We all drift along, silent, alone.

It's like a breath I'm lacking, that I continue to look for, driving around aimlessly, with eyes that see in the dark, matching profiles and desires. Desire fulfilled is a simulated death. And like every death, it examines the meaning of life retrospectively, transforming it into myth. Desire is the articulation of a solitude from which I will not emerge, except at the instant of an embrace. A moment, a caress, a body that responds like an object, in the unreasoning workings of sensation.

I have a powerful, expensive car. I pull up, knowing I've been spotted.

In Piazza dei Cinquecento, I drive around the heart, mine, that of the city.

At the drink stand, there's a fat, sweaty man. He is an actor made for the part, as if in the entire city, in all the stands of Rome, there were only variations of that same role, in male or female versions. Performing specters, full of life that I cannot think of as sentient, with open shirts, oil stains on their undershirts, hands gripping the glass, squeezing the life out of it before handing it to the customer. And the customer, a young man with heavy cigarette breath, his curls straightened to look more gorgeous and his beard pointlessly shaved to make him appear older, takes the glass without bothering to be polite. Rome is not polite. Rather, she is a slut, astute and well aware of her urges, who when caught with her hands in the till absolves herself by displaying her illustrious medals: Nero's crown, the Colosseum's stones, grass, cats, the Pope, political figures. They have all lied. All of them. Including the cats.

I have an expensive car, that is known here, which does not necessarily make me one of the family. I am the rich uncle: My eccentric manias are tolerated as long as I bring money. My gaze is not heavy. It skims, in order to procure what I need: targets with curly hair. Shoes with a wedge, to appear taller. Sweaters tight across the chest, in colors like small suns in the night. I wonder what life drifts through those heads. But it doesn't matter to me. It really doesn't matter to me. The thoughts are mine. The body I look for elsewhere.

The boys arrive, three of them, walking down the sidewalk from Via Volturno to Via Einaudi. They materialize out of partial darkness. Nights are never very dark in the city. There is always too much light to hide by, but not enough to see. I adjust my glasses, I turn the wheel, I am not thinking, I release a desire and a fantasy that proceed side by side, searching for someone.

The three boys arrive, but only one approaches, talks to me. A slight uncertainty, hesitation resulting from his young age. I am never afraid, I am not in a hurry, I do not have a primary need. This is a slow, philosophical city. It is not wise as some think, no. It wears a cloak of wisdom that has frayed over time but that still holds up, thanks to patching, and continues covering a king who will never be nude. We, or those who do not know better, will always see a jewel-covered brocade instead of a flabby, swollen, though still immortal body. The night envelops this body in a warm wakefulness, that inherits from the day an ancient lethargy: the mellow rhythm of one who has experienced magnificent times and conserves the memories, eyes closed. Thus the hesitation, the rejection, the slight wavering of the expression, the exaggeratedly seductive walk as he moves away—all fit in. The boys I love, I reflect, are the breath of this city.

It's like a breath that I am lacking. As I said, I am a foreigner.

And yet I know that it is a common situation, one that is shared. This piazza is thronged with ghosts who do not belong. It is a city of the world, Rome is, lost in the idea of an empire that once was. We all continue to look for it. It is a treasure hunt, tonight's hunt, and I can't find the ticket that will get me to the next station. The last stop . . . I can't even find a mate, a crew that will play with me.

The three boys are standing motionless in front of the drink stand. They're speaking in low tones.

The fat guy inside doesn't even look at them: You can only survive in these places by never really and truly being present.

One boy shoves another.

The third one laughs.

The curly headed one glances my way, turns serious, murmurs some more.

If I try to scan the syllables, I still can't manage to understand what they're saying. We adore conspiracies when we are young. Then we get old and we need proof, certainties, unclouded waters.

With the air of keeping a secret that he will not reveal, curly top advances boldly. He walks around the car and, without smiling, gets in.

I drive off swiftly. Via Cavour.

* * *

It unwinds like an artery through a body that is being drawn right now, before my eyes. The blood of the city throbs there, secretly. I try to grasp its rhythm as I listen to the words and breathing of the boy beside me. I breathe the scent of an aftershave that is cloying. I try to concentrate on what my momentary, hesitant companion is saying. I am unable to separate the sound from the dark throbbing of Rome's blood, which becomes deafening, arrogant, and obstructive when Via Cavour flows liquidly into Via dei Fori Imperiali. The wound has eviscerated the city. A knife slash, deep, precise, that severed memory at the beginning of the twentieth century, suturing the past to the present. There were gradual steps before this operation. The Medieval period was lost. The Renaissance was lost. What remains to us are only the past and the present, with a void in between.

But you don't know. You breathe beside me, ill at ease. You hide your uneasiness by dictating rules. You tell me what you want to do and what you don't want to do. You repeat that you are not a femme. You say you want to be paid well. Your laugh is strained. You smile. Then you act like a tough guy. You tell me to watch out because you're a tough guy. And you're not a femme. It's just for the money.

I say nothing. I listen to your breathing. I try to take possession of it. You have to understand: I don't want to hurt you. It's just that yours is a breath that I am lacking.

Empty.

The gaping mouths of the Colosseum are arresting desolation. I've always thought that it was the blood that made them noble. The death of others, especially if it is bloody, illuminates objects. The life that once was has left a spectral breath, captured in a thousand films. The gladiator, grown old, gropes in the dark, trying to stand up to the parameters of the battle. He has been there for a thousand years, waiting for an enemy, and all he sees, instead, is a swarm of lunatics equipped with cameras. He poses, flexes his muscles, yawns. In the beginning, he tried to tell people that none of it was true and that death in the arena was miserable and illegitimate, that a gladiator was brought there filthy and emaciated, that the savage beasts had no trouble devouring him, and that at times the gladiator almost failed to defend himself. His only desire was to die quickly, as soon as possible, and become a ghost. In the beginning, the gladiator-ghost wanted to unmask the lie, but later, like everyone else, he surrendered.

Now he roams around, gaunt, appearing in the dark cavities and passing through them silently. A cat tries to steal his mantle, but it's a just playfulness. Cats can recognize ghosts. It is we men who have a hard time doing so.

You busy yourself with your sweater, beside me. You take it off, pumping up your muscles. Your tang invades the car and I accelerate. I smile. I am never completely captivated. I am never entirely able to let myself go. I nonetheless observe myself succumbing to desire.

You take off a shoe as well.

The dirty feet of Rome walk on roads a thousand years old. Dirty feet run on improvised little soccer fields, wear shoes that are too tight, clamber on loose heels, get injured, heal, are liberated. In the end, they are sheathed again. Dirty feet inside clean shoes, with a heel.

History flows along in confused rivulets. It's an illusion that it is linear. We like to think so, to imagine a beginning and an end, because that way we can understand. History instead dupes us. It is a ball of yarn unraveled by a cat. I am the cat and I rush toward Via di San Gregorio with my prey in my teeth. I don't bite down though: I don't want to wound it. Only to allow myself, in the end, to become the victim. It is a subtle desire to imagine one's own death and transform it into legend.

No one knows what's in store for him. We try to imagine. But life is a master of fantasies. I am a disciple. As clever as I am, I will never be able to really understand.

At one time, chariots raced in the Circus Maximus. The echo of the shouting and applause remains in the air and is not erased. If you gather the dust, you feel how light it is and it slips through your fingers like the years that have gone by. But nothing has been erased. It is an illusion that the past disappears. Its strength lies in being transformed. Today's gladiators confront one another in a different way, but the taste of dust and blood remains, in the mouth, as the only reliable trace of the battle.

In this city, the body of a kidnapped politician may be found.

In this city, young revolutionaries and young policemen have died and will die.

In this city, we have seen and will see different weapons taken up with the usual rage inside.

The taste of blood is not erased.

There is no past. It is all, in fact, in a perpetual present.

You don't know.

That's what I like: Your mind does not know, your body cannot know.

The taste of blood is not erased.

* * *

Viale Aventino is another artery on which I speed along, a subtle virus in the body of the city. Houses of fictitious nobility conceal the Lungotevere from me, to my right. I miss the water. I want to go fishing for memories in the river. If I could rob corpses of their memories, I would.

But there is no time, there is no time.

The water flows along, immutable. Rubbish has accumulated, making the flow heavy and sluggish, deceptively harmless. There are treasures at the bottom of the Tiber, which has cushioned blows and concealed sins. The river does not disguise itself. From the bridges, we see ourselves in the filthy water for what we are: aggregates of mongrel desires that we are ashamed to confess.

You, however, are not ashamed. There is a straightforward, simple artlessness in the awkward gestures with which you open the window and lean your elbow out. You watch me out of the corner of your eye, proud to be in control of the situation. You interpret my silence as acquiescence, and in fact it is. I am ready, my boy, to do anything to have you: You are certain of this. The defiance you show is a performance that I am gladly willing to humor. Under your skin, your tense muscles prevent fluid movements. You are a young puppet, resisting the strings that control him. But the strings are strong and the puppeteer shrewd and determined.

Is it me?

The puppeteer has no emotions. He is lucid and stern. He is not seeking memories but money. He has no desire for flesh. He does not love you and is not attracted by you. He is not prepared to caress you. He does not think of you as the body of this city. He does not drive around at night scouring Rome in a luxury car. He has no money to spend on you to make you happy. He does not want to make you happy. He does not want to feel your skin beneath his fingers. He is not speeding along Viale Aventino (or is he? Is there a car following us? Maybe.). The puppeteer is a stern, organized individual. He could never fall in love, even for a minute. He is the ideal executioner, because he believes in punishment as education. It's his mission.

The puppeteer is the black heart of this city.

It's not me.

I'm not pulling your strings.

Rather, it seems, you are pulling mine.

The body grows. The city expands beyond its confines. Toward its confines is where I'm bringing you.

Via Ostiense: It is an evening of great roads that lead where I want to go. The street dwellers slacken. We are few, we nocturnal travelers, closed within this private world of metal and glass, silent with our thoughts.

The houses become different, Rome removes her false dignity and exposes bits of skin. Smooth, dark, wounded, filthy, soft, young skin. The skin of a body chasing after a ball. The skin of a mouth screaming. The skin of a hand that grasps, caresses, strikes, pinches, scratches.

Skin.

The skin of Rome begins to be exposed.

That is what I want, madam: to expose you in order to reach your heart.

But you are hungry, and heart, yours or mine, matters little to you. You are hungry and restless. You look around, look behind you (is there a car following us? Maybe.).

I'm not concerned. Young boys are anxious and nervous. I'm not concerned. I never am.

The fact remains that you're hungry.

I stop.

Eating is a rite. The food enters the body, intriguingly prepared. The gestures recall other sensualities. The eyes allow a pleasure to surface, this time permitted, that alludes to other less licit pleasures. And it is not the mind that does all this.

Your mind does not know that you are eating this food as if it were, for me, a preview of the moment when you will eat my body.

I am silent, watching you. The November night evokes ghosts, but it is quiet. The trattoria has no indiscreet eyes: a simulation of a broken family, where everyone hates everyone but doesn't show it. Around us, time has passed, and in a more evident way than in the city. Even the darkness is more worn and tired. Poverty wearies everyone. Those who have always been rich don't know it. But we know it well. In our veins, as in those of Rome, plebeian blood flows.

Hearts beat at close distances. In deeper silence, I try to measure your emotion, to feel the throbbing that drives the thin blood into your hands as they fret nervously. You chew, forgetting to close your mouth. A bit of food falls out.

Rome is layered with remains.

You pick up the bit of food and put it back in your mouth. Now it is you.

It is time to go. The city that never really ends pushes us out. I can't resist the urge. I speed along in the car. I am the virus in this city's blood. And you accompany me, without my having truly captured you.

Via Ostiense runs parallel to the river, and like the river, glides inexorably to the sea. I do not resist the current. I go where the water of desire leads me. Curiosity takes shape, side by side with your fear. I feel it, your fear, though I do not understand the reasons for it. I will not do you any harm. How could I?

Via Ostiense and its secret ways. Something leads me where we both want to go. Of this I am certain: We both want to get there.

The place is waiting for us.

The city can be seen from outside, mirrored in the garbage that it has pushed out.

The city appears unfinished and ongoing, in houses never completed but left waiting for better times. Brackish water has rusted what remains of old industries, looming shadows in the darkness that has deepened. It is a darkness that has teeth, this one: dangerous. It devours, leaving only stripped bones that shine in the sunlight. The skeletons of unfinished buildings are also bones, which someone will hasten to cover with the flesh of bricks, and then fill in the spaces with wretched lives.

I turn off the Lungotevere onto a lesser road, a small unknown blood vessel that you and I know. Fields and piles of refuse on both sides. Rummaging there, among the garbage, we learn many things we don't know about the city. It is a necessary rite in order to understand. As disgusting as it is, it's the refuse that tells us the most: What people don't want is more significant than what they keep, because we are afraid of waste and hasten to get rid of it. Over time, the refuse grows and invades and expands and breeds and is transformed. Into what, I don't yet know. But it interests me. It interests me to rummage through the scraps of these insignificant lives.

Through the small piazza, glimpsing the absence of movement. Exploits declaimed in small, out-of-the-way bars, the shabby trick of a con man who dupes people, wondering fruitlessly why they are here. The road I am following, that suddenly seems to turn back toward the heart of Rome, is also a rotten trick. And now it's a fraud. That's not where we're going.

And the heart that interests us is another.

There are soccer fields, poor simulations separated from the road by only a net. They contain the echo of a thousand little matches, a ritual that fascinates me, in practice and in memory. It is a mythological ritual, that of the game: Playing on a mangy field amid piles of garbage, we all feel like champions, and we will earn lots of money, we will be applauded, we will marry a model and bring beautiful children into the world. It is a fairy tale, a bag-lady version of the noblest myths, and it helps us. That's what fairy tales are for: to give meaning to the throbbing of a heart that is otherwise useless.

We are lives that occupy very little space in the world, you and I. We go unnoticed. The throbbing of our heart is only important to me and to you; no one else can hear it.

Here, the city has become silent, turning into a village of illicit lives, plaster and cardboard models of a well-being that does not exist.

This is a group of houses built piece by piece, over time, with scavenged materials. Closed within them, miserable solitudes dream of recouping by the weekend a wealth and power that they will never have. They won't find it. Rebellion is like these streets that don't go anywhere and end at some point without really leading to any specific place. Small dead-end vessels that pour blood into the mud.

The Romans are builders of roads, but over time they've lost their direction and their use.

Ours is a government that builds roads, but does not know how to pursue a course sensibly.

The Romans, over time, began to build roads not to get somewhere, but just to show that they could do it. Then, without having completed the project, they ended up stopping halfway, stranding themselves in a desolation without trees, a small unpaved piazza bordered by a fence of pink and green stakes.

I'm not a femme, you say.

I breathe. Air and an intense taste.

We do what I want, you say.

I don't take off my glasses. I never take them off.

What about the money? you ask, your eyes looking for something outside.

Ghosts. I try to hear rustling. But all I hear is the blood flowing, in your body and mine.

Because if you don't give me the money I'm not doing anything, you explain.

I scratch around in my residual rationality, trying to return to reality.

In the meantime, you open the door and get out.

It's not true that all places are the same at night, because you don't visit places only with your eyes. All places have odors (this one is briny, and permeated by the smolder of cheap barbecue with traces of smoke and sweat close by—yours, I think). There are colors as well. As I too get out, following you, I find myself staring at this fence of pink and green stakes. I am distracted.

I don't sense the taste of death approaching.

It is a city that has known gladiators. They weren't what they say, those men. They weren't people of great skill, courage, and valor. Rather, they were muscular wretches bent on surviving, and violent, so much so that they sharpened their teeth to protect themselves from the lions. They felt the earth beneath their feet, and it was the last vestige of this world.

Gladiators, whose legend I like to imagine. They fought in the Circus Maximus, getting high on the crowd. I hear those cries, surpassed by the throbbing of a heart that is my own. There is a noise as I follow you toward the net.

Desire and fear.

A heart. Throbs.

I don't hear the ghosts arrive.

Then, there they are.

I do not step back. The body is not alien to me. I fight.

Ghosts with sharp weapons.

A ghost shatters the fence. The stake is a jagged surface. I want to touch it, stop it, before it touches me.

I don't run away, and I can't hear anything except the blows. Is it the throbbing of a heart? This crazed heart of mine.

Blood flowing out of my body now, from the cut on my head. Blood that throbs. I take off my shirt, wrap it around the wound. On my knees.

I could pray.

I could.

I know.

Too far from God to pray.

I know.

This makes me, forever, a danger.

During a fight, you don't have a real awareness of fighting. You protect the body because with that gone, the soul will no longer know where to live and will go away, lost.

The ghosts want my body. You don't do anything. I try to guess your thoughts, I sense only fear, yours.

It's not true that at a time of danger one feels fear. The only thing that you perceive is the urge to survive, against all logic.

And the throbbing of a heart.

Mine.

Let's step down from the stage and watch.

Let's watch the victim who defends himself like a gladiator of the past.

Let's watch the insipid ghosts: There are too many of them for us to defend ourselves.

Let's watch the victim on his knees, wiping up his blood.

Let's watch the ghosts who grab him again.

Let's watch the victim who escapes, who runs away.

Let's watch the splinters of wood on the ground, slick with blood.

Let's watch the sand stuck to the victim's face.

Let's watch the ghosts who become spattered with blood.

Let's watch the victim falling forward.

Let's watch the blows.

Let's watch the victim who doesn't move.

Let's watch the ghosts run to the car.

Let's watch a bloody hand resting on the roof of the car, leaving a mark.

Let's watch the car start up, confidently, without haste.

Let's watch the victim stretched out, motionless.

Let's watch the car approach.

I can feel the taste of blood and sand on my lips. Like a gladiator.

Those times are over.

They never existed.

Let's watch the car approach, without hesitation, driven by ghosts.

I have not lost consciousness.

I hear the throbbing of my heart.

I have not lost consciousness.

I am here.

I hear it.

The throbbing of my blood.

My heart.

The car. Is. Here.

The heart bursts.

Silence.

Time stops.

The car drives off, carrying the ghosts.

To Rome. The city of roads.

ETERNAL ROME

BY Antonio Scurati

Colosseum

Translated by Anne Milano Appel

I

The spring breeze was still blowing but there were no longer nebulas of fine, powdery dust rising from the ground. The sand had become heavy. It was drenched with blood.

The entire expanse of the arena, more than 3,600 square meters, had been bloodied by hundreds of dead animals. The carcasses of forest predators—bears, tigers, leopards, panthers—lay next to the herbivores whose flesh they had been tearing at just moments before. A few hung on, in the final shudders of their death throes. Below the marble galleries, a disemboweled lioness, though soaked in her own blood, persisted in sinking her teeth into the femur of a wild ass. At the opposite end of the elliptical arena, a lion with its throat ripped open widened its mouth in a suffocated roar, searching for air and its enemy at the same time. The tragic bulk of a slaughtered elephant, already flayed by hooks, dominated the space, surrounded by heaps of ostriches with their necks broken. Nearby, a litter of baby pigs sprang from the belly of an eviscerated sow. The animal gave birth and died. The death blow from a double-edged blade had made her a mother. The piglets, slick with blood and placenta, came into the world in a cemetery at its peak, among the remains of a hecatomb of beasts. They themselves would not *last long: All around them, dogs, intoxicated by the blood, howled madly—the only creatures still living besides the sow's offspring. Along the edges of the arena, in the stands, seventy thousand human beings, intoxicated in turn, were no less mad than the dogs.*

It was at that moment that the human forms appeared on the sand. Three males. One wearing a cuirass and additional armor from head to toe, and two half-naked, covered only by loincloths. After making his way through the animal carcasses to the center of the arena, the soldier gave one of the two prisoners a short sword. The armed man immediately began chasing the other. When he caught him, he disemboweled him. Then he returned the sword to his jailer. A third prisoner was brought in. The newcomer was given the sword, still bloody, and, after a short chase, slew the first killer with it. The scene was repeated numerous times, always the same. On that blood-drenched sand, victim and executioner were one and the same: a slave in a loincloth prostrated in death before thousands of satisfied spectators.

Then everything became confused. Two crosses appeared in the arena. One more than three meters high and a smaller one, both planted in the sand. A man on each cross. On the taller one, a body nailed head up was set on fire. The flesh, smeared with pitch, flared up like broomcorn. On the shorter cross, a man hanging upside down was offered to a leopard. The leopard tore off his face; swallowed it.

At that point, seeing the face of the condemned man disappear in the leopard's maw, Donald McKenzie, a fifty-six-year-old citizen of the United States, on a pleasure trip to Rome, fainted. The man, a native of Shelbyville, Indiana, where he managed a Wal-Mart, woke up in a bed at the San Camillo hospital, in a private room, with an intravenous drip stuck in his right forearm and an electrocardiograph attached to his chest to monitor his blood pressure and heartbeat. From time to time the patient, though he was safe and far from the place he had visited in that terrible vision, still displayed arrhythmias and brief fibrillations. A few hours earlier, as he was visiting the Colosseum amid the group with whom he had traveled from the United States—and in the company of a thousand other tourists from around the world—a vivid hallucination had brought that scene of carnage to Donald McKenzie's eyes. Though once he recovered from the fainting spell he was able to report the details of what he had seen with calm and precision, McKenzie's fixed stare proclaimed that, from that day on, this peaceful resident of Shelbyville, in the state of Indiana, would never again believe his eyes. For him, the ancient bond of trust between the eye and the mind was broken. Irreparably.

The extent of the trauma was immediately clear to all those who had just heard McKenzie's testimony: at his bedside were the head of the hospital's intensive care unit, the chief of psychiatry, a senior official from the Italian Ministry of Foreign Affairs, the American vice-consul, John D'Anna, accompanied by a uniformed officer of the U.S. Army, and Angelo Perosino, a young researcher of ancient history at the University of Rome. A man and a woman in dark suits and dark glasses, who had not yet identified themselves, stood apart, next to a window covered by Venetian blinds. The woman was looking out, toying with the rays of light filtering through the slits.

They all gave the impression of knowing perfectly well why they were there. All except the unfortunate Donald McKenzie and Angelo Perosino, who had been picked up a few hours before by Italian police at his tiny office at the university—"my loculus," he called it—and taken to the hospital. Along the way they had explained only that his

Antonio Scurati // 39

counsel was required. They had chosen him, he was told, not only because of his expertise on the gladiator games of Imperial Rome, but also because he spoke perfect English, having earned a Ph.D. in paleography at Yale University.

After hearing the gruesome story, Perosino, frightened by the American's delirium and close to an attack of claustrophobia, felt a nostalgic yearning for the amber light that at this moment would be spreading over the hills of Rome, heralding evening. So the researcher gently took one of the two doctors by the arm. He got what he was looking for.

"Professor Perosino, you are here because our friends at the American embassy suspect that some psychically unstable subjects," the psychiatric chief explained in Italian, "strongly affected by the ruins of the Colosseum and overcome by the intense heat, may have developed hallucinatory visions of scenes that, based on what they were told by the guides, they imagine took place in antiquity on the sand of the arena."

"Why do you say 'subjects,' doctor?" Perosino replied, irritated by the absurdity of the situation. "There's only one patient that I can see."

"This is not the first case," the doctor whispered.

"English, please!" The demand came from the far end of the room, from one of the two individuals in dark suits: the woman.

"Yes, Professor Perosino, perhaps it is only fair for you to know that this has also happened to others in recent weeks. Persons very different in age, social class, and profession, who have never met one another." Speaking now, in a soft, refined English, was Vice-Consul D'Anna. "In this case, however, there is something that doesn't add up. And it is for this reason that we would like your advice, which will be well remunerated, I assure you."

Perosino studied the two figures at the back of the room, then gestured for D'Anna to continue.

"What we cannot explain, apart from the nature of these visions, is their content. The atrocities described by Mr. McKenzie do not at all resemble the gladiator matches . . ."

Angelo Perosino shook his head, visibly annoyed by the man's ignorance. "You see, sir, on any given day of the spectacles, in addition to the actual skirmishes between gladiators that took place in the afternoon, the Colosseum presented animal hunting and fighting during the morning program. The beasts were brought to Rome from every corner of the Empire and, sometimes in the space of a few hours, hundreds of them were exterminated. Furthermore, the scenes of torture described at the end of the story recall the executions of murderers, fugitive slaves, Christians—spectacles that filled the interval between the morning and afternoon programs. During the break between the *venationes*—the animal hunts—and the gladiator duels, while the populace feasted in the stands and the well-to-do left to go eat in taverns, some were slaughtered. Just like that, to pass the time."

"Are you telling us, then, that the hallucination experienced by Donald McKenzie corresponds to the scientific knowledge we have in our possession about what took place in the Colosseum in the days of ancient Rome?"

"Absolutely," Perosino decreed, hoping to be able to regain his freedom this way. "A philologically correct hallucination, I would say."

As Angelo Perosino was escorted out, he noticed that the two individuals in dark suits were whispering animatedly to one another. They appeared to be in open disagreement about a matter of utmost importance. The man was arguing with barely contained passion in favor of some hypothesis, while the woman responded with cold, decisive gestures of denial. The researcher managed to catch only a few words, spoken loudly by the man, who was obviously vexed by the woman's dissent.

". . . remote viewing . . . remote viewing," he nearly shouted at her, taking off his dark glasses for the first time.

II

Angelo Perosino had been wandering for hours among the ruins of the Colosseum along with the two mysterious individuals who had introduced themselves to him as Agent Stone and Agent Miller, obviously fake names. A telling incident had reinforced the young scholar's conviction that they were agents of the CIA. After a brief huddle with the Italian police stationed around the metal detector at the entrance to the Colosseum, the weapons that both Miller and Stone carried in underarm holsters had been returned to them. And so Perosino found himself acting as guide to two armed agents in what remained of the largest theater of antiquity, a structure built with the blood of tens of thousands of slaves on two imaginary axes of 188 and 156 meters, for an overall perimeter of 527 meters.

As they wandered among crowds of tourists in shorts and bogus Roman centurions in cheap costumes posing for pricey souvenir photos, Perosino could not help mentally reviewing the information about "remote viewing" that he had acquired on the Internet. A brief search had been enough to discover that the term referred to a variety of techniques and protocols used to produce and control extrasensory perceptions. In remote-viewing phenomena, it was believed that a "viewer" could acquire multisensory information on an object situated anywhere in space and time without having previous knowledge of it. The pseudo-scientific explanations for these para-psychological phenomena referred to the alleged ability of the individual consciousness to connect to a supposed "matrix," a field of pure information, which, like the realm of the mythical ether, is said to be found beyond the illusory space-time continuum that we conventionally call "reality." A conceptually elaborate form of clairvoyance, whose scant credibility had, however, been reinforced by a top secret project financed by the American government during the Cold War years. The project, initially launched in the early 1970s with the name Stargate, under the supervision of the United States Army Intelligence and Security Command (INSCOM), was intended as a response to experiments that had been performed by the Soviets with clairvoyants, psychokinetics, telepathics, and child prodigies in support of espionage and counter-espionage activities and security systems associated with them. Later, the project passed to the control of the CIA, under the name SCANATE, and then, in the mid-'90s, was shut down. This according to official versions. But on the many websites devoted to these topics, fans of parapsychology claimed that, following the attacks of September 11, research in the United States had resumed, with even more advanced and more covert protocols and projects.

Angelo Perosino was almost run over by a small horde of ecstatic Japanese tourists on a photographic safari. The more the researcher contemplated the reasons he found himself at the Colosseum on a muggy August day, the more they seemed like a load of nonsense. Instinctively, he turned his back to the arena and directed his gaze toward the exit. A hand gently harpooned his right forearm. Agent Miller, beautiful and icy as always in her mannish Armani suit, was staring straight ahead at the stands on the other side of the arena.

Surrounded by a small group of fellow travelers who were making useless attempts to reassure him, a man of sturdy build, apparently terrified, was shouting as if possessed and pointing to a spot in the middle of the arena where, two thousand years earlier, gladiators had duelled to their deaths. In that spot, only a mound of dusty soil parched by the August sun could now be seen.

"Iu-gu-la! Iu-gu-la! Iu-gu-la!"

Seventy thousand people were shouting in unison, chanting the invocation with a hypnotic three-syllable rhythm. As if with one voice, seventy thousand men, women, old people, and children, of all social classes, turned to the Emperor's dais and let the guttural sounds rise up in that single voice. A hoarse voice. The stands of the Colosseum had been sprayed with a mixture of water and wine spiced with aromatic essences, and the sweet fragrance of saffron was married to the acrid odors of sweat and blood.

In the center of the arena, a man kneeling in utter despair awaited death, his torso bare, his muscular arms hanging loosely at his sides, his head thrown back to offer up his throat, eyes closed and mouth gaping. Until just a few seconds earlier, the man had fought vigorously. He had challenged, attacked, and threatened his adversary. He had even mocked him, displaying his genitals with the hand that gripped the sword. Now he was offering the second man his throat. He knelt before him like an object discarded in the dust.

After kicking aside the double-edged sword, the long rectangular shield, and the broad-visored helmet taken from the defeated man, the victor stood towering over him. He was bare-chested as well, and wore leg pads up to his thighs to protect his lower limbs; in his left hand he gripped a small round shield; in his right, a short, curved sword, like a dagger. His features were hidden by a helmet that covered his entire face, leaving only two small openings for the eyes. The victor raised the blade of the curved dagger to within a few inches of his own nose, as if a bestial myopia drove him to smell the adversary's blood on the weapon that would kill him. The crowd worshipped him. He reciprocated, hardening into the unmoving madness of a stone idol.

"Iu-gu-la! Iu-gu-la! Iu-gu-la!"

Everything remained fixed for a few interminable seconds—the despairing defeated man, the exalted victor, the ululating public—a moment suspended in time as in a horrific infinity. Then, suddenly, that picture of unyielding savagery came to life again. The Emperor rose from his throne and held his arms out before him as if to embrace the entire amphitheater. A silence fell. Absolute. The most powerful man on earth, who could dispose of anyone in that arena however he wished, turned to the people, taking their views into consideration. At that moment, even the lowest of the excrement-befouled plebeians could express an opinion. The decision depended on him as well. He, too, was called upon to decide life or death. The Emperor radiated divine power, shedding it over everyone in the Colosseum. The people would be part of the spectacle, would descend into the arena and decide the match.

"Iu-gu-la. Iu-gu-la. Iu-gu-la."

Once again the cry broke the silence. The people had decided.

Even before the Emperor, coming down from his dais surrounded by vestal virgins, turned his thumb down, the defeated gladiator moved. Advancing on his knees, he clasped his hands around the victor's legs. Then he bowed deeply and, with exasperating slowness, bent his head forward. As soon as the head's arc reached the end of its course, the victor, gripping the knife with both hands, plunged it straight into the victim's neck. Up to the hilt.

"Ha-bet, hoc ha-bet!"

From the stands, a howl like thunder greeted the death.

* * *

"What does *iugula* mean?"

One of the two presumed CIA agents, the male, approached the bed from which the man attached to the drip and the electrocardiograph had just finished describing his vision. His name was John Dukakis, and he was a forty-three-year-old former soldier, who had joined the Army after his college education was paid for by ROTC scholarships; he was a veteran of the two Persian Gulf wars, and a native of Medina, a town in the western part of New York State.

Agent Stone waited for the man's reply in a room in a mysterious, small underground hospital connected to the U.S. embassy, on Via Veneto. Dukakis had been transported there after he fainted. Now, after he had been given the necessary care, and the medical personnel had been dismissed, he was being questioned. The only other people in the room, besides the two CIA agents, were the Army officer who had been present at the San Camillo hospital, Angelo Perosino, and an artist who specialized in sketching storyboards for film directors at Cinecittà, that Hollywood on the Tiber where all the great Italian films had been produced in the '50s and '60s by the likes of Fellini, Visconti, Rossellini, and De Sica. The artist was busily translating into images the story he had just heard from Dukakis, but the former soldier seemed to have nothing further to add.

"What does *iugula* mean?" Agent Stone repeated.

"I don't know," Dukakis said finally. "I only speak English. Those fiends in the stands were shouting it as though possessed." Then he turned his head away, swallowed with difficulty, and half-closed his eyes.

"It means *sgozzalo*, 'cut his throat.'" Perosino chimed in. "The public at the gladiatorial contests shouted it when they wanted to demand the death of one of the two combatants."

"And that cry at the end?" the agent inquired further.

"*Habet, hoc habet?*"

"Yes, that one."

"It means 'He got it.' It refers to the sword thrust into his neck. The people shouted it when the defeated man 'got' the sword."

The illustrator had finished. He handed the sheets to the two agents. The woman took them. A series of quick sketches perfectly reconstructed the entire scene that Dukakis had described, alternating long shots and close-ups, as in a film sequence.

The woman gestured to the others to follow her out to the corridor. She shook her head: "He's a soldier who fought in the front lines, probably suffering from the trauma of a grenade or some variation of post-traumatic stress syndrome, and he must certainly be a fan of action films like *Gladiator*. The one with Russell Crowe as a Roman general sent to do combat in the arena. He is probably superimposing the film's images on the scene of the real Colosseum."

"But Dukakis doesn't know Latin!" the other agent interrupted.

The woman quashed the objection with a quick hand gesture. Now she gazed severely at Perosino, her blue eyes like ice. It seemed that she would not allow her hypothesis to be proven wrong.

Perosino regretted having to do so: "I'm sorry to contradict you, but that's not possible. The patient's account is much more faithful to the historic reality than the film is. In a number of details. Even if you ignore the issue of Latin, Dukakis's description of the death ritual does not appear in the film and his details about the equipment are much more accurate. For one thing, Russell Crowe, in the role of Maximus, appears in the arena with armor that was worn not by gladiators but by soldiers of the Roman legions. The gladiators in Dukakis's vision, on the other hand, fought bare-chested, as they did in actuality—"

"Then you, too, Professor Perosino," Agent Stone interrupted "believe that these subjects have 'seen' the past?"

Little by little, as the conversation continued, Agent Stone was assuming an increasingly animated air. He stared off into space as he spoke, as if he were expecting at any moment to be visited himself by one of those visions.

Perosino began to feel anxious. Though compelled to say that Stone was right, deep inside he sympathized with the skeptical position taken by Agent Miller. He decided that it was his turn to ask questions. "Do you think that what we have here are cases of 'remote viewing'?" he asked point-blank.

"Our driver will accompany you back to the university. The agreed-upon sum will be credited to your bank account. You have been a great help to us. Good day, Professor Perosino," Agent Miller said as she moved off down the corridor. Agent Stone followed her without another word.

III

"It's happened again."

Angelo Perosino looked up from his Negroni. Standing in front of him in his Armani suit, Agent Stone stared at him from behind the shield of his inevitable sunglasses. Once again Perosino took offense. He had always gauged the meagerness of his salary as a university researcher by the cost of an Armani suit. *It would take a month's pay for one to buy an Armani suit. But only on sale at the end of the season.* This is what Angelo Perosino thought whenever he felt discouraged about his work, and this is what he thought now when Agent Stone appeared before him.

"Have something. Can I offer you an apéritif, Agent Stone?" He spoke as though defying poverty. His own poverty.

Stone looked around. They were at Café Fandango in Piazza di Pietra, in the very heart of Rome, behind the Pantheon and opposite an impressive colonnade that once marked the boundary of a pagan temple but had later been incorporated into a structure less than a thousand years old. Café Fandango, owned by a successful independent producer, was frequented by writers and film people. Perosino went there often, hoping to be able to market one of his many stories of ancient Rome for a film.

"There's something you definitely have to see, Professor Perosino."

Stone was peremptory, as usual. Once again Perosino followed him.

During the drive to the covert hospital attached to the embassy, Stone and Perosino did not speak. Their silence was broken only when the driver deviated from the route and took Via dei Fori Imperiali in order to pass by the Colosseum.

"Do you like the Colosseum, Professor Perosino?" Agent Stone asked, indicating the seven concentric circles of arches that had once been adorned with huge slabs of travertine marble.

"The Colosseum is Rome. I was born here. These are things that happen to you. You don't have the option of liking or disliking them."

"You don't believe that the past can reappear, Professor Perosino?" Agent Stone asked him after a brief pause.

"Rome is the Eternal City, I imagine you've heard it said, Agent Stone. When you live in eternity you don't believe in anything," Perosino replied.

Yet even as he spoke those words of deliberate cynicism, the researcher, confused by the noise of the traffic, had the momentary impression that he was seeing his city on the night before a spectacle, two thousand years ago. The blaring car horns sounded to him like the infernal din of the carts making their way from the animal parks of the imperial gardens, carrying the beasts toward the inevitable, their sole performance in the arena. Locked in dark cages, they would wait in the underground crypts of the Colosseum, already buried under the earth's crust.

In the hospital room where the most recent hallucinator had been treated, Perosino and Stone found only Agent Miller awaiting them. This time the person shattered by the visions was a woman. A young woman, exceedingly pale, with huge green eyes, lying in a state of persistent catatonia. Maybe because she was covered with a white sheet, maybe because she was so beautiful and unreachable—like the ancient priestesses of the goddess Vesta, who took a vow of eternal chastity and were buried alive if they broke their vows—for a moment the American girl seemed to Perosino like a vestal virgin dressed in white. One of those eternal virgins who surrounded the Emperor on his dais during the gladiator games. In the end, Perosino said to himself, she, too, seemed to be buried alive in the grave of a psyche lacerated by the apparition.

"What do you see in these images, Professor Perosino?"

Agent Miller interrupted the flow of the researcher's thoughts as she placed before him the visual transcription of the girl's account, which must already have been heard before his arrival and recorded by the Cinecittà sketch artist.

Perosino looked at the drawings. He looked at them and was horrified. They portrayed a woman prisoner who, wrapped in a cowhide in the middle of the arena, was made to couple with an enormous white bull. In subsequent images, the body of the woman, already mutilated, was pierced by the tip of a red-hot spear, brandished by someone wearing the winged headdress of the god Mercury. Appearing next in the scene was someone with a bird's beak, wearing a clinging garment and pointed leather shoes, holding a large hammer with a very long handle. This monstrous creature had seized hold of the unfortunate victim's corpse and was smashing the skull with the hammer. Finally, the Colosseum workers, using big hooks, dragged the corpse out of the arena. The hooks were lodged in the flesh of the woman's belly, already perforated by the bull. In the stands, surrounding the scene of carnage, the public was in ecstasy.

"What do you see in those images, professor?" Agent Miller repeated.

"I see the myth," Perosino replied, casting a compassion- ate glance at the girl lying on the bed. She might be more or less the same age as the torture victim, and to have witnessed that scene must have been severely traumatizing.

"What do you mean, professor?" Agent Miller pressed.

"The scenes are mythological. The coupling between a woman and a bull recalls the myth of Pasiphae, the wife of Minos, king of Crete, who became infatuated with a bull she was given by Poseidon, and had herself shut up inside a faith- ful reproduction of a heifer, constructed by the architect Dae- dalus, in order to copulate with the beast. The creature with the bird's beak is Charon, the demon who ferried the souls of the dead to the other side of the river Styx in Hades. In the beliefs of the ancient Romans, this figure, inspired by Charu, the Etruscan god of death, was almost always accompanied by the god Mercury, who appears here armed with a spear."

"Now it's all clear!" Agent Miller was elated. "This proves

that our patients' so-called 'visions' are actually inspired by concepts and images derived from previous knowledge. In this instance, the girl, a student of archeology at Stanford, drew upon sources of the classical myth that she must surely be familiar with."

Angelo Perosino glanced again at the girl shattered by the apparitions, lost in sympathy. Then he shook his head vigorously. "Unfortunately, that's not the case, Agent Miller. These mythological performances were actually staged in the Colosseum at the expense of some poor unfortunate. The violent copulation between the woman and the bull was made possible by the fact that the cowhide in which the victim was wrapped was first smeared with the blood of a cow in heat. It was the ancient Romans who believed in the reality of myths, not us."

At that moment the girl was shaken by a paroxysm and began thrashing around in her bed.

"Maybe she's trying to tell us something," Perosino suggested.

"She hasn't spoken since yesterday. She stopped talking right after finishing the account of her vision," Stone informed him.

"Why did you wait until now to call me?" Perosino asked.

"Agent Miller felt that your advice was no longer needed," Stone explained.

Using gestures, the girl asked to see the drawings. When she had them in her hands, she threw all except one to the floor. She turned the single sheet over to the blank side, took a pencil from the bedside table, and, with some difficulty, wrote a few phrases in Latin.

"Would you translate them for us?" Miller asked Perosino.

The researcher hesitated, still somewhat offended, then took the paper and read:

As long as the Colosseum stands, Rome will stand. When the Colosseum falls, Rome will fall. When Rome falls, the world will fall.

"What kind of nonsense is this?" asked Agent Miller, more intractable than ever. Her colleague Stone, meanwhile, clasped his hands in his lap, almost as if he were praying. He awaited Perosino's answer with an eager gaze.

"It's the prophecy of a wise man of late antiquity, who has come down in history by the name of the Venerable Bede." Perosino moved away from the bed toward the other end of the room, where a halogen lamp gave off a faint light. "Unfortunately, it never came true," he added. Then, not knowing what else to do, he turned the paper over and looked again at the drawing. "To be fair, perhaps there is an inconsistency," Perosino concluded after a few seconds' observation.

Agent Miller immediately rushed over to him, followed by Stone.

"Look here, in the stands, among the spectators," Perosino said to Miller, indicating a woman, one of the vestals who surrounded the Emperor in their immaculate white garments. Like everyone else, the young priestess was staring at the scene of the woman and the bull. But unlike the others, she was watching the torture through a strange device that she held ten centimeters from her face, at eye level. The gadget, a slim metal rectangle from which protruded an oblong cone with a lens at the end, was some sort of optical device. Upon closer inspection, the mysterious object appeared to be a camera.

Agent Miller sighed with relief. "Did the girl also describe this detail to the artist?" she asked her colleague.

"This too," Agent Stone was forced to admit.

"Excellent, there's your proof that these are hallucinatory fantasies rather than remote viewing of the past," Agent Miller ruled outright.

At that moment, however, the girl behind them began gurgling. Stone, Miller, and Perosino hurried to the bed. The girl was trying to say something, but the words were incomprehensible sounds burbling in her throat, almost choking her. Perosino, thinking she was spitting up blood, moved to ring the bell that would alert the medical personnel.

Agent Miller stopped him: "Hold on, professor." The agent again handed the young woman the paper and pencil.

The unfortunate girl, her face waxen as a lily, scrawled a brief phrase: *What appears in the visions is not the past. It's the future.*

THE MELTING POT

BY TOMMASO PINCIO

Via Veneto

Translated by Ann Goldstein

It all began right in the middle of that endless season that went down in history as "the Great Summer." Suddenly, without knowing how, I found myself in Vietnam. I was watching American soldiers fighting and dying in the jungle. Above me helicopters roared amid clouds of napalm. Then I looked up and saw the fan that hung from the ceiling of my room in the Hotel Excelsior.

It was only a dream and I was still in Rome. But it felt like a jungle in the tropics. The fan blades fluttered through the oppressive air of the room without providing any relief. They turned uselessly, like my life.

I was dripping with sweat; I had slept more than eight hours but I was still exhausted. It was an effort to get up. I ate breakfast listening to the same things the radio had been repeating every day for I don't know how long. The daytime temperature never went below 110 degrees. The health department recommended not going outside before sunset.

I looked out the window as I finished drinking my coffee. It was getting dark, and throngs of foolish Chinese had begun to invade Via Veneto. I observed the rows of red lanterns and the signs crowded with ideograms whose meaning

I didn't know. Another torrid night of hell awaited me in the city of the apocalypse. Hardly the Dolce Vita. Now there was only summer, and Rome had become a world upside down, an enormous Chinatown where the heat forced people to live like vampires, sleeping by day and working by night. I should have left like everyone else when I still had the chance.

I went back to the bedroom and discovered that, just as they say, the worst has no limits. A girl had appeared out of no-where and was lying motionless in my bed. She was half-naked and lay inert, on her stomach, her legs slightly spread, her arms extended along her sides, palms turned up, her face sunk in the pillow. She certainly looked dead. I hadn't the slightest idea who she could be; it had been quite a while since I'd been intimate with a woman.

When I tried to turn the girl's head I made another crazy discovery. Her face seemed to be stuck to the pillow. I tried several times. I finally took her by the hair and pulled her head, pressing the pillow against the bed. Nothing, the face wouldn't come free. And in continuation of this theme that the worst has no limits, just at that moment someone knocked on the door.

With a corpse in the room it would have been wiser to pretend not to be home. What in the world would I have said if I had found myself facing the police? But I opened it anyway. Something compelled me to. Don't ask what because I don't know. Luckily it was Signor Ho, the manager of the hotel.

"I have the bill for the overdue rent," he said. I glanced at the papers and gasped. He had nearly doubled the rent, holding me responsible for, among other things, the air-conditioning. I protested. The increase was robbery. As for air-conditioning, the system had never worked. Almost noth-ing worked in that lousy hotel.

"There are new rules now," said Signor Ho. "Everyone pays for the cool air now. If your system broken, my worker fix it. If you don't like new rules, you out. If you don't pay, you out."

It was pointless to argue, that Chinaman had a head harder than an anvil. Not to mention the business of the dead girl in the bed. I certainly couldn't risk having him call his lackey in to repair the air-conditioning. So I tore the papers from his hand and told him not to worry, I would take care of everything as soon as possible.

"When is as soon as possible?"

I told him I didn't know, but before he could reply, I said, "Tomorrow." Then I slammed the door in his face. I went back to the bedroom with the hope that the corpse had disappeared. Maybe I'd had a hallucination. Unfortunately, the girl was still there. So I lay down on the bed next to her. I realize that lying down next to a dead woman may seem depraved. But I was exhausted from the heat and the stress. I needed to stretch out to get my ideas in order, and that was the only bed available. I spent several minutes staring at the girl's hair. It was smooth and long. The shiny black made me think she was Chinese or one of the many other Asians who hung out in the neighborhood. Suddenly it moved. The hair, I mean. At first I thought it was the fan. But when it rose, and began to wave in the air like tentacles, I realized that there was something alive in it. The tentacles became an enormous octopus wrapped around the girl's body. The whole room was now immersed in a blood-red ocean.

The thought that I was still dreaming barely surfaced; fear had gotten the better of me. I would have liked to get up and flee. Go I don't know where. But I was paralyzed. I don't mean metaphorically. I couldn't move in the literal sense of the word.

It was terrible being present at such a spectacle while having to remain as still as a statue. Then everything went dark and when I reopened my eyes the girl had disappeared.

There are people who give dreams a lot of weight. They believe all dreams have a meaning. They waste time analyzing them, thinking they'll discover something or other about themselves or even their future. Nonsense. For me, dreams are only dreams, images that the mind seizes randomly in sleep, like the numbers that blindfolded children pick out of a lottery wheel. This has always been my opinion, at least. And, in fact, that night I got up without attaching too much importance to the strange nightmare I had woken from. I went to the bathroom as if nothing had happened and washed my hands and face. I avoided meeting my gaze in the mirror as I stretched my arm out for the towel. I knew I didn't look good, I almost never do when I wake up. The deadly heat of the Great Summer didn't help; it made me seem at least five years older, and, considering that I was no longer a boy, this bugged me.

I tried not to think of the heat or of the years gone by and wasted. I tried not to think at all. It wasn't difficult; with the weather I had become quite good at emptying my mind. Not that I didn't have things to think about. Money, for example. I was drowning in debts that I couldn't pay. Someone else might have gone crazy. Not me. I took bills, requests for payment, injunctions, and all the other papers in which money I didn't have was claimed from me, and I stuck them on one of those gadgets you used to see in trattorias. They're called check spindles, I think. Or something like that. They consist of a big metal pin fixed to a wooden base, and you feel an almost sexual pleasure in sticking a bill on them. Don't think badly of me, but it was like deflowering the economy. For me, there's never been much difference between the economy and a woman. In the sense that I have never understood either one.

Yet I was very fond of my pin. I kept it in plain sight on the table in front of the window. I still have it, in fact. Only now it's on the night table. If I spoke in the past tense it's because I wish I had thrown it away. Things would have gone differently without the pin in the picture. On the other hand, not necessarily. Basically, the fault is not the pin's but mine and the dream's. Why in the world did I go around telling it? To Yin, in particular. I knew very well that there's nothing to joke about with girls like her. And yet . . . Wait, I'm going too fast. I should begin at the beginning. Yes. But is there really a precise moment at which things begin? Like the Big Bang, so to speak.

I knew a guy years ago. I'll spare you the details, but I saw him go downhill overnight. Let's say he went to shit. I was surprised, because he had always seemed to me one of those people who know what they're doing. I asked him how he'd gotten into such a state, how it had happened. "The way everything happens," he answered. "Little by little at first. Then all of a sudden." I wasn't sure I understood. But now I know. Now it's clear to me. Little by little at first, then all of a sudden. It's like the Great Summer. Now it seems normal. The heat was infernal, the Romans had all escaped to the north, and here there were only Chinese and Bedouins. Plus some unlucky jerks like me. If I look at Rome now, it seems as if it was always like that. But when I think back to how this city was before the famous summer, I wonder if maybe I'm crazy. It seems to me that I live in a nightmare. And yet no. It's all true. It was all true before and it's all true now.

I remember the beginning of that famous summer very

well. I decided to stay in Rome. I liked the deserted city, liked not having to wait in line at the post office or the supermarket. During the day I worked and at night I went to see the films that were shown in Piazza Vittorio. Coming home, I smoked a joint and fuck the rest. I wasn't rolling in dough but I had a peaceful life, without bumps.

It began to get hot. But really hot. You, too, will remember. Old people died. The newspapers and television said that such a heat wave had never been recorded before. Every day they interviewed some expert who went on and on about climate change, pollution, melting glaciers, and emissions standards. We all nodded our heads yes, but we weren't really listening. It was something in the future. In less than fifty years there will no longer be annual snowfall even on the highest mountains, said the experts. And what did we care about what would happen in fifty years? The only thing we were interested in was when the heat wave would pass. We waited for the storms of late August.

August passed. Then September passed, and October. Of the storms, no trace. The heat increased. When Christmas came, the temperature hovered around a hundred degrees. Not knowing what to do, people went to the beach. They thought that after New Year's winter would finally come. Instead, the fires began and at that point people began to get seriously pissed off. They demanded answers, wanted to hear that sooner or later everything would go back to the way it was before. The experts said that such a phenomenon had never been recorded. But this was not an answer or reassurance.

In the end, people began moving to the north. More or less in the same period the first waves of Chinese arrived. People sold their houses and the Chinese bought them for cash. After a year it seemed like Shanghai in the days of opium smoking and bordellos. It was fascinating, from a certain point of view. So although I no longer had a job, I figured I'd stay.

My boss had decided to shut down operations. Business was getting worse and worse, and without ceremony he gave me my walking papers. In retrospect, it seems to me he behaved rather badly, but right then I didn't care. The job had always been shitty, I wasn't at all sorry to lose it. I took the severance pay with the firm intention of scraping by. It wasn't a huge sum, but, thanks to the Great Summer, prices had tumbled. With a little economizing I could afford not to work for several years. If I moved to the north, that money would be gone in a few months and I'd have to start seriously slogging. I had no desire to do that.

Every so often my mother called, worried. She said that sooner or later the money would run out. "And then? What do you intend to do then?" she asked. A good question. Only I had no intentions. I told her I would think about it at the proper moment. According to my mother, I should join her in Lambrate, outside Milan. It seems there is a lot of work in that area. I was in Lambrate once. You have no idea what a god-awful place we're talking about. Total desolation. "I'll think about it, Mama," I said. Then I hung up and rolled a joint or drained a couple of cans of beer. Not infrequently I did both together.

At the time I was not yet living on Via Veneto. I had taken a studio not far from Piazza Vittorio, in the middle of the historic Chinatown. I led a peaceful, orderly life. I got up, ate breakfast, and leafed distractedly through a book, waiting for the temperature to go down. Around midnight I went out. I wandered through the neighborhood, ending up inevitably at the market, and, with no real goal, struggled to make my way among shouting vendors and old Chinese women examining the greens displayed in the stalls. Often I stopped in front of a shop selling tropical fish and killed time watching those strange creatures circling the aquariums. I ate around 2 in the morning, usually noodle soup. Soon afterward the Forbidden City opened.

It's there that my life changed forever, there that I met Yichang. The Forbidden City was a go-go bar. There had never been places like that in Rome before the Great Summer—I think because of the Vatican. Usually I stayed almost until closing time. I drank beer, watched the girls dance, waited for dawn. It was my favorite time of the night. Maybe because in my life I didn't do much, while there it seemed to me that a lot of interesting things happened. I wouldn't be able to say what things, exactly. Basically it was just a place where men went for whores.

One night Yichang sat down next to me. I had now been going to the Forbidden City regularly for several months and had the impression I hadn't seen him before. I was wrong, because he knew me. In the sense that he had noticed me.

He asked if I liked the place and I said yes.

"I thought so," he said.

I didn't know what to say.

"Where did you come from?"

"Nowhere, I'm from Rome."

He widened his eyes; I might have said I was a Martian.

"A Roman in Rome—a real rarity. May I buy you a drink?"

I shrugged. I had no desire to talk. I was used to minding my own business. I looked at the girls and my head emptied out in a pleasant way. This man was inserting himself between me and the best moment of my night. But I couldn't refuse. He was Chinese, we were in a place run by Chinese and frequented by Chinese. Few Italians came to the Forbidden City, and those few were almost all northerners on vacation and often they were down-and-out.

"May I ask why you've stayed in Rome?"

I was about to say, *No reason*, but I stopped myself. The Chinese are busier than ants, they don't trust idlers. "Business."

"Ah," he said, and shook his head as if to consider the answer. After a pause he asked, "And what do you do?"

Another good question. The world was full of people who were concerned with what I did. I said that I was a journalist, the first thing that crossed my mind.

"Really? And who do you write for?"

"A little here, a little there. Reports from the Roman front." The truth is that I hadn't the faintest idea how a newspaper works. I've never written a line in my life, not even a shopping list.

"I suppose you do well."

"Not as well as you think. Let's say I get by."

He smiled, touched my bottle of beer with his. Then he changed the subject, luckily. I couldn't go on shooting off my mouth about something I knew nothing about.

"Do you come here often?"

I took a swallow and nodded my head yes.

"You like this place, eh?"

"Yes, it's not bad."

He was silent for a while, looking at the girls rubbing their bodies against the steel poles.

I was under the illusion that the conversation had ended there, when he said, "And why do you like it?"

What the hell sort of question was that?

"You know why I'm asking? I'm asking because I've seen that you come here every night. You sit down, you have a couple of beers, you stay till closing, but you never ask a girl to your table. And I wonder why."

"I don't like to pay for sex." It was true, but only in part. The real reason is that I couldn't afford it. A night in itself didn't cost much then. Thirty euros to the bar and fifty for the girl. Plus another twenty if you needed a room. But I knew how it worked. The girls were experts. Rarely was it a one-time deal, then over. A hundred today, a hundred tomorrow. Not counting gifts. Like nothing, at the end of the month you find yourself poorer by several thousand euros. Those girls could become worse than a drug—once they had hooked you, you couldn't shake them off.

I could tell you a bunch of stories about people who squandered fortunes at the Forbidden City. Maybe that was why I liked going there. To watch others slowly go to ruin made me feel wise, someone who knows what's what. I'm not sure if I'm explaining it well, but this, too, was a reassuring dynamic.

Life for me has always been a mystery; in fact, I've never done anything very well. At the Forbidden City, however, things seemed clear as daylight: Watch and don't buy. If you understood this simple rule you could come back whenever you wanted. Every night, even.

"I understand, but then why do you come?"

Can you believe it? I said that it helped me put my ideas in order. Looking at the girls I was able to concentrate, focus better on the pieces that I had to send to the newspapers I worked for. At dawn I went home and typed out on the computer what I had mentally written at the Forbidden City.

"You're saying that you come here to work?"

"In a certain sense," I confirmed shamelessly.

"Then my conversation has disturbed you."

"No problem. You have to disconnect the plug from time to time."

"Very true." At that point Yichang introduced himself. He told me his name and I told him mine. We shook hands.

We toasted our meeting with our beer bottles.

"I must confess something to you." He paused, then: "I've studied you closely over the past few months, you know."

I looked at him. Part of me foresaw that this man had in mind a precise plan.

"Your detachment is admirable. I wonder how you manage not to let yourself get involved in the situation. I mean, many of these creatures would be capable of bringing a dead man to life. What's the matter, don't you like women?"

"Oh no, I like them a lot. I told you, I come for other reasons."

"Yes. You will agree, however, that your behavior is not like everyone else's."

I shrugged.

"However that may be, it's good for you. No offense, you Italians risk being stung by those creatures. You're not used to a certain type of woman. You let yourself be fooled by their childlike behavior, by their tender, defenseless ways. But they're not at all defenseless. They're whores. I've seen many Italians like you come here sure of themselves, they choose a girl, and take it all as a game. They end up badly. Then there are those who fall in love and end up worse. They get it in their heads to take the whore away, they think that underneath they're good girls. They couldn't make a more serious mistake. There are no good girls here. Chinese, Vietnamese, Laotian, Cambodian. All the same, all whores. And whores are like scorpions. You know the story of the scorpion, I imagine."

"Of course," I said distractedly, trying to convey that all

this talk was starting to annoy me.

"With these girls it's the same. You can't expect them to change their nature. It's something that you Italians tend to forget because of appearances. You know what some of them are capable of doing?"

"Cutting off your dick," I said brusquely. I couldn't take it anymore. The little lesson on the traps of the Forbidden City was really too much.

Yichang felt the blow, or at least so it seemed to me. "I see that you are informed."

What had he taken me for, one of those fools who came down from the north in search of exotic adventures? I didn't speak Chinese, but certain stories reached my ears anyway. Stories of girls who castrated clients because they hadn't paid, or maybe simply because they'd begun a relationship with another whore, as if a man can't have all the girls he wants. When they established that they had to break it off with you for good, they took you to bed without letting anything show—Asians are masters of hiding their rancor. Between one caress and another they gave you something to drink, and within a few minutes you were paralyzed.

It seems incredible that concoctions like that exist, and yet it's true. I don't know where they get it, but these girls have a kind of drug that immobilizes you. You're conscious but you can't move a finger. And while you're in this condition, they . . . well, you understand, they reserve you a front-row seat so that you can enjoy the show.

I got up, intending to go home. The night was ruined.

"You're leaving?"

"Yes."

He detained me by resting a hand on my arm. "I hope I didn't bother you with my conversation."

"No, I'm just a little tired. Besides, I have an article to finish for tomorrow."

"I understand." Then, as if it were an afterthought, he asked me, "Do you live far away?"

I thought he would continue to bore me with his talk as he walked me home, so I told him the truth. "No, just around the corner."

"You live in this neighborhood?"

"Yes, why?"

"Nothing, it's just that a journalist . . . This is a poor neighborhood, dirty, noisy. Not exactly elegant."

"It's convenient," I said.

"Convenient for what?" He didn't give me time to answer. "Sit down. I have a proposal to make that might interest you. What would you say to living on Via Veneto? You know the Hotel Excelsior?"

Of course I knew it, a luxury hotel far beyond my reach.

"It's no longer a hotel, and I'm sure that a professional like you can afford to pay a hundred euros for a suite."

I was open-mouthed—it was less than half of what I paid for the one-room apartment, three hundred square feet, in Piazza Vittorio. Yichang explained that the Excelsior, after having been closed for several months, had been bought by a friend of his who had converted it into apartments. Almost all the apartments were already rented to very fashionable Chinese people. There was one, however, still free. Yichang's friend was having difficulty finding a tenant because years ago a famous person had killed himself there. "One of those rock stars with long hair and torn jeans. I don't remember his name."

"You mean Kurt Cobain?"

Yichang snapped his fingers. "That's right. You know,

we Chinese are a superstitious people. Many of us believe in ghosts and don't like to sleep in a room where someone took a gun and blew his brains out."

I avoided explaining to him that things hadn't gone exactly like that. It was more convenient that he and his Chinese friends continue to believe that Cobain had killed himself in the Hotel Excelsior.

"So do you think it might interest you?"

It might, yes. The prospect of moving to Via Veneto, of living in the city where I was born like a Russian prince in exile, attracted me quite a lot. And for only a hundred euros a month!

Yichang said he would introduce me to the manager of the Excelsior as soon as possible, maybe the following night. I didn't know how to thank him. I wanted to repay him in some way, but Yichang waved his hands and shook his head, he wouldn't even speak of it. He ordered another beer, made some comments about a girl, then wrinkled his forehead as if he had suddenly remembered something.

"There might be one thing," he said. "Would you like to play a little card game?"

"Cards?"

"Yes. You know how to play poker?"

Obviously I knew the rules of poker, but I wasn't at all the typical player. To tell the truth, cards had always bored me. But Yichang insisted, and when I tried to demonstrate my indifference to games of chance, he said, "What a lot of big words. I'm just proposing a little game among friends to pass the time. Nominal bets, just small change, enough to add some excitement. Come on, you can't say no."

Little game, big words. His way of speaking in diminutives and augmentatives made me uneasy. But he was right,

I couldn't refuse. Not if I really wanted to move to Via Veneto.

I returned home at 9 in the morning. I lay on the bed and, staring at the blades of the fan rotating above me, I thought over the bizarre events of the night. Or rather, the events that I should have found bizarre but that at the moment appeared to me only manna fallen from heaven.

First of all, it should have seemed bizarre that a Chinese guy was so expansive with a stranger, and, furthermore, a Westerner. Then there was Yichang's perfect Italian and the business of the suite at the Hotel Excelsior. Even a child would have been suspicious. But as I said, at that time I had a tendency not to think too much. In a single stroke, while drinking beer and looking at whores, I had found a new place to live and won two hundred and fifty euros: I confined myself to thinking this.

Yes, because between one thing and another the little game had gone on for hours and, in spite of the fact that the bets were limited, I had left the Forbidden City with a tidy sum in my pocket. I may not have been a great player, but Yichang showed himself to be even worse. Above all he was obstinate. In the sense that he seemed purposely to do his utmost to lose. And this was the thing that should have made me suspicious. But I was intoxicated by the ease with which I was winning money.

Yichang kept his word. That night we went together to the Excelsior and he introduced me to Signor Ho. There was no problem. After a few preliminaries and a handshake, the suite was officially mine. For a deposit I left the two hundred euros that I had won at cards. With a warm smile, Yichang said that I couldn't refuse him the right to recoup.

I couldn't, as a matter of fact. We decided to meet at the Forbidden City at 3 in the morning. I won that night, too, but a little less, because Yichang succeeded in taking a few hands himself. I discovered that losing, rather than worrying me, increased my desire to keep playing. For reasons that in time I understood but which were then completely obscure to me, winning a hand after having lost one made me feel stronger. So that I even considered losing some on purpose, a little out of vanity and a little out of pure enjoyment. In spite of the money I won, however, cards still essentially bored me. I never changed my ideas on the subject. For me, there's nothing more tedious or foolish than poker. Maybe that's why I remained a terrible player.

You understood perfectly, I said terrible. Little by little, I don't even know how, I began to lose. And the more I lost the more I raised the stakes and the more I wanted to keep playing. Every night I went to the Forbidden City, I sat at a secluded table, and I played. I played and lost. From time to time, raising my head from the cards, I'd find my eyes meeting those of a girl who was dancing, and for an instant I'd feel nostalgia for the time when drinking a beer and looking at whores had been the crowning moment of my daily routine.

But it was really just an instant. In less than a second I was plunged back into the idiotic questions that assail the mind of a cardplayer. Pass, bluff, stand. All bullshit, and the moral of this bullshit was that I lost and Yichang won.

Yichang and his friends. Because a couple of other players always joined us, and none spoke a word of Italian. They won, too, but less than Yichang.

In the space of two months I accumulated debts of nearly two hundred thousand euros. A sum I had never seen in my life.

Yichang seemed to take it lightly. We played with chips and when, at dawn, the accounts were settled, Yichang wrote everything down in a notebook, but he never asked me for a cent. In fact, he told his friends that he would be my guarantor. He said that there was no problem. That I was an established professional who wrote for the papers. When he said that, I trembled inside.

Then came the crash, the devaluation, or I don't know what. As I said, I've never understood anything about the economy. The fact is that prices began to rise, including the rent on the suite at the Excelsior. So my debts spread like an oil spill, and with that we finally come to the time when I had the strange dream of the dead girl in the bed.

Later that night, Yichang asked me if by any chance I could lend him a thousand euros. I had gotten to know these people a little and I am well aware that when a Chinese person circles around a problem, it means that he's presenting the bill. He had said "lend" but in effect he meant *pay*. And not only a thousand euros but also the rest of my debt, or at least a considerable part of it. I had no idea where to go to get fifty, let alone a thousand and the rest. I told him that he must excuse me but I was a bit short.

"A bit short in what sense?" He couldn't understand how a journalist like me didn't have enough to lend a friend a thousand euros.

I had to tell him the truth. I would have been better off making up some more nonsense, but I saw no way out. And then I'd had it up to my ears. The situation was tearing me to pieces. I wanted to go back to my old life and stop playing, stop losing, stop fooling a friend. Because Yichang had behaved like a true friend, he had shown that he trusted me. And how had I rewarded him?

I would have liked to see him outside of the poker game. Have a few beers and talk about this and that. Yichang was in fact an amiable companion, a cultivated person. While we played, he often recounted interesting details about the history of Rome. He was a real expert. He had read Gibbon's *The History of the Decline and Fall of the Roman Empire* five times. Before meeting Yichang I didn't even know the names of the seven hills, but thanks to him I learned a lot of things. For example, that the greatness of Rome consisted above all in its eternal decadence.

I wonder if my life went as it did because I'm a Roman. It's consoling to be able to convince ourselves that our ruin is a kind of predestination, something genetic, or some such nonsense. It relieves you from the obligation of being sorry for all you have not done or could have not done. Like telling Yichang the truth.

I didn't expect him to take it so badly. I imagined that he would be pissed off, of course. I owed him a boatload of money, basically, and maybe he had already made plans for how to spend it. But what happened caught me off balance. He made me understand that I had understood nothing, excuse the wordplay.

On the table were the cards, the bottles of beer, a couple of ashtrays full of butts, and the piles of chips. Yichang raised his arms, held them suspended a moment, then pounded his fists down violently. The objects tottered, tipped over, fell to the floor. The two other Chinese guys gave signs of smiling. I bit my lower lip and hung my head.

"Look at me," said Yichang.

I did.

His face was a mask of tension. He was breathing hard through his nostrils. He stared at me for moments that, it seemed, would never pass, then he pointed at me with his index finger and uttered my full name.

"Tommaso Pincio. You . . . you . . . you . . ."

He never said what he was about to say. He got up abruptly and went off somewhere. The other two Chinese sat motionless in their places, staring at me. I thought it was best not to move, either.

At the Forbidden City, no one noticed a thing. All was proceeding as usual. The girls' bodies swayed lazily to the rhythm of the music. One of them came down from the stage to sit on the knees of a client, an Asian man of around fifty.

I recall that at that moment they were playing a remix of "San Francisco (Be Sure to Wear Flowers in Your Hair)." The one by the Global Deejays, you know it? A rather silly tune, but then the Chinese are not very sophisticated. Every so often in the song you hear a female voice saying the names of various cities. Paris, London, Los Angeles, Tokyo, and a bunch of others. Even Baghdad. And I would have liked to find myself anywhere, including Baghdad, but the Forbidden City.

Then Yichang returned to the table. He gathered up the cards, lit a cigarette, and said, "Okay, let's get back to the game."

The expression on his face was indecipherable. He seemed to have calmed down, but I glimpsed a light in his eyes that I didn't like. I tried to say that I would rather not play. I wanted to go home. I felt like a shit. I had lied. I had accumulated a mountain of debts that I would never be able to pay.

"Nonsense."

"No, seriously. I lied to you and I can't forgive myself."

"It's true, but for that precise reason you can't withdraw."

I didn't understand.

"You see, if you withdraw now I'll be forced to have your dick cut off by one of the girls." He stared at me for a few seconds, then: "I was joking, obviously." But he didn't have the tone of someone who was joking. I tried to show a hint of a smile. We played. Every so often I glanced at the other two, but they gave no sign of having understood what Yichang had said, and he hadn't uttered a single word in Chinese. I had a lot of ugly thoughts. I think it was then that I began to use my brain again, a little. However, I promptly got into another one of my usual messes.

Incredible to say, but I had started winning again. Yichang didn't seem at all disturbed by this. In fact, he began to make some jokes and he told a story about the origins of Rome, as if nothing had happened. I felt tremendously embarrassed and wanted to contribute to the conversation. Since I was short of subjects, I had this bright idea of recounting the strange dream I'd had the night before.

Yichang listened attentively but said nothing. He continued to lose. When we stopped playing he was down by almost three hundred euros. It wasn't much compared to the two hundred thousand I owed him, but at least it was something. He took his notebook and updated it, saying that we would see each other the following night at the usual time.

I don't know if it had something to do with telling Yichang my dream, but the following night there was something new. Sitting to one side, near our table, was a girl. Yichang introduced her. Her name was Yin. Like all the girls in the Forbidden City, she was very pretty. I didn't remember having seen her before, but that didn't mean much. Ever since I had thrown myself body and soul into cards, I had stopped paying particular attention to what happened on the stage.

Yichang said that she was there to serve us. He asked if

I had anything against it. All this was rather odd. Usually, when we finished our beers we raised a finger and immediately more were brought. Our needs were always limited to this. I didn't see how this girl could serve us. But could I make an objection?

The first few nights slid by smooth as glass. I continued to win big. I had recouped almost half my debt. Within two weeks I found myself ahead by a hundred euros. From the stable to the stars.

"You see, Yin brings you good luck," Yichang said every so often, smiling in that strange way he had on those nights. And when Yichang made these remarks, Yin smiled too, staring at me with a look full of meaning.

I shielded myself, embarrassed. I had discovered that I was not at all immune to Yin's charm. She was beautiful, but there was something else. I don't know how to explain it. Maybe it was the fact that she sat near our table the whole time without saying anything. She didn't even bring us the beers, as I had imagined she would. She was just a presence. She seemed to be there only to be looked at, and, indeed, I looked at her. I couldn't help giving her furtive glances. And every time I did so, I found that her eyes were on me.

I felt good. I was winning, and having a girl gaze at me the whole time made me feel . . . how to put it? Stronger, more of a man.

The cards had extinguished in me any desire, and so it had been an eternity since I'd been with a woman. But now it was different. I felt reborn and was beginning to have thoughts about Yin.

This didn't escape Yichang. At the end of one night, in Yin's presence, he said, "Why don't you take her home?"

I pretended not to understand.

"Yes, you should celebrate. You've started winning again. You're ahead by seven hundred euros. It's a whim you can satisfy. I've seen how you look at her, what do you think? And I bet Yin wouldn't mind. Right, Yin?"

Yin smiled without saying anything, as always.

I, however, felt different. I told you, I felt as if I'd been reborn. So the words came out of my mouth by themselves: "You would really come with me?" Only an idiot would ask a whore a question like that.

She nodded her head yes and I brought her home. We made love all day, heedless of the heat and the sweat. At sunset we went out. I asked her if she wanted to have breakfast with me. She nodded. What did I expect her to say? We didn't speak. We only gazed into each other's eyes as we ate. We had no need for words, we felt satisfied. Then again, maybe I shouldn't use the plural. It was I who felt satisfied. She had simply done what she was paid for—something I began to forget, despite the fact that I had always boasted that I knew how things worked at the Forbidden City.

The fact that I'd paid nothing so far had its weight. I supposedly had seven hundred euros available. Yichang scrupulously noted my winnings in his famous notebook, but he had not yet given me a cent and I hadn't found the courage to ask him for anything. How could I demand that he pay me after what had happened?

Nor did Yin demand anything. When I raised the subject she shook her head and said, smiling, "Me know you many money Yichang. Me not care. Me like you." I was struck by hearing her speak in the broken English of Asians. I realized that until then I had never heard the sound of her voice. A sound that I would not hear again for a long time. We stayed together. It became a kind of routine. I played, I won some euros, I said goodbye to Yichang and went home with Yin. We made love and then watched television or simply lay on the bed. Without ever saying anything. Or rather: It was she who didn't open her mouth. I sometimes did. For example, I made comments on the heat or asked if she felt like something to eat. Sometimes I mentioned that I liked her. Whatever I said to her, Yin nodded her head yes. Which didn't bother me. In fact, I found it relaxing and, in a strange way, I began to fall in love with her. I say strange because I knew nothing about Yin. Where she came from, how old she was, what went on in her head.

In time I began to make grandiose speeches after we made love. I talked to her about myself, about how my life had been and how I would have liked it to be. I told her my opinion on all kinds of things. If there was something after death, if I believed in God or extraterrestrials. Ideas. She seemed to listen because from time to time she nodded. But the truth is that deep down it wasn't so important whether she really listened. Otherwise I wouldn't have spoken in Italian. What the fuck, the only words I had heard her say were "Me not care. Me like you." There was a serious probability that she understood nothing.

One day I felt in a particularly romantic vein and told her the dream. I don't know why, but it came to mind. Suddenly, I realized that after that absurd dream my life had changed. I had begun to win and I had met her. Maybe dreams had a meaning after all. She nodded yes without saying anything. She didn't seem at all moved by the fact that the girl in the dream was dead. A detail that I noted only later.

Some more weeks passed during which everything seemed to keep running smooth as glass. I was becoming richer and richer, if only in Yichang's notebook. Sex with Yin was fantastic and every day I was more in love with her. I was convinced that she felt the same, because from the beginning she had never asked me to pay her. In my screwed-up brain I had conceived the idea that her "Me like you" was worth more than "Me know you many money Yinchang."

Until one night, after months had gone by, she decided to open her mouth, and she did it to ask for money. In her broken English she said that, between one fuck and another, I owed her something like fifty thousand euros. If I considered the request in purely virtual terms there was nothing to worry about. According to Yichang's notebook I was nearly a millionaire. But in my pocket I had barely a hundred euros and my bank account wasn't much better off.

Yin told me I don't know what nonsense about her family in Cambodia; in other words, she really needed money. She wanted actual money, not numbers written in a stupid notebook, and she wanted it right away. Suddenly I saw her for what she was, a whore from the Forbidden City. Maybe she loved me, in the animal-like way that binds those girls to their source of income. Nonetheless, she was a scorpion, as Yichang put it.

I began to fear for my lower regions and I explained the problem to Yichang. I said that if it had been for myself I would never have asked. And, in fact, for myself I asked nothing. Only a couple of thousand euros for Yin. A laughable sum compared with what he owed me.

"Laughable, you say. Once I asked you for only half that, you remember?"

"I know, I behaved very badly. But so much time has passed. Let's not dig it up again, please. Now it's different."

"You're right, it's different. Now I'm the one who finds myself a little short. Actually, I'm very short."

"You're kidding."

"Not at all."

"You mean you won't give me the two thousand euros?"

"I can't even give you a cent."

"But what do I tell Yin?"

"Tell her you love her."

"Do you take me for a fool? What's a whore going to do with my love?"

"Until today I never heard you speak of Yin in those terms."

"You know what I mean."

"No, I don't know. Anyway, I'm afraid there is no other possibility." With that, Yichang said goodbye, leaving me alone with my problems.

Overnight I had become broke again. There were a lot of Chinese people I owed money to, who had given me credit because Yichang guaranteed me. I understood that from now on everything would be different.

But the more immediate problem was represented by Yin. At least, so I saw it at the moment. Maybe I was getting too paranoid, but that girl's long silences suddenly seemed to me threatening.

I explained that Yichang was a little short.

"You not have money you?"

I tightened my lips and shook my head. I told her I was sorry.

It was a bad moment but things settled down. I told her that I loved her and that I would stay with her.

"Me big problem now."

"Yes, I know."

"You take care me?"

"Of course, Yin."

She peered at me without saying anything. I knew the meaning of that look. I stuck a hand in my pocket and gave her everything I had.

"Only this? You not take care me if you only this."

I said again that I was sorry and that I loved her.

She stared into space for a very long time. I saw that her lips were trembling.

"You not good with me. You very bad," she said finally, her eyes bright. Then she got up and left. I didn't try to stop her.

I wish this ugly story had ended there. For a while I thought it had. Yin didn't appear. I stopped going to the Forbidden City and had lost sight of Yichang. I no longer drank, I no longer smoked marijuana. I had even found a job. Not much, but little by little I was able to pay my debts and get back on my feet. I had put the pin with the bills on the night table so that I could look at it before going to sleep and meditate on my past errors. I would become a new person, this was my intention.

Maybe I would even have succeeded if Yin hadn't knocked at my door one day. She said she wanted to talk to me. I let her in. She came straight into the bedroom, sat down on the bed, and, with her head bent, waited for me to join her.

I sat down beside her. "A lot of time has passed," I said.

She nodded in her usual way. It wasn't so long, really. Only a couple of months. But my style of life was so changed that to see Yin again was like diving into a distant past.

"You're well?"

She nodded again.

"I've thought about you a lot." I don't know why I said it. Yes, the memory of her occasionally surfaced but only as one of the many things that had happened, one of my many mistakes. It wasn't true that I had thought of her a lot. Not in that sense, at least.

She said nothing.

I felt embarrassed at having lied to her, and since the silence that fell after my words was unbearable, I asked what she had come to talk about.

She let some more moments pass, as if she had to gather her thoughts, then she raised her head and, looking me in the eyes, said, "Me like you. Think only this very long time."

We made love as in the old days. The next day neither of us said anything, but to me it was clear that we were together again. Yin moved in with me. Or, rather, that day she stayed in my suite at the Hotel Excelsior and never left.

At sunset I headed off to work and when I came back at dawn I found her where I had left her, lying on the bed. She got up only to take a shower or get something to eat from the refrigerator. She never opened her mouth, just as in the old days.

I didn't think of asking her what had impelled her to return to me, nor did I ask if she had resolved her problems or how. It was enough to find her there, ready and available only for me. Of course, I wondered what was the sense of a relationship like that. Because the fact is that I no longer loved her as I believed I once had. Yin was now like a bed dog. A kind of domestic animal, something comfortable to have in the house. Maybe my feelings were not very uplifting, but I decided not to beat my brains out. If it was all right for her, why should I have to make a lot of trouble for myself?

The end of this bad story came when I had stopped thinking about it. About the past, I mean. It happened sometimes that I remembered my nights at the Forbidden City, the girls who danced on the stage and the things that were said about them. But it happened less and less frequently, and anyway it was something so distant that it felt alien. It was as if neither Yin nor I had ever been the person of that time.

I began to think of us as a real, if somewhat peculiar, couple. I even considered asking Yin if she would like to have a child. This, because she seemed more and more affectionate. Not that she did anything apart from being silent and lying on the bed. I don't know, it was something in her habits, in the way she made love. She seemed—how to put it?—really in love.

I felt serene. Until one day I found her sitting cross-legged on the bed waiting for me to come home from work. On the night table, beside the old pin with the bills, there was a bottle of red wine with two glasses. She poured the wine and offered me a glass.

Nothing like that had ever happened. Her proposing a toast, that is. So I asked her if there was something I didn't know that we had to celebrate.

She shook her head smiling. And then: "You know everything. Me like you." She touched my glass with hers and drank.

"I love you," I said. I don't know if it was true. I was happy that she had made the gesture, and was happy that she was there for me every day, on my bed, waiting for my return. If this can be called love, then I loved her.

I drank the wine, and was about to kiss her, but she moved her face. She grabbed me by the hair and pushed me down, on her breast. I began to kiss her there, then on the neck and behind the ear. I tried again to bring my lips to hers, and again she moved. Suddenly, in a flash, I understood. And in understanding I lost consciousness, with an acid taste in my mouth that wasn't wine.

I came to as in the dream, paralyzed. And what else can I say? It's not true that before you die you see your life go by in an instant. This didn't happen to me, at least. In that final moment, I thought only of how blind and stupid a human being can be. I'm referring to all the things I hadn't realized in those months. For example, the way I began to win again after telling Yichang that I was in no position to pay my debts.

Then I also wondered if anything would have been different if I hadn't told her and Yichang my dream. And I almost reached the conclusion that certain things would have happened anyway. I say almost because when Yin took the pin with the bills and stuck it in the pillow, I understood that she was about to do something different from what I thought. She didn't intend to emasculate me. I saw her sit on my stomach. Then she raised the pillow over her head and stared for a moment at a precise point between my eyes. Everything lasted less than a second, and maybe that's why I didn't see any film go by. I thought only that it's really astonishing how a person can be capable of not thinking things through.

LAST SUMMER TOGETHER

BY CRISTIANA DANILA FORMETTA

Ostia

Translated by Ann Goldstein

I'm not dressed properly. I realize it from the way the other passengers are staring at me.

They're right. The train headed to Ostia-Lido is gritty, dust-coated, and none of them would dare set foot in it wearing a white linen suit. Here in Rome, dirt has a fascination with soft colors, insisting on the palest tints, and enjoys removing from them every trace of whiteness. My suit will soon be covered by a thin patina of grime, but that doesn't matter now. I no longer distinguish colors or the faces of the people around me. I no longer hear their voices, I have no desire to listen to their words, what they say, what they think.

English, that man in shorts and flip-flops said when he saw me arrive. And the fat woman next to him nodded her head yes.

English. Of course, that explains everything. My clothes, my composure, even the indifference I show toward the curious gazes of the other travelers. For them, my detachment is not the result of a natural disgust for a rude, vulgar segment of humanity. No, if I'm like this it's because I'm English. If I act like this, it's because I was born in a place where to sit silently reading a book is not yet considered a crime. Criminal, if anything, is the insistence with which a girl keeps asking me question after question, in an absurd mixture of English and Italian. She thinks I'm a tourist, she thinks I'm here just to dive into the dirty waters of Rome. And she won't stop talking to me about the Colosseum, about the marvels of the city, about places that in her view I really cannot do without seeing. Stupid girl. If she only knew how much beauty I've seen, and how much pain I've felt in the face of its enchantment. But she's incapable of understanding. She's young, but already she has the obtuse gaze of an old woman. And, just like an old woman, every so often she loses the thread of the conversation, wanders, and no longer knows what she's saying.

"You know Pasolini was murdered at Ostia?" she asks. Then, without waiting for an answer, she adds, "Of course, he was asking for it . . ." Then, as if unconsciously, I got up and left the compartment, overwhelmed by the brutality of that statement, but far more disturbed by the rapidity with which the recollection of a long-ago crime had brought back to mind other crimes, other horrors.

There's nothing odd about it. The history of Rome was written in blood. Every street, every building of this city conceals within its walls the sighs of executioners and their victims. And if everyone on this train stopped talking, even just for an instant, those moans would be heard here too, on this dirty train. But for now the noise is louder. It covers up the voices. It suffocates the cries. Just as you did, my dear Charlotte. Only you had the power to banish evil thoughts. You did it for almost thirty years. Thirty winters and thirty summers together, the last right here in Rome, visiting museums, walking on the beaches at Ostia, like a happy young married couple. That summer, you smiled, Charlotte. The way the child smiled who came and sat beside me. You, too, looked at me and smiled like that, while Alzheimer's was already eating away your brain. A simple, pure smile, and yet so distant, letting me understand that I was losing you. And you were losing the power to keep those voices at bay. Soon, my love, your smile would no longer rein in desire, the call of the young bodies that crowded the beaches of Ostia that summer. Male bodies. Bodies of tall, tanned youths. Memories of a past that you, my sweet wife, had been able to erase, giving me the illusion that nothing had ever happened. Yet it took so little to make my confidence crumble. A look, a few words were enough. It was enough that he told me his name.

Mario. Yes, his name was Mario, I haven't forgotten it. And Mario is the name I've given my shameful act. Mario is the name I've assigned to my lies.

I just bought him a drink, Charlotte. There's nothing wrong with having a soft drink together, a Coke. And yet in the depths of my heart I already knew that the years of peace you had given me were about to end.

You had changed me, Charlotte. You had transformed me into an adult who lived in a world of adults, a world where there was no room for young men with crew cuts and tanned skin.

Thank you, sir, the boy had said, taking big gulps of his Coke. He must have been barely fifteen, but already the expression of a scoundrel was painted on his face. Of a little adult. The bartender at that kiosk on the beach, Antonio, or whatever the hell his name was, seemed to confirm my impression.

"This kid here is a rogue," he said in a friendly fashion. "He always finds a way of getting something from the customers." At those words, I was tempted to withdraw, to make a prudent retreat, as if I feared that a stranger could read my mind and discern my guilty thoughts. Because, Charlotte, I had done something ugly. I had looked at that boy a moment too long. And in that moment all my desire returned from where I had buried it, leaving me like that, like a Lazarus come back to life, wandering alone on the beach, anxious to see that boy again, to hold him in my arms.

Charlotte, I don't understand why you had to die first. I surely deserved such an end more than you. But destiny tricked us both, and now I'm certain that you're looking down at me. So go on looking. Look at me, on this train again, when I had sworn to myself that I would never return to Rome, that I would never walk the white beaches of Ostia. And yet now I'm here, and now not even you can slow my descent into the Underworld. If I could, I would have done it two years ago. And even then you didn't stop me. You, Charlotte, you let the darkness enter my life like an unwanted guest. You opened the door to the night that made me a murderer. You gave it the keys to my house, my life. A curse, Charlotte. Why did you do this to me? Why did you let me believe that you could give me peace, when in reality you granted me only a truce. If you had told me the truth, I would not have done what I did. I would not have waited for Mario at sunset, with the excuse of buying him another Coke; I would not have followed him home, just to know where he lived; I would not have bought him that ball just to see him happy. I swear, Charlotte. If I had known I couldn't stop, I wouldn't have done any of the things I did in the days of our last summer together.

I wouldn't have told Mario that I would take him to a nice place for a pizza that night, a place here in Rome that only I knew, and that he was not to say a word to anyone. It's a secret, Mario. Don't tell anyone; otherwise, no pizza.

My God, why did a scoundrel like him pay any attention to me? Why on that particular night were you sicker than usual, did you seem scarcely aware of me?

There are many questions that I can't answer, and even today, Charlotte, I wonder why I didn't take Mario to have a pizza *for real*. It would have been so simple to get to central Rome, I had even rented a car. But at the last minute I changed my mind. I changed course, and brought Mario to the Idroscalo, the old seaplane station. I stopped the car and sat peering at the darkness all around.

You don't know it, Charlotte. Tourists don't go there. It's an unreal place of mud, garbage, and weeds. And it's been like that for thirty years, from the day of Pasolini's murder. A place abandoned by God and man, where the voice of that violence still sounds in the silence. The voice of an ancient violence, which Rome has never ceased to conceal. And that night the voice was heard again, like an echo, in the deserted fields of the Idroscalo. Loud enough to cover Mario's words, his protests. *What are we doing here, let's go*, he kept saying to me. But I couldn't hear him. I took him by the arm. I hit him to make him shut up. Then Mario got frightened and ran away. He opened the door and began running through the fields. He ran like a rabbit, Charlotte. Fast, like a frightened child. I started the car and went straight after him. I called to him to stop, but children, you know, they never do what they're told. Children are never still. Children are never quiet. They can't keep a secret, even if they've promised. I alone could silence him, I alone could stop him. I pressed my foot to the gas. Faster. It was essential to stop him. Before Mario could tell anyone what had happened. I had to end his life. End his world there, in those fields.

* * *

My world today goes on turning, Charlotte.

No one knows, no one has ever suspected.

Mario was always out, and his parents were not too concerned about him. Likely he fell victim to someone with evil intentions.

The fault is the family's, society's.

The fault is this city's.

Rome was born in blood, and blood always calls forth more blood. I believe it, Charlotte. The voice of violence shouts every night through these streets, but now among the victims' cries I seem to hear my name too. And it's Mario's voice that accuses me. A voice louder than the others.

It was you, he says. And yes, it was me. I killed that poor boy. It's no use turning your head and pretending that nothing happened. I tried, but it was all in vain. Two years have passed, and the sound of those broken bones still echoes in my head. That sound is my company day and night, it won't let me sleep, won't let me think.

He asked for it, Charlotte. From that day, I've been repeating this, over and over, but I'm not persuaded.

Mario's voice has followed me everywhere. It pursued me over land and sea, until I was exhausted, until it made me say Enough. Enough now. I'm too tired to escape again.

I'm dying, Charlotte. In the end his voice found me. It crossed the silence with which Rome remembers its dead, and murmured in my ear the word "cancer." And at my age cancer is unforgiving, as you well know. I'm going to die, my dear. And I'm going to die here at Ostia, where everything began. I'm going to die on the white beaches of this blood-colored city, like an old whale that has lost its way in the ocean. And in a way, my love, that's just how it should be.

PART II

IN THE FOOTSTEPS OF CAESAR

DON'T TALK
TO THE PASSENGER
BY DIEGO DE SILVA

Fiumicino

Translation by Anne Milano Appel

I get off the plane in enviable physical shape, proud of feeling and above all looking like I'm in sync with the wealth-producing world around me, not at all nostalgic, stylishly dressed, immune to politics, to freedom of the press and freedom of expression in general, to culture, to global warming, to Muslim terrorism, crime reports, the Democratic party, model towns of quiet living where low-level clerks massacre their neighbors and families for no reason, to rampant pedophilia, the never truly ascertained extinction of the first republic, to world championships, soccer bribe scandals, paparazzi who blackmail public figures, to the uncertainty of work, to Family Day, to Rights for Cohabiting Couples and the Catholic Church's meddling in the political life of the country and the private lives of individuals. I am a man of my time, having achieved a truce with the world. Not that it took that much, a wink was enough to send the signal: You mind your business and I'll mind mine. We're all adults, after all.

In the shuttle that brings us to the terminal, I look around (no one escapes the gaze of others in the airport shuttle: find me another public place where strangers pay so much attention to one another) and declare myself the most attractive man on this flight that just landed in Rome. For a moment I fear competition from a couple of young studs who are flaunting their gym-buffed physiques in tight T-shirts, but seeing that an attractive piece of tail with a child is looking at me and not them, my concern quickly eases.

We arrived right on time, which reassures me about the little game I intend to play before putting myself in circulation. As usual when I come to Rome, I group my engagements. Not that any one of them preoccupies me very much, but it's the sum of them that adds up, as the well-known joke says—and though it doesn't make me laugh, I find myself citing it often, a little like a bad tune that sticks in your head the more you try to forget it.

I retrieve my suitcase from the carousel (a job I detest, but since the antiterrorism measures have been in force, they make a lot of fuss, even for us) and before the shooting range I go and have a caffè macchiato, because I find the combination of foamy milk and espresso intoxicating. The cashier, a skinny brunette with delicate features, looks at me in an explicitly inviting way when she gives me my change. At first I think it would be fun to tell her that I'd be delighted to pick her up if she tells me what time she gets off, and then not show up, but her soft little face inspires such tenderness that I choose to spare her the humiliation.

When I finish the coffee I go to the men's room to complete the job, using for the occasion one of the business cards that I got printed on recycled paper, because it rolls up better. I lay the line I do not have out on the sink counter, prompting the silent disapproval of a family man washing his hands a couple of sinks down. I thin it out with a credit card, I snort noisily with my right nostril, tap my nose with my forefinger, throw my head back, stick my left pinkie in the nostril, then rub the fingertip over the upper gum arch, run my tongue over it, and swallow. The man continues staring at me, mesmerized. He has probably seen that there was nothing on the sink's marble, but ingenuous as he appears, he must be wondering if maybe they've invented some new type of invisible cocaine in the years since he gave up social activity. I can barely keep from laughing in his face. He dries his hands and moves away disgusted. I find myself irresistible, I congratulate myself at length, and finally I go take a leak. While I'm at it, I stop to read the little notes stuck to the outside walls of the urinals, handwritten by a semi-literate homosexual. I find them ridiculous and depressing. I give a little shake, I go wash my hands, I hold them under the jet of hot air from the dryer on the wall, curse the photoelectric cell that doesn't work, use the other dryer, get bored, finish up, open the suitcase, check that it isn't missing anything. At first I find myself thinking that I wouldn't mind strolling around the airport with the handle sticking out of my jacket pocket to cause a little outburst of panic and then apologize to the colleagues who would surround me with their weapons drawn ("Hey, guys, I don't know what to say, I'm really embarrassed, hasn't this ever happened to you? After you wash your hands, don't you sometimes just stick it in your pocket without thinking?"; "Never happened to me"—some idiot itching for a fight would surely respond— "you risk getting yourself killed, doing something stupid like that"; to which I would reply: "It depends on how stupid the one who shoots you is"); but I'm forced to reject the idea because I don't have much time, so I put it back in the holster, wet the palm of my right hand again, smooth my hair back, and finally get out of there.

A black attendant with a cart greets me in English, for

some reason. I reply, *Bonjour*, do a little airport shopping not geared toward buying, reach the exit, head over to the taxis. I locate the first free one, signal to the driver, he nods, I open the back door and am about to get in.

—Excuse me.

—What?

—Your suitcase, please.

I look down at my suitcase.

—What about it? I ask, confused.

—Do you mind if I put it in the trunk?

I shrug.

—No, I guess not, I reply, still not understanding.

—Okay, the guy says.

He gets out of the car. I look him over. Tall, bald, barely fifty, a little overweight, strong jaw, well-shaped goatee, fake Ray-Bans, open-necked shirt, NN jeans, street-market ankle boots. He is chewing gum, a habit that has always annoyed me.

I hand him the suitcase, he sets it in the trunk, motions for me to get in, gets back in the car, says good day, I reply good day, tell him my destination, and eventually we start off.

At first I think I will keep my mouth shut, convinced as I am that speaking to taxi drivers means allowing them to talk your head off until the time they let you out, but then I cannot suppress my curiosity.

—How come you asked me if you could put the suitcase in the trunk?

He rolls his eyes (I can see him in the rearview mirror) as if to say: *I knew you'd ask that.*

—It's a precautionary regulation, he says defensively; it's not as if he invented the rule.

—Precaution against what?

—Accidents.

This I didn't know.

We take the ring road.

—And how long has it been in effect, this regulation?

—For me, since the day a model almost broke her neck in my taxi.

It's beginning to get on my nerves, this explanation in bits and pieces.

—See, he continues, she had a big portfolio, you know those ones you put drawings in, like the kind architects use? She probably kept photographs of herself in it. Such a knock-out, I can't even tell ya. So, she puts it there on the ledge, in back. She says: *They won't run into us, will they?* Such a looker, I still remember her. Well, to cut a long story short, the model gets the portfolio right in the back of the neck. Her eyes pop out of her head. Such a blow, I thought for sure she was dead.

—Wasn't she wearing a seat belt?

—The model, yes. The portfolio, no.

—Oh, I mutter. His eyes search for me in his small mirror, probably expecting me to laugh (I think he had some wise-crack ready); but since I do not give him the satisfaction, he goes on.

—Well, now I have to deal with a lawsuit, get it?

Who knows if it's true.

—It's not your fault they ran into you, I comment.

—Sure. Go tell it to the model's lawyer.

Now there's the kind of answer that makes me see red. A person tells you something distressing, you make a suitable observation showing that you're on his side, and he answers you as if you were wasting his time. You're the one who told me all your business, imbecile, what did you expect me to say,

It's your fault, the lawyer was right, let's hope you lose the case?

—Do you have the number? I ask, irritated.

—What number?

—The lawyer's. Give it to me, that way I'll call him and tell him.

He peers at me in the little mirror.

—Oh! he says. I guess he didn't find my joke amusing.

Score one for me.

He's stopped talking. Wonderful.

—Excuse me, he then says, as if he is reading my mind.

—Hmm?

—You have to put the seat belt on.

I saw a film, as a boy, where Renato Pozzetto played the part of a poor devil who establishes a fetishistic relationship with a taxi. Like before going to bed he checks the car's water, oil, brakes, and tire pressure, polishes it, caresses it, falls asleep beside it, and when he goes on duty he subjects the passengers to a series of behavioral rules that border on the abusive (obviously, during the course of the film, the taxi falls apart). The fool behind the wheel of this taxi is unfortunately making me think of that character. Among the things I despise are nasty resemblances. I don't yet know how, but this involuntary superimposition will end up on my driver's account.

—The seat belt? I say.

—Yes, of course, this Font of Knowledge replies self-importantly, it's compulsory.

I lean forward so that he can see I'm raking him with my eyes, observing a not so insignificant detail: He isn't wearing one either.

—In case they try to hijack us, the jerk says, we have to be able to get out of the car quickly.

The response of a true bumpkin, more tactless than rude,

He stops a moment to catch his breath. Naturally, so much crap all at once requires a surplus of oxygen. It's exciting, though, sitting there listening to him try to provoke me.

From his tone, when he picks up again, I figure my silence is beginning to make him nervous.

—But things didn't go so good for one of them. He ran into me.

I knew it. Go for it, Rambo.

—When he got in, I knew right away what his intentions were. He had me drive around a bit, *Go this way, go that way,* he couldn't make up his mind. I was already losing my patience. At a certain point he goes: *Listen, can you take me to Saxa Rubra for five euros?* The meter was already showing twelve euros. So I says to him: *What the hell, are you kiddin' me?* And he goes: I *don't really give a fuck, you're the one who's going to give me money.* And I find the knife in front of my eyes.

But . . . I think.

—Well, I was so mad I couldn't see straight. I floored the accelerator so hard I still don't know why we didn't roll over. Then I jammed on the brakes and made that shitty Albanian go smashing against the window. I got out in a hurry, and grabbed him by the hair: *Out, you bastard!* And I beat the living daylights out of him, Christ did I give it to him. Lucky for him a police car came by, or else he'd have been pushin' up daisies instead of sittin' behind bars. But I left my marks on him, ya know.

I wonder how he can go on talking, given the fact that I haven't deigned to say a word since he began his pathetic story.

—You can't work anymore. Believe me, it's become a jungle. If the police won't protect us, then they should just say so. No problem, we'll take care of it. At night, instead of staying home, we team up and do justice on our own. After

one that would give me permission to become indigna
burst out with a who-do-you-think-you-are-and-who-d
think-you're-talking-to, but at this point I get the urge
a little fun, so I remain solemnly silent.

After a while he looks at me once again in the little
ascertaining that I have not put the seat belt on.

—It's become very dangerous work, this job of our

The idiot trails off, probably realizing what an
made of himself.

—Now, see, since they came up with this disgrace
don," we taxi drivers have become mobile ATMs fo
immigrants.

I don't say a word, letting him go on destroying
with his own words.

—Just think, he resumes heavily after a painful
in the span of a week, a couple of Albanians took ou
that's *seven* drivers. A knife to your throat, and you'
for. One of us reacted. Not that he wanted to be a hero
that it came to him instinctively. It's a miracle he wasn

I continue to hold my tongue.

—And to think that these sonsofbitches had thei
us for two months. The police had reports and more
descriptions, all the clues you want. Nearly every day
would go to the police station to report another one. I
what does it take to catch them, a couple of shitty Al
You think they arrested them? Not a chance! It's
problem. We're the ones out on the street, at the
everything and everybody, what the hell do they care
end of the month they collect their paycheck. To c
story short: The police are asleep, the judges are bus
ing on TV, let's not even talk about the politicians.
end we gotta organize things ourselves, right?

He stops a moment to catch his breath. Naturally, so much crap all at once requires a surplus of oxygen. It's exciting, though, sitting there listening to him try to provoke me.

From his tone, when he picks up again, I figure my silence is beginning to make him nervous.

—But things didn't go so good for one of them. He ran into me.

I knew it. Go for it, Rambo.

—When he got in, I knew right away what his intentions were. He had me drive around a bit, *Go this way, go that way*, he couldn't make up his mind. I was already losing my patience. At a certain point he goes: *Listen, can you take me to Saxa Rubra for five euros?* The meter was already showing twelve euros. So I says to him: *What the hell, are you kiddin' me?* And he goes: I *don't really give a fuck, you're the one who's going to give me money.* And I find the knife in front of my eyes.

But . . . I think.

—Well, I was so mad I couldn't see straight. I floored the accelerator so hard I still don't know why we didn't roll over. Then I jammed on the brakes and made that shitty Albanian go smashing against the window. I got out in a hurry, and grabbed him by the hair: *Out, you bastard!* And I beat the living daylights out of him, Christ did I give it to him. Lucky for him a police car came by, or else he'd have been pushin' up daisies instead of sittin' behind bars. But I left my marks on him, ya know.

I wonder how he can go on talking, given the fact that I haven't deigned to say a word since he began his pathetic story.

—You can't work anymore. Believe me, it's become a jungle. If the police won't protect us, then they should just say so. No problem, we'll take care of it. At night, instead of staying home, we team up and do justice on our own. After one that would give me permission to become indignant and burst out with a who-do-you-think-you-are-and-who-do-you-think-you're-talking-to, but at this point I get the urge to have a little fun, so I remain solemnly silent.

After a while he looks at me once again in the little mirror, ascertaining that I have not put the seat belt on.

—It's become very dangerous work, this job of ours . . .

The idiot trails off, probably realizing what an ass he's made of himself.

—Now, see, since they came up with this disgraceful "pardon," we taxi drivers have become mobile ATMs for illegal immigrants.

I don't say a word, letting him go on destroying himself with his own words.

—Just think, he resumes heavily after a painful silence, in the span of a week, a couple of Albanians took out seven, that's *seven* drivers. A knife to your throat, and you're done for. One of us reacted. Not that he wanted to be a hero, it's just that it came to him instinctively. It's a miracle he wasn't killed.

I continue to hold my tongue.

—And to think that these sonsofbitches had their eye on us for two months. The police had reports and more reports, descriptions, all the clues you want. Nearly every day a driver would go to the police station to report another one. I ask you, what does it take to catch them, a couple of shitty Albanians? You think they arrested them? Not a chance! It's not their problem. We're the ones out on the street, at the mercy of everything and everybody, what the hell do they care? At the end of the month they collect their paycheck. To cut a long story short: The police are asleep, the judges are busy appearing on TV, let's not even talk about the politicians. So in the end we gotta organize things ourselves, right?

all, we know who the crooks are and where they live, we don't need no warrant.

I'm about to say something, but he keeps going.

—Me, when they tell me to believe in the law, I say: *Excuse me, what law?* Because I know only one law: an eye for an eye, a tooth for a tooth. The one that's written in the courts, the one that's supposed to be equal for everybody, not even young kids believe in it anymore.

At this point I interrupt.

—Listen, speaking frankly: Have you made any raids yet?

—Any raids?

—Right. Any . . . punitive expeditions, let's say.

—What d'you think, huh? the idiot replies.

—Come on, are you serious?

—What, you think I'm jokin'?

—How many are you?

—About twenty, give or take.

—How does it work? How are you set up?

—Helmets, chains, iron bars. Sometimes I even use a corkscrew. And then we go lookin' for 'em one by one. After a while you get a taste for it, ya know?

—Oh, sure.

—Yeah. It's a little like hunting.

He chuckles.

I don't.

—How come you're interested? he asks me, bewildered by my icy silence.

I let a few seconds go by before answering him.

—Well, it's nice to know there's someone who can help you in your work.

—Come again?

I shove the badge in front of his eyes. His jaw drops.

He turns pale. He actually pivots around to look at me. We swerve (a pickup truck blares its horn), then the imbecile regains control of the car.

—Watch the road. You're a cab driver, don't you know that's how accidents happen?

—Look, I'm sorry, I was only kiddin', I swear.

—Imagine that. He was only kiddin'.

—I'll swear on whatever you want. On my kids. May I drop dead right here in front of you if it isn't true.

—So then what you told me was a bunch of crap.

—Yeah, yeah. All of it.

—Why should I believe you if up till now all you've told me is a bunch of baloney?

He falls silent, terrorized by his future.

I take out the gun. I smooth the barrel with the tip of my forefinger. He spots it out of the corner of his eye and begins to sweat. At a rough guess, I'd say that his saliva flow rate has gone from one to thirty.

—What are you doing, drooling? I say.

—Please, officer, I'm sorry. Look, I'll get down on my knees if you want. Should I come back there with you? Huh?

—Don't try it or I'll shoot you right here.

I mean his right side, into which I've just stuck the gun.

He doesn't breathe. He's sweating like a pig now.

—Jesus, look at you pissing your pants, aren't you ashamed?

—Okay, I'm an idiot, a moron, a real shithead, my whole life I've been talking bullshit, God Almighty should strike me dead for all the crap that comes out of my mouth.

—There's no need to trouble God Almighty, I'll take care of it.

—Excuse me? What did you say?

—You heard me.

—You wouldn't really shoot me for the few lies I told, would you?

—Why not?

—Listen, let's be reasonable. I haven't done a thing. I'm a decent working man. There are a ton of unpunished criminals out there, who act like swine whenever it suits them, and you take it out on me for some stupid boasting?

I shove the gun back in his side.

—What now, back to badmouthing others? So then it's not true that you were telling lies.

—No, no, I'm sorry, you're right, I didn't mean to say that . . . oh, sweet Jesus.

We remain silent for a while. The imbecile is probably afraid of making the situation worse if he opens his mouth.

—What's your name? I ask him at a certain point.

—Mar . . . Marcello.

—Well then, Mar-Marcello, you're not actually all wrong, since it wouldn't be very sensible on my part to shoot you. First, because shooting idiots serves no purpose, meaning it's like shooting mice, and we know that shooting mice doesn't solve any problem; second, because it would be crazy to risk a charge of willful homicide to knock off a moron who talks just for the sake of talking.

—Right. Exactly, the idiot says, relieved. The return of hope must have reactivated his blood circulation, since he seems to have regained some color. So I quickly move to throw him back off guard.

—Unfortunately, however, it's turned out badly for you, I add, you know why?

—No, why?

—Because I hear voices.

—What?

—Naturally, I'm a schizophrenic.

—Excuse me, what does that mean?

—You don't know what a schizophrenic is?

—No.

—Ignorant too, besides being a jerk.

He wipes his dripping forehead with his hand. When he puts his palm back on the steering wheel, it leaves greasy marks.

—Well, let's simply say that I have a sick mind.

—Oh, holy Virgin, the imbecile says, as hope once more abandons him.

—So, I continue, if the voices I hear give me an order, I have to obey, you see how it works?

He thinks it over a bit, the poor devil.

—And you . . . can't you talk to them, to these voices?

—Talk to the voices? That's a good one.

—Why? Can't you try?

—No, of course you can't talk to the voices.

—I see a lot of people in the streets talking to themselves.

—Those people are not schizophrenics. And even if I could, what am I supposed to say to the voices?

—What you told me before about how it isn't worth it to shoot me. I mean, there's no reason to shoot morons.

—In other words, you want me to put in a good word for you.

—Right.

I consider this. And I think that I can indeed pretend to give him a shred of hope.

—So you think that if I tell them, I can convince them?

—Yes! Yes! Definitely! In fact, I'm sure you can!

—Could be. Maybe you're right. Wait, I'll give it a try.

I wrinkle my forehead, squeeze the bridge of my nose be-tween my thumb and forefinger, forcing myself to appear as absorbed as possible. Out of the corner of my eye I see the imbecile watching me in the little mirror, full of expectation. I let the operation go on until I see the sign for the exit *Campo Nomadi*, a local gypsy camp.

What fucking luck, I think.

I come out of my trance. I open my eyes.

—I'm really very sorry, Marcè, I tell him with a heavy voice, but your request was turned down.

—What do you mean, turned down? Why was it turned down?

—I don't know why. It's a surprise that they even an-swered me. That's never happened before. In a certain sense I'm grateful to you, I didn't know I could do it.

He turns around. He looks at me, desperate. We're about to swerve again.

—Do you mind watching the road, dickhead? I scold him, even raising my voice a little, I must admit.

—Sorry.

—Don't worry about it. Drive, go on.

—Please, officer, don't hurt me, I got a family.

I put a hand on his shoulder.

—No way, Marcè. I have to shoot you in the ear, they tell me.

He instinctively covers the part in question with his right hand, and begins crying like a baby.

—Hey, look, I can shoot you in the ear even through your hand, you know. It doesn't change much.

But I don't know if he even hears me, he's so disconsolate.

—Take this exit, go on, I tell him, indicating the gypsy camp, I'll shoot you there.

He obeys, with a kind of resignation to the awful day he's having.

I tell him to drive to a particularly squalid area with some really ugly trailers.

—Get out, go ahead.

He complies. He is still crying, though less than before.

From their ratholes on wheels, a couple of gypsies are watching us like hyenas hoping for prey.

I get out too. I make him walk two or three yards from the car, then I tell him to turn around. Though it is a rotten thing to do, I let a few seconds go by.

I take his place behind the wheel. I close the car door.

The sound makes him turn around.

—Hey, Marcè, I say loudly, do you have your wallet?

He pats his back pockets.

—Y-yeah, he answers automatically.

—Did you hear that? I shout in the direction of the gypsies, who have just stepped out of their shitty vans. —He has his wallet on him, this guy!

Marcello looks at me in shock. He probably hasn't understood a damn thing, demented as he is from everything that's happening to him.

I start the car.

I pass alongside him.

He looks at me, incapable of any reaction.

—And now they're your problem, I say, tossing my head back toward the gypsies who are beginning to approach.

Then I drive off.

In the rearview mirror, I see the hyenas starting to circle.

The two have already become four.

ROMAN HOLIDAYS

BY ENRICO FRANCESCHINI

Villa Borghese

Translated by Ann Goldstein

Settled at a table in a café, I check my watch: It's still early for our appointment, but I'm already anticipating her arrival. I like to stretch out the tension, up until the moment I see her, suddenly, in the crowd, head high, with that unmistakable gait, which distinguishes her, and, I would say, elevates her above all others. Today, however, I know in advance how I'm going to spend the time that separates me from the first glance, the first furtive kiss, the first thrilling moment of the day we'll spend together. I've brought a notebook with me, here to the café, a small book with a black binding, held shut by an elastic band: a handsome object with uncut pages, whose first lines I am filling with an old pen. Now I've taken a break, ordered a beer, lit a cigarette. What could be better, on a warm spring afternoon, than to sit in a café in the heart of Rome, have a sip of cold beer, take a drag on a cigarette, and prepare to write about the woman you love, knowing that in a couple of hours you'll see her?

My name is Jack Galiardo, I'm fifty years old, I'm an American citizen of Italian ancestry: My grandparents emigrated to New York in the early part of the twentieth century—they came from the countryside right around here. I'm a lawyer, a criminal defense lawyer, and I have a professional bias toward writing: When I accept a new case, after studying the details I need to slowly construct the line of reasoning that I'll use to defend my client, and the only way to do so effectively is to take notes, otherwise I can't think. *Cogito, ergo sum.* Paraphrasing Descartes, I could say: *I write, therefore I think.* It's valid here, too, at the café table, although the case I have to think about now is my own.

Two years ago, I was sitting on a plane next to a woman, an Italian. I was going to Rome to meet a witness who might be useful in a trial. She was returning to Italy from a short working trip to the United States. The flights from America to Europe generally arrive at dawn, so the majority of the passengers try to sleep; but that night the two of us weren't tired and we got to know each other. I had recently begun to study Italian, drawn by a sudden curiosity about the land of my forebears, which had never much interested me as a boy; so the conversation unfolded mainly in her language. After a couple of drinks and the initial chitchat, I revealed something about myself: that I had been married and divorced twice, had two children already in college, two houses, one in New York and one in Florida, two cars. "Two of everything," she commented, laughing. Then she told me that she was a journalist, that she was married, and that her husband was also a lawyer, in Rome; unlike me, he was not a criminal lawyer but, rather, worked in commercial law. They had three children, two boys and a girl, the last still small. Giulia—that was the name of my traveling companion—must have been forty, but she looked at least ten years younger. I soon discovered that she loved to talk: She did almost all the talking, jumping from one subject to another, telling endless anecdotes, little stories, situations— quite entertaining, I think. I can't be sure, because after a while I had trouble following her, given my limited knowledge of Italian. But the sound of what she said, the tone of her voice, the rippling laughs with which she punctuated her speech fascinated me. I would have liked her never to stop.

The truth is that she could also have stayed silent: The effect on me would probably have been the same. I was in love with Giulia from the moment I saw her. I've never believed in the classic thunderbolt. I've had a certain number of women, some of whom—including the two I married—I liked a lot at first, but I've never really lost my head. I suppose that as a boy I must have had, like everyone else, a crush on the cutest girl in the class, but as soon as I reached the age of discretion I left romanticism behind; love songs, for one thing, have always seemed to me banal, foolish, excessive. I found all those sighs, that agitation, vaguely comical; they seemed a pose, an attitude, rather than expressions of true feeling. With Giulia, however, it was like plunging into a state of adolescent regression. To please her, win her, possess her suddenly became my only purpose in life. Every other concern or consideration disappeared. I had to make an effort, that night on the plane, not to make myself look ridiculous by kneeling at her feet and declaring my love, then and there, in front of stewardesses and passengers.

When we landed, I asked for her phone number, and proposed that we see each other the next time I came to Rome. My stay this time would actually be very short: I had to leave within twenty-four hours so that I wouldn't miss a court hearing in New York. "I'd love to," she said simply. And we parted.

Phrases that are repeated an infinite number of times, in an infinity of casual encounters, in the course of a life. We might never have seen each other again. But I couldn't stop thinking about Giulia, and after just a few days I called her from New York. "Ciao, it's Jack Galiardo . . . I'd like to see you again," I recall myself saying, emotionally. I got immediately to the point: "I could come to Rome next week, if you have time."

She had a moment of hesitation. "You'd come to Rome just for me?" she asked.

"Yes."

She paused again, then said, "All right."

Our first meeting was at Villa Borghese. Sitting on a bench, I made the declaration of love I would have liked to make on the plane. In a mixture of English and Italian, I described my image of her: alone, in a state of crisis with her husband, desperate for affection, for a man who desired her as no woman had ever been desired. And that man was me. Slightly put off, she said that I had misunderstood: She had agreed to see me, but that didn't mean that her marriage was in trouble. I apologized. I added, however, that this suited me as well. That is, I was still happy to be there, on that bench, near her, even if she wasn't having trouble with her husband and I was, at most, just slightly likable. It wasn't a strategy to induce her to yield. I really felt that way: I felt that my love was so great that it was enough, at least at the beginning, for both of us. We got up from the bench and walked in silence for a little while, barely brushing against one another. In the square overlooking Piazza del Popolo she let me kiss her. We had lunch on the terrace of the Hassler. We continued to kiss, and then to touch, on the sofa of a deserted drawing room in the hotel, after lunch. We took a room there at the Hassler, although I was staying in another hotel. We made love until late afternoon. Then we descended to Piazza di Spagna, where she hastily said goodbye and got in a taxi. Walking as if in a trance, intoxicated with happiness, not knowing where I was or where I was going, I got a message on my cell phone: *I already miss you.* At that moment I knew: I had been knocked down. And I've never gotten up.

Rome, from then on, became the fixed destination of my vacations. As soon as I have a few days, I get on a plane and fly to Italy. Every so often, it happens that I can stay for a week, and then I manage to see Giulia two or three times. More often, they are whirlwind holidays: I leave at night from New York, arrive in Rome early the next morning, stay a day and a night, leave the following morning: a weekend in all, including the nine hours in the plane to get there and the same coming back. But it almost never happens that my Roman weekend coincides with an actual weekend. In fact, on Saturday and Sunday she has to be home, except for one weekend a month, when it's her turn in the office, and so she's just as busy. On some pretext, she can take a day off during the week as compensation, and devote it to me. Usually we see each other a couple of times a month. It works like this. I arrive and take a double room at a luxury hotel: the Hassler on Trinità dei Monti, the Hotel de Russie on Via del Babuino, the Plaza on Via del Corso, the Raphael near the Pantheon, the Excelsior on Via Veneto: These are my favorites. I earn a good living, enough to afford them, and besides, I love five-star hotels: They're the only luxury I indulge in. But in this case I choose them for other reasons. They're in the center, first of all, and Giulia lives in a residential neighborhood in the south of Rome, so it's less likely that she'll meet someone she knows. Furthermore, in these hotels the doormen are worldly, used to looking the other way in exchange for a generous tip, if in the late morning a woman accompanies a guest to his room without presenting her documents, as is usually required in Italy. Thus I spare her the embarrassment of disclosing her identity, of leaving traces. Finally, since we spend most of our time together in the room, I like it to be large, comfortable, elegant. I always wait for her in a café near the chosen hotel. When I see her coming, I get up and pay the bill, and she follows me, like a stranger, brushing my hand, pausing to give me a kiss in the doorway of a building, then immediately starting to walk again. Arriving at the hotel, we begin kissing in the elevator, start again as soon as I've closed the door of the room, and almost never stop. We take off our clothes quickly, we fall into bed, we make love—in every possible way—until evening. Maybe we fill the bathtub and spend awhile there. Sometimes we have room service: When the waiter comes in with the table, she goes into the bathroom, even though it's obvious, from what we order, from the unmade bed, and from the *Do not disturb* sign hanging on the door, that there are two people in the room. Sometimes, at night, we have dinner in a tourist trattoria in the neighborhood between the Pantheon and Piazza del Popolo. Rome is full of these trattorias; they are places where no Roman would ever eat and so there, too, the risk of running into someone who might recognize her is not so high. It's a system that guarantees eating badly, or at least not especially well, but it's not the food that interests me. For Giulia and me, it's enough to sit together in a dark corner, our knees touching, hands seeking each other under the table, letting ourselves be dazed by wine, only to hurry back to the room as soon as we've finished eating.

There have been exceptions to the rule of these encounters in the two years since we've been seeing each other. Once we went together to the Sistine Chapel, she hidden under a scarf and a pair of big dark sunglasses—well camouflaged among the legions of foreign tourists. Another time we took a car and went to Fregene, out of season, to stroll on the beach. It was sunny, we tumbled among the dunes. We also went to the movies one afternoon, not for the film but for the excitement of finding ourselves in the dark, in a half-empty theater, doing everything that is forbidden. Occasionally, I climb up behind her on her motor scooter and she drives me around, with no set destination: Since we're wearing helmets we're both unrecognizable. And since so many Romans travel around the city the same way—two wheels are the only alternative to the slow pace of cars and the inevitable traffic jams, Giulia explained. Protected by the mask of the helmet, holding onto her, I traverse the Eternal City like an invisible man to whom all is granted.

But it is in bed that we spend most of our time together. Partly we stay in these hotel rooms because ours is an illicit, clandestine love, which can't be lived in front of others. The main reason, though, is that we like it. However nice it is to eat together, walk together, go somewhere together, nothing seems better to us than staying in bed together. I've never felt anything like that. I've had other women who excited me, but I've never spent eight, ten, fifteen hours in bed with one of them—at a certain point, desire always ran out. With Giulia it's different: It never ends. Even if I'm tired after we've made love for a long time, an electric current impels me to caress her butt, lick the inside of her thighs, kiss her mouth, trace the line of her teeth with a finger, bite her ear, and on and on, without stopping. I can never have enough of her. It's like a universal truth that was suddenly revealed to me: For the first time it seems obvious, as it never had before, that things should always be this way between a man and woman who are in love. That or nothing. No half-measures. The idea that a couple can lie together, I don't mean for ten minutes but for an hour or two, and that each prefers to read a book, watch television, sleep—that is, do something else—now seems inconceivable, sad, wrong. If two people are in love, if they want each other, love should be the way the two of us live it: uncontainable. Morbid. A disease. Now I believe that the moment this passes and excitement turns into routine, love starts to end. Rather, it's already over.

Eventually, however, a worm began digging a hole in my obsession with Giulia, very tiny at first, then larger and larger: the thought of her husband. I'm a free man, without ties; I could be with her, if we wanted, all the time. And I would like it to be all the time. But Giulia isn't free; she's a married woman. For months, after that first meeting at Villa Borghese when I said that I saw in her a neglected and unhappy wife, we never returned to my mistake. Besides, it seemed to me that the facts expressed our wish to be together. Mistake or not, I thought I had understood everything: Giulia and her husband were the typical couple who married very young, but after twenty years things had cooled. As an explanation it suited me. I had no doubts, residual questions, uncertainties. But the worm, quietly, slowly, continued to dig. The hole got bigger. And I fell into it. I had to admit to myself that the classic roles of the triangle were reversed: I, the lover, was jealous of the husband. Of course, every so often Giulia mentioned his egotism, the fact that he never listened to her or that he dumped on her shoulders as wife and working mother all the responsibilities for the house and the children. But she said it as a simple fact, without much complaint, without expecting to change him or the situation. Of him she never spoke with malice, never.

Now Giulia had someone to listen to her: me. As in our first conversation flying over the Atlantic, it was always she who did more of the talking, telling me an infinity of stories great and small, about the articles she commissioned or wrote for the paper, about the minor incidents of life in the office, petty feuds, jealousies, injustices, the confidences of friends, the problems or successes she had with her children, the things she bought for the house, the vegetables she got at the market, the delicious meals she cooked. There—that's where my uneasiness made itself felt for the first time, I remember clearly, at the table. One of those evenings when Giulia couldn't stay with me, but had to hurry home at dinnertime—breathless, in her constant struggle with time—as if she were coming from the newspaper. Suddenly, as I was eating dinner alone in a squalid pizzeria, I saw her at the stove, preparing food for her family, and then at the table, laughing with her children, telling her husband something, receiving compliments from them all for the wonderful meal she had made. I felt a pang of jealousy. From that day, I began to desire Giulia not only in bed. I began to want to share with her the little rituals of daily life: dinner with friends, an outing with the children, a vacation, shopping at the supermarket. I thought how, in all those situations, it was the husband who got to be close to her, who enjoyed her presence continuously: not me. And I wondered how she really was with that man. I wondered if, and when, and how, they made love: odd, I had never thought about this before. Giulia talked so much, she told me so many things, but about him, and what she really felt, she said little. Was it reserve, a need to protect the privacy of her marital relations? Or perhaps only timidity, a difficulty in opening up? I then realized that she had rarely said to me, "I love you," "I adore you," phrases typical of lovers. It seemed to me that I could see love in the way she looked at me, but she measured her words, as if she distrusted them. She was much freer with text messages. She wrote: *What are you doing to me? I'm yours more and more, I miss you, I want you, I think of you, dream of you, you're inside me, part of my life.* And yet when, having received the message, I called her, I had the sensation that it was a different person who had sent it, that she was retreating, that she no longer wanted to talk about it. And the worm, planted inside me, kept on working. I would have liked to ask her: *You, what do you really feel? What is the difference between me and your husband? Would you leave him if I asked you to? How would you react if I asked you, for example, to marry me? Would you run away with me to New York? Or, if I moved to Rome, would we live together?* But I couldn't: It was stronger than me: I couldn't. These were the sort of questions that, the other way around, women had always asked me, in the various relationships I'd had. Relationships without love. Relationships in which I listened to those plaintive questions—*What about you, what do you feel? Do you love me? Do you care for me, think of me?*—with an increasing sensation of nausea. With the wish to silence their mouths, flee, never see them again.

The Italians take long summer vacations: usually an entire month. During the second vacation after we met, which Giulia spent at the beach with her whole family, we talked very little on the phone. It was complicated, her husband or children were always around. When finally we saw each other again, during a hot September in Rome, Giulia was more stupendous than ever: tanned, polished by the sun, slightly rounder, from days of repose and, I imagined—in vexation—from the food she had lovingly prepared over the four weeks. We made love furiously. Then I pounded her with questions. All the questions that the worm had burrowed into my body. Giulia didn't expect it. She was stunned, almost frightened. Then she answered. She said that her husband wasn't perfect, that their relations in twenty years of marriage had obviously changed, but that he was a good father whom the children adored, a good man, intelligent; certainly he neglected her somewhat, but not out of meanness or insensitivity—he just was like that. Once she had thought of leaving him, of divorcing, she admitted, without specifying if it had been after we met or before, but she had abandoned the idea: It wouldn't be easy, it would have been too painful for too many people, the children would never forgive her. Then, speaking of the two of us, she asked me point-blank if I would really be willing to leave my law office in New York. She knew that I loved my work. Before I could answer, she said that she loved hers as well. She said she needed me, that she was happy when she had me near her and heard me on the phone, that she didn't want to lose me—but life was a magical accord made up of many things: love, work, children, the city where she was born and raised, family ties. And she didn't want to lose any of them. Then she went silent, exhausted by all these explanations that she evidently wasn't used to.

Was it really like that, as she had said? I didn't know. But instead of making me angry, instead of her seeming egotistical or evasive, that speech made me feel a tenderness toward her. "When your children are grown up, will it be less painful?" I asked, laughing. "When you're old. When you're eighty. When you're ninety and I'm a hundred. Then I'll carry you off. Then we'll run away to the south in a convertible. Then you'll be mine and only mine."

She laughed too, relieved. "Idiot." Her voice trembled. We embraced. We made love again. We didn't talk about it anymore. The worm, for that day, vanished.

She hadn't answered all my questions, but she had said something. And I myself had always theorized, when women assailed me with questions, that words count for little in a relationship; what counts are actions. Promises, explanations, confidences mean nothing; in fact, they're a sure way to begin poisoning a relationship. Giulia was the proof of it. I thought of her as of a splendid jungle animal, guided by instinct. There were many components to her life, and the part that I played was crucial, but it didn't exclude or cancel out the others. That was it. In meeting, we had received from destiny a talisman of happiness—and only *we* could damage it, destroy it, lose it. Besides, I wouldn't have wanted to change places with her husband. How many times, proclaiming that love should always be like this, crushing, enveloping, like a dream or a drug, did I reflect that if I lived with Giulia I wouldn't rush to leave a bouquet of flowers in her office with an anonymous note; coming home from work, I wouldn't fling myself at her, since we would have fought because one of us had forgotten to buy toothpaste; we wouldn't exchange phone calls punctuated by sighs, or erotic text messages. So it was better this way. The question of jealousy seemed to me closed.

Some time afterward, however, I had the temptation to do something. I was spending a week in Rome, rather than the usual two days, and, not being able, naturally, to spend it with Giulia, I found myself with a lot of free time. Some I spent walking in "our" neighborhood, up and down Via del Corso, wandering between the Pantheon and the Trevi Fountain, sitting first in one café and then another, letting myself be pulled along by the river of foreign tourists until I lost any sense of where I was. Even today, after two years of Roman vacations, I get lost in the center of the city as soon as I leave the perpendicular line of the Corso. For someone accustomed to the perfect symmetry of Manhattan, the twisting streets of the Italian capital seem a labyrinth of squares and narrow alleys, all the same: a fountain, a column, a flaking wall, a café, a market stall, a wild dog, a motorcycle, a beggar, a group of American or Japanese tourists, another fountain . . . And in appearing to me indecipherable, impenetrable, Rome reminds me of Giulia: mysterious, seductive, majestic, happy, talkative, endowed with an ancient wisdom, breathtakingly beautiful, capable of making you lose your head and then demolishing everything with that laugh of hers . . .

But I've lost the thread, I was saying something else: that at a certain point I had the temptation to do something. I wanted to see her husband. I knew his surname. I knew he was a lawyer. A couple of phone calls were sufficient and I knew what day he would appear in court. I went with my heart beating madly. What impression would he make? What if he was hideous, the man for whom Giulia lovingly made dinner every night? Or what if, on the other hand, he was incredibly handsome? When I finally saw him, and heard him speak in front of the judge, I realized that he was neither. He was a normal man, with the face of a decent, respectable person. Against every expectation, I found him congenial. Yes, jealousy really seemed to have passed. To ask her and myself too many questions would only ruin everything. I became even more careful than before not to compromise the secrecy of our love. Giulia was no longer alone in protecting her marriage. Now I, too, wanted to help her.

I would never have imagined, as I was thinking along these lines in the courtroom, just a short distance from her husband, in what way I was to find myself helping her. Three months ago, while Giulia was following me along the route from a café near the Pantheon to the entrance of the Raphael, a storm broke. Umbrellas opened, tourists fled, streets emptied. I turned to look at her: With her rain-wet face she was beautiful, terribly desirable. I committed an imprudence: I pushed her into a doorway and kissed her for a long time, as if in a trance, slipping my hands under her skirt, where, I knew—she had promised me—she wasn't wearing panties. When we came out again into the street, embracing and running in the rain, someone saw us without our noticing. A man. A journalist. A colleague of Giulia's, who had worked for years at the same newspaper, and who had tried in vain, for years, to get her into bed. He followed us to the entrance of the Raphael. Maybe he waited for us there, maybe he simply gave the doorman a tip, more generous than mine, or maybe he even had an informant. The fact is that the next day, when they were both at the office, he sent Giulia a message and began to blackmail her. Either she slept with him or he would tell her husband everything. "You're scum," Giulia said to him when they met in a corridor at the office. "Yes," the man answered, and I imagined him drooling. Let me make it clear: Everyone—at the newspaper and outside it—courted Giulia. I would like to explain the reason for this fascination. She's beautiful, of course, but it's not only that. It's that Giulia has a particular sensuality which certain women are granted, and by virtue of which she emanates an eroticism without realizing it, without even trying. She has the air of a woman who is ready to flirt with anyone, whereas in reality she doesn't think about it at all. The result is irresistible. Men fall at her feet. I know because, with that innocent laugh, she told me herself. But when one of them, like the colleague in question, insists, and the pursuit becomes annoying, she won't play, she coldly cuts it off. That man, therefore, detested her. He was like a hungry beast who follows his prey for months, years, and knows he will never be able to savage it. Giulia in spike heels. Giulia wearing boots. Giulia in shorts. Giulia with her navel showing.

He was going mad. And when he saw her with me, he thought that he had finally found his chance to capture that prey. "I'm not in a hurry," he told her, excited.

As I feared, Giulia changed. We didn't see each other for three weeks. Whereas before we talked on the phone practically every day, in that period even phone calls became rare, brief, monosyllabic. Giulia felt stalked, pursued, spied on. She was afraid to see me. To provide the blackmailer with further proof. To be accused by her husband, lose the love of her children. Finally we met, but we were together only for a few hours, in a car with tinted windows that I had rented, and for the first time I saw her cry. She didn't know what to do. She didn't want to lose me, but even more she didn't want to lose her family. She didn't want to break the magical, fragile accord that held her life in balance. I dropped her at her scooter, saying, "I'm going to the airport, I'll call you tomorrow from New York," and I left in a screech of tires. But I didn't go to the airport.

I took a room at the Excelsior, I telephoned New York, putting off all my appointments indefinitely, and stayed in Rome. Without even needing to think about it, I had found the solution, the only one possible. I knew the name of the journalist who was blackmailing her. I easily found a photograph and information about him on Google. His father, a businessman, had died some years earlier, leaving a substantial inheritance. He didn't have money problems, or real career aspirations. He wasn't a famous reporter, having been stuck at a desk all his life. Every so often he was interviewed on television about the activities of the secret services: from there, I imagined, came his propensity for blackmail. I discovered where he lived with his wife and two children—on the Lungotevere, a few hundred meters from the Pantheon—and that was how he had happened to see us on that cursed afternoon. Giulia had told me what sort of man he was. He didn't get along with his wife, treated her badly, seemed to enjoy making fun of her in public, as if to demonstrate his superiority. The poor woman, at dinners of colleagues that Giulia had sometimes attended with her husband, took it and took it, then every so often they had a tremendous quarrel. One Saturday, I posted myself near the man's house and saw the whole family go out together, father, mother, children. They went shopping in a small supermarket in the neighborhood. I didn't at all like the way he behaved with her, not bothering to help her carry the heaviest bags, and, with the children, grumbling with irritation at their innocent whims. In my rented car with the tinted windows, I waited near his house another couple of evenings. He would come home on his *motorino*, as so many do here in Rome, a little after midnight—always at the same time. A time when the Lungotevere is deserted.

I have to digress here, in order to make what happened next understandable. I was the first in my family of Italian-American immigrants to get a college degree. My family would not have had the money, or the patience or the desire, to send me to college. When I finished high school, I enlisted in the Army. I went to the military academy, became an officer, and, with the rank of lieutenant, served in the Special Forces, the Green Berets. Besides teaching me to kill, the Army paid for the college education that my family could never have afforded. After I got my law degree, I waited a short time, then I resigned and returned to civilian life. Of my years in uniform, what remains is a medal for valor—I prefer not to speak of how and where I got it—and the techniques of hand-to-hand combat. My specialty was the knife.

It was simple to get one. In Rome you can find knives of all sizes in hunting and fishing stores. I chose the one suitable for my needs: a short but sharp blade. The following evening, I waited as usual near the house. When he got off his scooter I came alongside him in the car, asking through the window, in my halting Italian, where was the closest hospital, and waving a huge map of Rome. I coughed, I stuttered, I looked like someone who was about to have a heart attack. He was obviously annoyed, but he opened the car door and leaned in to show me on the map. Under the map I held the knife. With a quick movement, from right to left, I cut his throat and pulled him in toward me. He fell without a cry. I had covered the seat with plastic, and I used a towel to stanch the blood. I closed the door and drove off. I parked a kilometer farther on, along the Tiber, near a bridge. Not a soul in sight. I took his wallet and watch. The body made a thud, and was immediately swallowed up by the water. I threw the knife and the wallet, emptied of money, into the river, much farther on, from two different bridges. I cleaned the car, took it to a garage, slept in the hotel. The next morning I got on a plane and returned to New York, but not before changing my victim's euros to dollars and destroying the watch.

Giulia, whom I hadn't heard from since the day of our last, brief encounter, called me three days later. She didn't want to tell me anything on the telephone. Only that she needed to see me urgently. I took the first plane. We met in one of our usual cafés. She followed me to one of our usual hotels. In the room, she told me everything: the mysterious disappearance of her colleague the blackmailer, the corpse retrieved from the river, the lack of a motive, the police groping for clues, the hypothesis of murder committed during a robbery by some tramp, drug addict, or radical—the only types who hung around under the bridges and along the banks of the Tiber late at night. No one had seen anything. The crime seemed destined to remain unsolved. Without another word we undressed, we made love, then we lay there, silent, close. Until, as if overcome by a profound weariness, we fell asleep. And when we woke, it was as if everything could resume exactly as before.

Like every Italian-American, I'd had a Catholic education. As an adult, I stopped going to church and confessing for Holy Communion, but I remember perfectly well that a man can sin and be forgiven. God has mercy for everything, even a mortal sin. It's necessary, however, for the sinner to repent. And I didn't repent. For some time I deluded myself: It was true, I had cancelled out a human life, but that man was a pig, an unworthy being, garbage. I took a husband from a woman who didn't love him, a father from children who deserved better, I said to myself. But the illusion didn't last. I had become a lawyer because the concept of justice fascinated me, the attempt by men to come as close as possible to the truth. And the truth, bare and crude, is that I killed a man, I executed him without a trial. And I did it all alone: I was prosecutor, judge, executioner. A monstrosity.

And still I do not repent. I am aware of my sin, and yet I do not repent. I say further: I would do it again. I've had many women in my life, many have loved me, but I never really loved any of them in return. As a young man, seducing women was a mark of distinction, a badge attesting to virility and courage. I was attracted to the two I married, but never really in love. With some others it was a fleeting infatuation. For the most part, not even that. Only now that my hair is turning gray do I truly love; for the first time in my life. And I don't intend to stop. If the seal of our love is secrecy, if the precondition is to maintain a magic circle that includes her husband and children, I will be vigilant so that the circle doesn't break. If one day someone else discovers us, I'll get another knife. I will protect my love, however I can, as long as I can.

As a member of the legal profession, I know that the perfect crime doesn't exist. Sooner or later almost all murderers are discovered. That's why I'm writing these lines, this memoir. To set down in black-and-white that Giulia had nothing to do with it. Giulia didn't ask me to do anything. Giulia would never have approved of what I did. She would probably leave me if she knew. But meanwhile, until then, until my crime is eventually discovered, Giulia is mine. Two days a month, twelve hours a day, in a certain sense always, Giulia is mine. My Roman holidays continue, they might continue like this for my whole life, I'd put my signature on it. Like the signature and date I now place at the end of this document: *Jack Galiardo, Rome, March 21, first day of spring, sitting in a café between the Pantheon and the Trevi Fountain.*

I check the time: My love is late today, ten minutes already. Could something have happened? If so, why didn't she call me? I pay the bill. Light another cigarette. I smoke it with rapid, deep inhalations, eagerly scrutinizing the faces in the crowd, in search of hers. I take the last swallow of beer. I push the chair back, I get up. There she is.

TIBURTINA NOIR BLUES

BY FRANCESCA MAZZUCATO

Tiburtina Station

Translated by Ann Goldstein

A second-class station, a station to put up with, then cast off. So it seems to some: sticky with worn-out expectations, sickening with the sharp odors of sweat, unwashed skin, and rotting food. For me it was vital, I feel bound to this piece of the city, this place of shipwrecked souls, with its sudden drafts, perennial construction sites, gritty, dirty stone walls. You hear the echo of the street outside, only one sound lost among the many in this tangled skein of balustrades, platforms, asphalt, iron, stairs, sad shops, and tracks that end who knows where.

"Look at this crowd, what a mess, this station is a bordello, makes you sick, yes, let's go sit down, let's move away, there are Poles, Bulgarians, and Romanians lined up outside waiting for some bus or other, going back to their countries whose capital cities aren't worth shit, cities that no one remembers, with names too crowded with consonants, they're going home or to some other country for their deals, and I could say a few things about those deals, things you wouldn't believe. Deals and relatives go together for the drifters of Tiburtina, but basically the whole world is home, don't they say? Come on, sister, it's what they say, it's pure popular wisdom, pay attention to me, I'm well acquainted with them, these Bulgarians and Romanians, these human rejects running away from everything, who make sweet eyes at you, then become predators—they have a brutality inside, a brutality that they spew in your face, you can't imagine the violence they inflict, I know it, I bear the marks, but you can't imagine, sister."

I don't even try. I've never tried to put myself in someone else's place, to think like others, and, lucky for me, life has coddled and protected me, it's spared me the violence you're talking about, life singled me out from birth, granted me privilege, inserted me among the elite, if it hadn't would I be here? She's following me, her high-heeled sandals, really hideous, are noisy and they attract the glances of some Sinhalese. One sticks out his tongue with a lascivious gesture, disgusting, and it's better if they don't even notice us. We should hurry. I try to camouflage myself; in the meantime we get to the bar and sit down.

"Let's have something to drink while we wait, all right?"

"Yes, perfect, I'm thirsty, order some wine, what was I telling you? Damn, there's gum stuck to my heel, disgusting, I paid fifteen euros for these sandals, to you, a lady, it won't seem much, for me it was quite a sum, usually I buy shoes at a stall, from Biagio, who charges three euros a pair, four at most, one time I gave him a handjob in his van and he gave me three pairs, can you imagine what a stroke of luck? A simple, quick handjob, just a matter of holding it, not even that bad; he has a hairy stomach but he doesn't smell, or make you do something you don't want to. I gave him this handjob and I was all set with shoes for quite a while. Eh . . . certain kinds of luck don't happen often. What were we saying? Yes, about these people here, these Bulgarians and Romanians, who now, if I understand it, can come and go without even showing their documents, Madonna, what a shithole politics is. Let them stay in their countries instead. Maybe in those countries, maybe there are even some nice things, but a person with her back to the wall, like me, doesn't have much time or desire to think about nice things, a person like me, sister, doesn't have the desire to feel tolerant, trying to understand is hard work, it's a luxury, a privilege for the rich. For someone who's alone, drifting, without ties, someone who lost her mother as a child and ended up with a goddamn drunkard of a father, nice things are a cigarette smoked with pleasure or a man who fucks you tenderly, or something like our meeting, sister, I mean it, or maybe something like Biagio and the shoes, those are the nice things, but I'm used to seeing garbage all around me, and these people are garbage. Don't make a face, I'm not mean, but it's easier to think of an enemy, to enjoy someone who seems worse off than you at that moment when solitude seizes you by the throat, gnaws at your guts, devours your insides. It's been years since I've tried to hold onto something, to make a regular life, but I always end up skidding off track, something doesn't work, it slips and slides away, it doesn't go right, then I have to vent, that's natural, and I have to unburden my mind, my thoughts. If you don't they're in danger of becoming a burden, you have no idea how certain thoughts can harass you, scream in your head, so I start observing those people and doing like everyone else, thinking of them as the enemy, shitty foreigners who come to steal our jobs and our opportunities, that's how I see them . . . Instead I should see them as a mirror reflecting my puffy face, the dark circles under my eyes, because—you wouldn't believe it—but I know I'm not so different, it's only that I don't admit it and never will, that's all. It's a shortcut and I take it; I hear the newspaper lady who, after pushing away a fat gypsy with a child in her hand and one at her neck, mutters, *Disgusting,* and if I think the same thing while I drink a glass of wine sitting on this uncomfortable chair, shooing off flies and intrusive glances, if I think the same thing I can delude myself that I'm not the totally marginalized person that I am."

She points, raising herself slightly from the chair; her body gives off a fetid odor. I look at them through the window, lined up on one of the platforms, in groups, holding tight to suitcases like the ones people used in the '70s. Some women are leaning against the wall at one of the side entrances to Tiburtina.

"With those packages, those old suitcases piled on top of each other, those boxes tied with string, they make me sick, and the ragged children, little tramps ready to stick their hands in your pocket or your purse. You get to hate them, it's not out of meanness, sister, you agree? You know, you know better than me that to say a thing is good or bad is difficult, sometimes certain situations impose choices that go back and forth between good and bad, and then what the fuck are good and bad? Sometimes there's not a big difference, right?"

When she speaks like that she scares me, but I know it won't last long, luckily; sometimes I listen, sometimes I pretend because her speech is more like a disconnected muttering, anyone would think she's a poor lunatic with heels that are too high and a confused mind, she eats her words or they're incomprehensible because of the spaces between her teeth and her pale, cracked lips. Every so often she spits and a tiny drop of saliva lands near my motionless, clasped hands, or on the table; she notices, and dries it with her sleeve, then continues her monologue, which is repetitive, like a litany or maybe a prayer, an invocation, a lamentation. Something indefinable and strange, I would like to shut her up but I can't. The truth is, she doesn't want to talk to me but to everyone and no one, and anyone who can pretend to pay attention will do. Outside, the platform areas are blue, a blue lacerated by the colors and noises of the city buses and the long-distance buses that sometimes sit for a while, sometimes arrive quickly, pick up passengers, and leave. Evening is coming, a pink and blue sunset, dotted with the lights of the streetlamps and some advertising billboards. I don't know if she's noticed. She asks if she can have another drink, I nod to the waitress, who wipes her hands on her apron, brings a carafe of wine with two glasses, and rolls her eyes as if to say, When are you leaving? But it's just 7:00 and the bar closes at 9:00, so she has to be patient. I know perfectly well that she's irritating, her body and her manner are irritating, especially when she raises her voice and speeds up the rhythm of the litany, speaking like a psycho and making the other (very few) customers in the bar turn. I'm sure, in fact, that the waitress is disgusted, and since I'm with her I have the same effect, because that waitress can't understand what in the world I'm doing in the company of this woman. She shouldn't speculate, or feel irritation, or ask us why we're together, all she has to do is bring the wine. All she has to do is take the money and bring back a handful of coins in change. That's all.

"It's a while since I felt so relaxed. I've had so many bad times and never anyone to give me a hand. I've always had clowns instead of men around me, good-for-nothings with no balls who ruined my life, and now their ghosts chase me, their voices echo in that shithole where I live, have you ever seen ghosts? Have you ever been pursued by irritating voices? No, eh, no, right? You're respectable, you've got money and an education, why would you ever be persecuted, you're a person who's got a nice life. I'm just unlucky, and, shit, now my nose is running, this damn allergy."

She sneezes three or four times, opens her purse and rummages for something, with the back of her right hand she wipes her nose, with the left she's still rummaging around, then, exasperated, she empties the purse on the table. The waitress turns for a second, hearing the sound of objects falling on Formica, but fortunately some customers come in. *Two Tampaxes, a glass bead necklace, and two rings that seem like a child's toys or old prizes from an Easter egg tossed out who knows when, a crumpled package of Winston blues, a red pen with a chewed cap, a felt-tip pen, a bunch of receipts, cards for masseuses, fortune tellers, and cleaning agencies, a wallet and plastic document holder, three matches, supermarket makeup, spilled and half-empty, and a tiny cracked mirror. I think of my expensive foundation in its precious case, tiny grains that make the skin opaque and smooth. I think of my wallet with all the slots for credit cards. I make a rapid mental comparison to reassure myself. I keep my hands away from all that stuff. Finally she finds the package of Kleenex and dumps everything else back into the purse that's leaning against her feet. I feel a sensation of retching after seeing her worthless things, horror that stinks of rot and sweat, of age and negligence, the traces of her devastated life, the weave of small useless things that mark her desperation. I breathe in and out and it passes. I can't let myself go, not now. I order another carafe of wine and two slices of pizza.*

"Yes, good idea, I wanted to tell you I was hungry, you could have asked me before, when the allergy attacks I get all puffy, my eyes tear, I sneeze, I can't taste flavors anymore, but now it's better and I'm really hungry. What, are you eating too? You're really eating too, keeping me company, you won't leave me to eat alone like a dog, like the maid who eats in the kitchen? You're not showing how you despise me, the way everyone always does?"

I nod.

"Good, pizza, then maybe a sandwich. Look there. You see that woman over there? She's Bulgarian, from a town in the countryside, I don't know the name. I met her here once, she's a prostitute, and a client brought her back to the station, she'd been beaten, her face was swollen, she had a black eye, her head bleeding, she was staggering, it was also lovely, the tracks in the early morning, with all the wires, the gray sky, the trains standing there, and only a few souls waiting, it was lovely, and I must have been there watching and smoking a cigarette, waiting for the train to Termini to go home; but, not even thinking about it, I helped that Bulgarian shit whore who was screaming in pain, I got her a pizza, I helped clean her wounds, she told me she needed something strong to drink and I ordered a brandy for her. I paid, goes without saying. You should have seen her, she was indecent, in a miniskirt with orange sequins stuck to her thighs, no underpants, and black boots with very high heels, threatening, like her expression, well, I didn't think about it, I took care of her and fed her and she, that shit whore who should go back to her disgusting country, she cheated me out of the little money I had when I went to the bathroom. Then they say . . . they say so many things, that you shouldn't be a racist, that we need solidarity, but what solidarity are we talking about?"

I order a bottle of water and another carafe of wine, still so long to wait, hours that pile up on one another, in the midst of this construction, it's already started, that's going to make this hideous station something difficult to imagine, for the future, glass everywhere. I let my mind wander, trying to picture commercial areas, a radical cleaning, police everywhere insuring the safety of middle-class people, luminous spaces for shopping—it will be beautiful someday. Now it's depressing, the way her words are depressing, the way even her tone of voice is somehow depressing, a melancholy that enters the bones and chills you. Luckily I just need a little patience, just a little patience and this agony will be over.

"I come here the same hours she does, the Bulgarian whore, not that I do the same work, let me be clear, my dear—I've given it away for money only three times in my life and it was a question of real desperation, but I defy anyone to say that Maria Grazia is a whore, I defy anyone to even think it. I come from a town in the south, it's true, my town is a dead town, all the young people have given up, thrown in the towel. My father's still there, that slobbering drunk, and four of my six brothers and sisters, but I haven't seen them for years, that's my past, I fled as a child. I've had two husbands, three, no, five children, given up first to foster care, then adoption, eh, my dear, some people are born with the maternal instinct and some aren't, and now I'm alone, I'm not hiding these things, but I don't want anyone to associate me with those people there, those dirty tramps who come to steal bread from us Italians."

I nod again, I don't know why but I do. I have the illusion, agreeing with her, that time is passing more quickly. Time has a strange rhythm in this place, it's like the flow of time in a hospital. The squalor is suffocating, choking, a squalor that, strangely, you soon get used to, it tames you, drugs you, bringing you back to an almost animal stage.

"This pizza is good"—*chewing, she drips tomato on her shirt, she doesn't notice, and I wipe it off with a napkin*—"really, they warmed it up, hey, what are you doing? Oh, sorry, oh, oh, okay, no problem, sister, happens to me all the time. I spill things on myself, I know it's because I'm greedy, I'm hungry, and I don't always have something to eat, I've struggled sometimes to get a meal, my life is a mess, my mother died when I was eight, shit, order something else to eat, look at that slutty Bulgarian, her lipstick is smeared, it's making me lose my appetite."

She won't lose her appetite; at my grandfather's house she cleaned out the refrigerator after she killed him with that sort of modern statue that he bought at auction in London, the old fool. He was so pleased when he came back from that auction with those horrible, expensive pieces. He was especially proud of that statue—to me it was repulsive the moment I saw it, but I pretended to appreciate it with him. I make a great effort to maintain a certain style of life: I knew that the will was all in my favor, I knew roughly the amount, I mentally calculated what I would soon get my hands on, but I felt an uncontrollable rage for all that money thrown away on a stupid statue. Grazia grabbed it and bashed his head in. She could've used whatever she wanted, that wasn't a problem, all she had to do was kill that disgusting old man who had stopped supporting me, and then plant her fingerprints everywhere. Besides, she didn't like interference. She urged me not to get involved, and I didn't, she said that she knew her business. I can't say she was wrong.

"Look at the tracks when evening comes, this station seems different, there are souls walking on the platforms, dragging themselves, look at them, fragments that have survived, lives torn to pieces and then put back together, like mine, look at the scene, it's changed suddenly, what a strange effect, the platform must be very slippery, an intercity train just came through, some others should be arriving soon and then your cousin's."

"More wine?"

"Sure, sister, let's have more wine, basically you're set and so am I. I should be fine, no? And there's no risk, right? I'll listen to you, I'll lie low, hole up in my house and put those things in a safe place, and they'll say it was a robbery by those disgusting Romanians . . . Those disgusting Romanians . . . People like when they make headlines in the TV news, the talk about the safety of the citizens in the balance, about the dangers of immigration. Aaah ahhaha! I mean, immigration is a horror and it's dangerous too, and those people, look, right there"—*she points like a lunatic at a group of women and chil-*

dren getting on a bus—"are criminals, but let's say that in this case they've got nothing to do with it, but who cares, no? One more, one less . . . Heavens, I'm only forty-two, maybe with the jewelry, the gold coins I took—oh, your grandfather cared about them, they were carefully hidden—maybe with all those things I can reconstruct a scrap of a decent life for myself, get out of this wretched poverty."

She's wearing a low-cut gray sweater. Under it you can see a dirty, threadbare flesh-colored bra. A thickset man with a mustache enters the bar, in a horrible brown-checked shirt, a type of man you never see even by mistake in the places I usually frequent, art openings, sushi bars, exclusive parties—a man who must have short, dirty nails and bread crumbs in his mustache, I don't see them but I'm sure they're there—passes by, looks at her, ONLY at her, and this causes me, in spite of my horror at this man, a strange pang of jealousy; he stops a moment, casting his eyes on her décolleté, they linger there, bovine eyes the color of eggs fried too long, observing her abundant flesh; I can read in his expression a pleasant excitement, but how is it possible to be excited looking at this wreck? This human refuse that thinks about rebuilding a life when she'll never have a life, when her life will be so brief she can't imagine it. Here's some more wine, she must be drunk, or at least tipsy.

"You want some, dear? It's good, this wine, I like sparkling white wine, one of my two husbands—wait, ever since they beat me up outside Tiburtina, trying to steal a necklace, I've lost my memory. I was three months recovering, you know, I didn't lose my memory completely, but I have trouble remembering—one, maybe it wasn't even one of my husbands but a man I was with for a while, told me I didn't know shit about wine and had a typical woman's tastes, stupid tastes. Well, I don't give a fuck and I've always, and only, drunk sparkling white wine like this—it's very good. I was telling you. I could clean myself up, find a job, eh, what do you say, maybe with all those things it might be time for life to smile on me, to start going well, it never has, I've always been so unlucky. So unlucky."

She's crying. Well, it means she's getting drunk. I don't say anything; I've noticed that she doesn't like to be touched, she hates caresses, sudden physical contact, she's terrified when anyone—man or woman, doesn't matter—she's terrified when anyone touches her, she gets defensive, and it's no good if she loses her total trust right now. Other people's hands scare her, and it's understandable, poor thing—if anything about her worthless life can ever be understood—she was badly beaten up years ago. Maybe even as a girl, she took a violent beating on the street, she mumbled something like this the day I met her. Then there were the husbands and various boyfriends, the violence that she doesn't even count, but they worked her over, they reduced her brain to mush, her whole face is a scar, but all you want to do is hit her, she is so irritating, I'm sure that waitress would happily hit her, me too. And yet I needed a drifter with a residue of innocence. I came here many times, to the Tiburtina station, a neighborhood far away from the one where the "operation" was going to take place. I couldn't find anyone for my purpose in the wealthy neighborhoods, those chic, fashionable neighborhoods that my family liked, where I grew up protected by a ring of private schools, by the sharp vigilance of governesses, restrained by the paralyzing block of solitude whose echo I heard, room after room, in that labyrinthine house where, as a child, I lost the map of doors, verandas, windows. I was looking for someone suitable to do the dirty work and I found the right person, I was really very clever about it, she was perfect, my grandfather's house is full of her fingerprints, her traces, I wore gloves and didn't touch anything. She didn't ask me why, she didn't even notice, she carried out my orders with her bare hands, like an idiot. At last I'll be able to pay back the person who provides the coke, those types don't have much patience—first they give you the top-quality stuff without a fuss, you spoil your lover, your friends, you all snort it with that marvelous Dolce & Gabbana exclusive designer straw that's only sold abroad, and not everywhere (I found them in Ibiza during a quick trip for a party, and I bought ten to give to certain friends), they arrive punctually with the white powder, and your parties become the most sought after, your invitations the most in demand; the only thing is, then they present the bill, it's okay to make them wait a little, then give them a down payment, a diamond necklace, another small down payment, and meanwhile they continue to supply you and your lovers and friends, and then the debt goes up, it rises, that old bastard couldn't understand how much I NEEDED to have MORE money available, he took the liberty of prying into my finances to make a point about how my lifestyle seemed excessive to him. Come on, excessive? I have friends who go around with Arab millionaires, you have no idea the life they lead, I'm like a bum compared to them, I told him, but he wouldn't listen, he muttered moralistic tirades about good sense, ethics, growing up, once he even talked to me about a JOB. I started laughing and walked out, but is this really funny? Anyway, now the problem is solved. Good, first the debts, then I'll be able to buy that splendid apartment the filthy old man wouldn't give me for Christmas; he wanted to enjoy his money, he wanted to spend his last years in peace, but how the fuck was I supposed to manage? As soon as I saw that apartment I let it be known among the "rich people" that they'd better keep their clutches off it, that it would be mine. Well, I can't care too much about my reputation now. Even Sandro said he was going to leave. He's used to spending time in the gym, snorting the high-quality stuff whenever he wants, free access to the joint account, restaurants every night, and I began to find myself in serious trouble—that stubborn old man, all his fault. Really, you could say he asked for it.

"I might try to see my children again, I know it's not right to go and look for them when they've been adopted, it's not right to disturb the equilibrium of young kids, but they might have the desire too, might like to know me, to understand that I wasn't in any condition to take care of them when they were born, that I had big problems, and the new families might have a bit of compassion and decide at least to let me see them, to find out if they're well. We're waiting for your cousin, right? There's not much time left, it's rushing by. I understand, see-ing what happened. On the telephone she believed it about the robbery, right?"

Of course she believed it. She believed it so completely that she repeated the special offers of my telephone service provider. There is no cousin to pick up, but in about fifteen minutes we'll go to the track where the regional train passes, and a slight push will be enough, you might even slip by yourself but I'll help you, hap-pily, you'll end up under the train, and they'll find your foul body mangled and almost unrecognizable. Almost. I've managed to stick a couple of Grandfather's coins in your purse and a card from the restaurant he always went to—it will be easy to connect you to him. I'll be set, and so will you, basically, you poor derelict, you'll have stopped suffering. You'll die knowing you've done the world, and especially me, a favor by getting rid of that old man. He ter-rorized my parents for a lifetime with his despotic claims, he made my father a worm, with no balls and no will power, my mother an unstable neurotic who kept herself going with drugs and clinics, he sent my brother off to the United States. He allowed me, it's true, a comfortable life, but it was always as if he were giving me a handout, as if I should be content like a dog that picks at a bone with a piece of rubbery meat attached; that's how I felt, that old man was throwing me crumbs the way you throw birdseed to the pigeons, he thought he could humiliate me with impunity, at his pleasure, with that sadistic, distant little smile. Now he's lying in the enormous living room of his gloomy but (it's true) very beautiful villa, all those super-sophisticated alarm systems were of no use to him, I've always known the maid's day off, she's been with him for decades, more a slave than a housekeeper. I showed up at the gate timidly, saying I was with a friend, half a bottle of sleeping pills in his usual glass of port (incredible how alcohol enhances the effect of benzodiazepine), and everything unfolded naturally, without a hitch. He's lying beside the desk in the big living room, I don't know anymore how many floors or how many rooms the villa has, set in its vast park, cared for by a crowd of gardeners, I've never been interested, maybe that will go to my mother, but I know for certain that all the real estate, the stocks, and the money in the bank go to me (my brother's had a trust fund for years). Mama can keep the villa, she and I never see each other, I can't stand her crises and her sense of victimhood, and I could never live in the same place where he lived, ate, burped, peed, and where now he lies with bits of brain matter scattered over the expensive carpet. Drowned in a pool of red blood. Oh, no, really, I couldn't.

"Excuse me, have you looked at your watch?"

I was lost in my thoughts. Grazia wipes her mouth and points to my wrist. She's right, it's time.

"Gracious, it's late. Shall we go to the track?"

She nods, sways as she gets up, perfect, she's tipsy, swaying, and more ravaged-looking than usual. The waitress must have finished her shift because, with my fifty-euro bill, I pay another girl, one I hadn't noticed, and she doesn't seem to really notice us either; luckily I put on this scarf. I take the change and head to the exit, I check the track on the board, she's dawdling, I take her arm, we can't be late, and in fact we aren't late, the timing is absolutely perfect, she holds on and smiles at me, she stinks of poverty and empty hopes, and I can't wait to be free of her.

"I told you my daughter must be fourteen by now? It's true I don't have a maternal instinct, but sometimes I wonder how she is, if she resembles me, what sort of life she has, maybe she even has a boyfriend, what do you think? Oh shit, I'm boring, eh, always talking, I don't shut up for a moment, you've offered me a chance to change my life and I'm annoying you, wait, I'm going to trip, don't hurry so much, please, not so fast. I thought your cousin always goes in first class, here I am, I'm coming, how beautiful Tiburtina is in the evening, it looks like it's wrapped in velvet. Look, the train's coming. Which car is your cousin usually in?"

I ignore her, I have to concentrate. The spot is perfect, I feel a drop of sweat beading my forehead, but I have taken a tranquilizer, I've got to maintain perfect self-control, I can't make a mistake now, or it would all be in vain. She's looking at the train, her back's to me, she keeps asking about my cousin, I have to shut her up, it's time, just a little push, I reach out my arm . . .

"Don't move, stand still!"

They twist my arms behind me, they're hurting me, the train's coming, my heart is pounding, but what the fuck is happening? My plan, my project?

"What's happening, sister, the police, but what in the world? Tell me . . ."

There are four of them, they've put handcuffs on me, they lead me out of the Tiburtina station, pushing me, separating me from her. Grazia disappears from view, I stagger, I feel lost, then I recover and confront them: I try to say that they don't know who they're dealing with, they cannot even REMOTELY imagine who they're dealing with, that I belong to one of the most important families in the city. They aren't listening to me, it's disgraceful, the whole station seems to be blocked off, everyone's looking at me, I'm a freak to all these derelicts, an amusing sideshow. An itching sensation spreads along my back. I was supposed to carry out an act that would allow me grandeur for the rest of my days, and I'm reduced to an ordinary criminal, even that despicable Bulgarian whore looks at me and laughs, she roars with laughter, showing broken yellow teeth, Grazia was right, she was really right about the Bulgarians, about the Romanians, about this woman who took advantage of her good faith and robbed her, oh, she was right, because Grazia is my friend, no, she's not human waste, I never thought so, I had respect for her, you shit whore, you hurt her, I'm yelling that she hurt my friend and shouldn't have, then I spit on her, and I don't care if the cop on my right gives me a painful slap, my family's lawyer will take care of her, a prince among lawyers, who will come and get me out of this mess, the spit hits her in the face, when I see Grazia I'll tell her, I want her to be proud of me; the truth is, I've never had a friend like her, not even in high school. Okay, I wanted to push her under the train, help her slip, drunk as she was, but I would have done it unhappily, the circumstances were beyond my control. I'm almost glad it didn't happen, I miss her company, let's hope that they don't put me in isolation, that they let me stay with her. I'm not very talkative myself but I really like listening to her, and she's never quiet, I unfortunately have this voice that talks to me inside and a different voice that comes out of my mouth and says almost nothing, so I'm confused, but she, Grazia, she's tough, someone who knows her business, she even got Biagio to give her some shoes, thanks to a simple handjob, a hundred points to my friend. I could never make grandfather understand how much I needed the increase in my monthly check, a bonus and that apartment, I could never explain to him that he HAD to get it for me, otherwise he was going to shatter my life, shatter everything I had, I insisted, I talked, I insisted; instead, life is so simple, a handjob at the right moment is all you need, all you need is knowing what to use when you have to do something, and

*when you have to do it you do it, she taught me all that, I MUST
see her again, hear her talk . . .*

"You're in trouble, signora, serious trouble."

*Night descends over the tracks at Tiburtina and if you watched
carefully you would see that it really looks like velvet.*

Epilogue

We're in an anonymous room at the central police headquarters in Rome. A policewoman is talking to a woman who, it seems, is forty-two years old and is wearing a scarf, along with high-heeled sandals, a low-cut sweater of a light color, under which can be seen a pale bra, and a peasant skirt. Concealed behind a tinted window, several people observe the scene: the lawyer for the woman, whose name is Selvaggia Torri Livergnani; the vice-commissioner; one of the policemen who found the body of the grandfather, the well-known Count Edoardo Torri Livergnani; one of the policewomen who made the arrest; and a psychiatrist called in by the lawyer. The vice-commissioner speaks first:

"Sir, we found Count Livergnani lying on his back on the floor of the living room in his villa. The maid informed us, she's still in a state of shock. We hurried to the place and found fingerprints all over the crime scene, obvious signs and clues leading to the granddaughter, without the shadow of a doubt. We wanted to be sure, and we located her as she was heading toward the Tiburtina station. We followed her; she sat by herself for more than an hour in the bar, talking to herself, a jumble of disconnected fragments that attracted the attention of one of the waitresses, whose signed statement I have here. Then we understood, with conclusive evidence, that Signora Torri Livergnani intended to throw herself under an arriving regional train that was headed to the Termini station. At that point we were obliged to proceed to the arrest. I hope you see, sir, of course we understand the family's grief and would like to treat the case with maximum discretion."

"I understand perfectly," the lawyer says calmly. "But you see, and you can hear too, that she keeps asking about this imaginary friend Grazia, and when she's alone she talks to her and she answers, addressing a 'she' who isn't there, as if 'she' were the one who had actually committed the crime. What do you say, professor?"

"There will have to be an examination, but it strikes me as a clear case of split personality. If she's faking, she's a phenomenal actress—she should win an Oscar."

"Yes," the policewoman comments, speaking up, "she should win an Oscar if she's faking it. While we were leaving the track at the Tiburtina station she spat in the face of a Bulgarian woman, saying it was for what she had done to Maria Grazia, but we found no trace of any Maria Grazia. In the car, as we were bringing her here, she kept asking about this Grazia. Then she became silent for a moment and in a strange voice said, 'Don't worry, sister, they won't separate us.'

"Furthermore, I should add that Signora Torri Livergnani had camped out at the entrance to the Tiburtina station for several nights, and had already been removed once by the transit police, who also checked her documents. That's it."

"You can see that this is a very disturbed person, especially with the addition of these details."

Most of them nod in agreement.

Behind the glass, the woman, left alone, smiles.

"Really, sister? You spat at that Bulgarian whore? I'm proud of you, you were great. Now it looks like we're going to have some problems, eh, I understand, I'm not stupid, but I'm sure your powerful, wealthy family will get us out of this trouble as soon as possible, filthy rich people like you certainly don't need a scandal. They'll give us a hand, right?"

You can be sure of it, Grazia, you can be sure.

WORDS, THOUGHTS

BY MARCELLO FOIS
Via Marco Aurelio

Translated by Anne Milano Appel

From here I can barely glimpse my soul,
nor do I know how long my sojourn may be,
since death draws near, and life is fleeting.
—Francesco Petrarca, "Canzoniere LXXIX"

I

Six hours later . . .

They took a break around 6 in the afternoon. Outside the window of the interrogation room a perverse sun warmed the stones of the Colosseum. Marchini was one of those people who endured the heat with a kind of depressed resignation. To Curreli that same heat felt like the overly doting embrace of an unwelcome relative. What can you do, the commissioner said to himself, glancing at his watch: ten after 6, 104 degrees in the shade, who knows what the humidity is . . . another missed flight.

—Weren't you supposed to go home? Ginetti said, in fact, coming over with a folder.

—I missed the flight, was all Curreli replied.

Ginetti was all too familiar with the tone of such responses.

So he merely handed over the folder without even opening it and said, It was her, I'll bet my motorcycle on it. Fingerprints everywhere. She tried to wash them off, but you can tell she wasn't too much of an expert on domestic cleaning.

—Is that it? Curreli asked, seeing Marchini arriving with a cold soft drink in his hand.

—I thought you might need one, Marchini said and handed the can to the commissioner.

—It's not all, Ginetti said, as Curreli began to feel the coolness of the can radiating from his hand to his wrist. A look of gratitude was the most Marchini could expect from the commissioner for his good deed, and indeed that was all he got.

Curreli nodded to Ginetti to continue. Marchini was fanning himself, holding his arms out from his torso and brandishing them as if he were a Sumo wrestler about to land a blow, or a king penguin ready to leap off the rocks.

—She wasn't alone, Ginetti informed them.

Marchini seemed surprised, then immediately concealed the fact, seeing that Curreli, by contrast, didn't bat an eye.

—That's what I thought, Curreli confirmed, gulping down the contents of the can. What was that stuff? he asked.

Marchini smiled. Chinotto, he replied expectantly.

—I like sour orange, Ginetti remarked.

Curreli made a grimace of disgust. I think sour orange is revolting, he said, but with no particular emphasis.

Marchini tried to make excuses: That was all that was left in the vending machine.

Curreli ignored him and looked at Ginetti.

—The house is full of partial prints that don't belong to either the family members or the girl. We ruled out all the prints from people in places anyone could have had access to: the mailman, the neighbor . . .

—I got it, go on, Curreli cut him short.

—Well, in the bathroom and in the girl's bedroom we found the same type of print . . . The mailman doesn't go into the bedroom . . . right?

Marchini smiled faintly and shook his head. The girl had an accomplice? he finally asked.

Ginetti nodded. As sure as we're dying of heat today, he said, then asked, What does the girl say?

Curreli seemed to be in a daze. You're asking me? he said in turn, but he moved toward the interrogation room without waiting for an answer.

Marchini and Ginetti watched Curreli close the door behind him, then looked at one another.

—He's pissed, Marchini tried to explain. They were expecting him home, had his ticket already bought, but his plane left half an hour ago. Some pretty bad luck, you have to admit . . . Anyway, the girl hasn't opened her mouth, hasn't say boo . . . Not a word.

—She wasn't alone. I'll bet my motorcycle on it, Ginetti insisted. Prints don't lie, but all these super technicians yank my chain . . . If you know how to read the prints, I'm telling you, super technology is a jerk-off.

—You need jerking off by any chance, Ginetti? Marchini said.

Ginetti raised the middle finger of his right hand. And walked off toward his office.

Marchini discreetly headed back into the interrogation room. Dr. Vanni, the assistant district attorney, was beginning to reveal signs of how tired she was. A V-shaped sweat stain had spread over Curreli's chest. Without speaking, Marchini lifted his arm to feel if any cool air was coming out of the air conditioner. It was hopeless: not even a breath.

An incredible silence filled the room. Marchini looked at the girl, she was seated exactly as she had been six hours earlier, when she was summoned to come in and "talk" to the DA.

Dr. Vanni sat down in front of the girl and leaned toward her. Talking can only do you good, she murmured, her voice hoarse from exhaustion.

The girl looked at her, opened her mouth slightly as if to speak . . . but didn't . . .

I remember that night, you couldn't see even a few inches in front of you. I remember all of it. Almost all. You were afraid, you were trembling, you kept asking: Are you sure? You lowered your gaze like a small, spent sun. I watched you, I watched your eyes and I said to myself: Is that all? A man in the making, an overgrown child, an accomplice, a weapon. Take that thing off, I whispered, indicating your bright white sweater, take off your shoes too. And so we spent the minutes in silence while you removed your shoes and sweater. The problem was filling that silence, those long, empty minutes loaded with unasked questions. Outside the windows it was pitch black, a dark curtain covered everything. Don't scream, I said, lightly brushing your lips, don't scream. Are you hungry? I asked you at a certain point, toying with your hair. You shook your head no, but you tightened your arms around my hips. Strong as a sun at its zenith, you offered your mouth. For the kiss you closed your eyes and breathed through your nose. You entered the dark, you entered the moonless night. I broke away, bringing you back to the light: Are you afraid? I asked, breathing against your lips. A little, you said, offering another kiss. You mimed a small pain, a kind of intense suffering, but it was a desire to return to the dark. For there are things we women have always known and you men have always been unaware of. It had to have happened that way, as soon as we saw each other in the corridor at school, between classes, in the video game arcade, at the parish cinema, who knows? It had to have happened that way: I knew who you were.

—Look, if you continue acting like that it will be harder to find a way to help you. Dr. Vanni's voice was a sequence of peaks and valleys like the graph of an electrocardiogram. Marchini hurried to fill a glass of water from the cooler. He handed it to the DA and she thanked him with a smile.

—We know you weren't alone, Curreli ventured, taking advantage of the pause while Dr. Vanni swallowed.

For a moment the commissioner's voice seemed to rouse the girl. Her eyes moved in perfect accord, like a cat hearing a suspicious sound, or an owl detecting the squeak of a mouse . . . but it was just for an instant. Then the girl reentered her mute state. She nestled there, she hunkered down there.

—We'll be here all night. Dr. Vanni spoke her words with just a thread of a voice.

II
You should see her . . .

I knew you forever, I knew every single inch of your skin as soon as it was exposed to life. I knew things about you that even you didn't know. I could stare at you unseen, waiting for my gaze to surround you. I knew that you would turn around looking for me among the others. I knew that you would turn to your friend and ask: Do you know that girl? *That girl was me.*

On the other end of the line, Commissioner Curreli's wife took care to let him know that she no longer took anything for granted, far from it, she said, it was normal: When on earth had he ever come home when he said he was going to?

Still, she said, she had heard the news on TV and had gotten really frightened. Curreli nodded his head as if his wife could see him. She went on: Hardly more than a child, dear God, such a cruel act.

—You should see her, Curreli interrupted. You should see her, he repeated. You wouldn't believe she could do what she did.

The commissioner's wife sighed over the line.

Curreli wanted to tell her that she was the same age as their oldest daughter, but he remembered that if his wife had seen the news broadcast she already knew that.

—She's a child, the woman remarked as if reading his mind.

—Sure, a "child" who massacred an entire family. Curreli imagined seeing his wife cross herself in fear.

—My God, she whispered. And now?

—And now we'll see what happens . . .

—Did you eat anything?

—With this heat?

—Of course, what, when it's hot you stop eating? Order something cool, and eat a lot of fruit, will you? You always forget to eat . . .

—Hmm, we'll see, Dr. Vanni gave us a two-hour break, since the girl isn't talking . . . Marchini says he knows a place that has pretty good food . . . Incidentally, let me talk to Manuela.

A few seconds passed during which it became clear that the commissioner's wife and Manuela were discussing whether his daughter would come to the phone.

Finally, in a hurried voice: Hi, Dad . . .

—Sweetheart, everything all right? Curreli asked.

At least ten seconds of silence from the receiver . . . Well,

Manuela finally grumbled. Look, Dad, I'm in the middle of something. She broke off, and before Curreli could say good-bye the receiver had already been handed back to his wife.

—What's wrong with her now? Curreli asked.

—Ah, *what's wrong*, Giacomo! She's seventeen, that's what's wrong . . . God help us . . . Nothing pleases her . . . One day she's too fat, the next day she's too short . . . Nothing fits her . . . What do I know . . . ?

—Put her back on.

—Giacomo . . . she doesn't want to, you know how she is . . . I'll talk to her . . .

—Don't tell me it's still because of that earring! Curreli snapped.

—I'll talk to her, his wife repeated. Go and eat something.

There was a full moon that absorbed your light. And you a rising star. The first time I took your hand, you looked straight ahead and continued walking, you didn't do a thing, you left it up to me. You barely responded to the pressure of my fingers. I studied you: You were stunning, with a beauty all your own. You were attractive like the beginning of a world can be attractive. Nothing more. And that wasn't why I chose you. You could have stopped me if you were a man, but you aren't, you've never been, and who knows if you will ever become one at this point.

—I've always wondered what goes through people's minds to make them commit such acts, Marchini said, sucking the meat of a clam directly from the shell . . . Fuckin' heat, it won't even cool off at night.

Curreli was stabbing an excessively oily seafood salad with his fork.

I was born on a luminous night; I struggled because I knew. I didn't want to come out: too much light, too much exertion, too much terror. Everyone looked so extraordinarily happy: What a magnificent baby, what expressive eyes, what delicate hands. *The rest is lived in silence, because my life has been coals beneath the ashes. My life has been trying to exist; it's been an indigestion; it's been seeing and hearing something that I was unable to grasp.*

You're in too much of a hurry, *they said,* you'll recognize that eventually . . . *How many times I screamed at my image in the mirror without opening my mouth:* I hate you, I hate you, I hate you! *I screamed this, because my life felt like a pair of tight shoes.*

In Curreli's dish the tentacles of the squid seemed like arabesques, the little coils of crab meat were pitiful, only the green of the sliced celery looked good and the orange fruit of the ripe mussel. Commissioner Curreli thought it was hopeless: The seafood salad was an aberration so far from the sea, in a trattoria for truckers in the center of Rome. Then he thought maybe this particular seafood salad was a painting by Miró, or maybe not, maybe Kandinski. Certainly Kandinski with Miró's curves . . .

—. . . to commit such acts . . . Aren't you hungry? Marchini's voice came from far away.

Curreli raised his head from his plate. I can't stand the fact that the girl isn't talking, I've never been able to put up with people who insult you with silence.

—Maybe she's simply realized that she has nothing to say.

—Sure, and by not talking she ends up exterminating her family . . . They always do that. You know, don't you, that I have a daughter who is seventeen?

Marchini nodded. Muzak was coming from the TV on the restaurant wall, meant to emphasize the day's news:

. . . The party responsible for the slaughter of the Amadesi family—the mother Laura, her twin children Luca and Denis, the paternal grandmother Erminia—has a face and a horrifying name: Deborah Amadesi. The seventeen-year-old was detained by the assistant district attorney in charge, Elena Vanni, after the young woman was summoned as someone having information about the matter. The interrogation, which has gone on for twelve hours now, does not appear to have produced results. According to investigators, the girl has withdrawn into absolute silence, overwhelmed by the circumstantial evidence. The area is being combed in search of an accomplice, who according to well-informed sources may have helped the girl commit this horrendous crime.

—You don't know what a child's silence means, you have no way of knowing how terrible it is. It's better not to have them at all, kids, Curreli blurted out for no apparent reason.

—You're talking like that because you're tired, Marchini responded.

III
Let me die.
That's how I implored, at night: I hate you, let me die.

Deborah Amadesi narrowed her eyes a little. Up till now she had not shifted position, she had endured the questions without losing her composure. Curreli had confronted her, looking her straight in the eye.

—You know, don't you, that what's happening here is just a farce?

It was then that Deborah Amadesi narrowed her eyes for the first time. So that she almost seemed to be forcing herself not to cry.

—*Everything* is a farce with you kids, the commissioner burst out.

Dr. Vanni looked at him with growing concern.

—Nothing is ever enough, right? the commissioner continued. There's always someone who has something that you don't have and as luck would have it that thing is vital!

The girl went back to her catatonia, but her expression had totally changed: She seemed watchful now, and riveted, like a gazelle ready to sidestep an attack or a lioness ready to launch one.

But everything moved forward relentlessly. Time went about its business in the tedious recurrence of days. I had one persistent thought: I wanted it to end. I was afraid of that void disguised as everything. And I was afraid of becoming like my mother. Who was a terrible model, who was both suffering and joy, who was pain and sacrifice, who was sweetness, who was a rising moon, luminous, full of expectation. She would have understood and would have been willing to die for me. Like the time when I suddenly felt that cramp in my stomach. Then blood. And everything I had ever known came to an end. I ran to my mother's room and wept. And Mamma smiled a broad smile. I remember very well what she said to me. It's like dying a little, she said, because women safeguard the mystery of death: It's the price they have to pay to give life.

My breasts grew, then it was a matter of dissembling. Though maybe it was only a way of existing. In school, at the gym, in church. Eating in the evening, smoking in the afternoon, drink-

ing in the morning. Testing the limits. Screaming at night. Ready to sacrifice myself. I had already been dying a little for some time. And she, my mother, was already dead, only she didn't know it. My father, no, he was a scorching hot sun, a constant, merciless high noon. Pure power, truth and justice. Far away, who knows where. Why aren't I him? Why aren't I his? Why don't I have that satisfied, contented gaze? Why did he go away? He could have loved me, but like all men, he was afraid. Because men's power lies in not having any power: That's how they win all the time. They make us think that their weakness depends on us, but they are weak to begin with and that's all there is to it. It's simple. Killing him would not have been necessary. A waste of time. Again.

Silence. Dead silence. Curreli leaned forward until his nose was almost touching that of the girl.

—A farce, he repeated. Because we know all there is to know. Do you hear me?

The last question was an octave higher. Marchini jumped in his chair. Deborah Amadesi did not budge, not even to avoid the commissioner's heavy breath.

—We know you have an accomplice and we'll find him within a few hours . . .

Then, unexpectedly, you arrived. You who were there at the beginning of it all and breathed my breath.

—Then, unexpectedly, you arrived. You who were there at the beginning of it all and breathed my breath, Curreli read, showing the girl a twisted strip of paper. You had it in your pocket. What is it, a rock song? If you would be kind enough to tell us which "you" you were referring to, maybe we'd lose less time and maybe the DA would also keep this in mind.

The girl didn't bat an eye. Absolutely nothing.

I remember that night well, it wasn't even romantic without a moon like that, it was filthy and shabby. We made love in my room and you said how great it would be if it could always be this way. Without knowing it, you said something dangerous. I repeated: If it could always be this way? You looked at your watch: What time does your mother get back? you asked. She won't be back, I replied, she won't ever be back.

As she smoked a cigarette in the corridor, Dr. Vanni shook her head. Time is running out, she said. As soon as the attorney arrives, we're done.

—What could happen? Marchini said ironically. The witness stops talking?

Both the commissioner and the assistant district attorney found the line rather funny, but by some unspoken agreement decided not to show the inspector, who laughed on his own without missing his associates in the least.

—What does Ginetti say about the prints? Vanni asked.

Curreli shook his head before responding.

—Partial and too deteriorated to tell us anything. If the girl doesn't talk, all we can do is speculate about the accomplice . . .

—Maybe it *is* only conjecture, Marchini remarked. This time Curreli and Vanni laughed heartily . . .

IV
What did you do?

Then, suddenly, it was all over . . . and she'll never be back. My mother didn't even have time to suffer. We embraced each other, I embraced you. In the night that was vanishing, I saw too many things that were vanishing with it. It was at that point that I thought about it, and it was as if I understood everything: that it wasn't her, that it wasn't freedom, that it wasn't continuing to strike her, covering her mouth so she wouldn't scream, that it wasn't even my mother, that body on the floor drenched in its own blood. I embraced you; you, as usual, looked at me, your eyes half-closed.

I begin to laugh because you're strange and you don't want me to talk. You ask yourself so many questions, seeing my mother there on the floor. I hear them banging around inside your head, I feel you taste them on your palate and try to remove them from your teeth with the tip of your tongue, like a candy that is too sticky. For my dear little brothers and my grandmother, it was like fulfilling a duty, you know? See, the worst thing was discovering the pointlessness, discovering that all my thinking and thinking and thinking wouldn't affect anything . . . discovering that the enemy had not been defeated. I'm laughing because I see that you're uneasy, an uneasiness that is new . . . you, who believed blindly, now begin to have doubts . . . and night is collecting its things and day arrives and the light returns and the void comes back to life and nothing seems important anymore, not even this fiction of ours.

Seeing the girl's faint smile was a strange experience. In the interrogation room, Curreli, Marchini, and Vanni, after sixteen hours, felt like the survivors of a silent shipwreck. That place, that table, every single floor tile, had heard all types of confessions, voices, lies, but never such stubborn silence. Curreli instinctively returned the smile, as if all those sixteen hours spent together were nothing but a long, grueling prologue.

—Did I tell you I have a daughter your age? the commissioner suddenly asked.

The girl couldn't help briefly shaking her head.

Curreli sat down: I was wondering if you could help me.

See, my daughter won't talk to me, she wants to put a diamond stud in her nose . . . Well . . . you seem knowledgeable
about these things.

Deborah thrust her head back until you could hear the
bones of her neck snap.

—How can we help you kids if you won't speak to us,
huh? What, exactly, have we done to deserve so much hatred?
What? Curreli implored with feeling. The face of his daughter
Manuela had suddenly superimposed itself on that of Deborah seated before him.

The girl looked at him with a mix of astonishment and
affection. Dr. Vanni and Marchini could not believe their
eyes when she reached out a hand to caress Curreli's stubbly
cheek.

*Then something extraordinarily clear appears in your eyes. What
did you do? you ask. Just like that. As if you had realized that, in
the tedious course of things, it is nevertheless impossible to get away
with a slaughtered body scot-free. And I know what's left. What's
left is to end it. Get dressed and go, I say. And you? you ask. Me,
I'll manage, I say. I'll manage. I stand waiting to hear the door
close behind you as you leave. I glance around me, looking for . . .
looking for a plausible finale . . . and it all seems clear to me . . .*

With incredible lightness the girl rose from the chair, leaned
toward the commissioner, and whispered a name, just a
name.

PART III

PASTA, WINE & BULLETS

CHRISTMAS EVES

BY GIANRICO CAROFIGLIO

Stazione Termini

Translated by Ann Goldstein

I t was Christmas Eve, in the vast concourse of Stazione Termini.

Marshal Bovio, his mood grim, his hands deep in the pockets of his big regulation overcoat, swam against the current of a desolate river of men and women. Small groups of pinched dark faces; lost gazes and a few laughs—too loud—to summon up cheer; the faces of vagrants, of old women bent over shopping carts, pushing their little piles of possessions. Unmindful—or unconscious—of everything around them. Normal faces, having ended up there by mistake, on Christmas Eve, in the cold of the station rather than the warmth of their own houses.

The marshal leaned against the locked door of the information office, looked at his watch—7:30—and took out an MS from the crumpled, half-empty pack, lit it, and inhaled deeply.

Many years earlier, he recalled, he had been on duty on Christmas Eve when a traveler was knifed to death, near the track where the last local for Nettuno departed.

The whole night had been spent interrogating the derelicts who lived in the station because they had nowhere else to go.

The murderer had been an illegal taxi driver, a slightly disfigured little man whose name the marshal couldn't remember.

The man's face, however, he remembered clearly—a sick-looking face, the jaw shaken by a silent weeping, an animal sob after the last smack. The first gray light of Christmas Day was mixed with the yellow streetlights and the bitter odor of humanity, of fear of officialdom after a night of interrogation. Robbery and homicide for the disfigured taxi driver. Life in prison. Bovio had heard nothing more of him after the trial.

He inhaled the last drag of his cigarette, smoked down to the filter, and let it fall to the ground.

At home they must all be gathered by now for the big dinner—a southern family, traditions still strong—and for the exchange of gifts, after the flavors of Christmas, fragrance of homemade sweets, brilliant colors, and comforting warmth.

The newspaper seller near the information booth was preparing to close. He chaotically piled up newspapers and magazines inside the kiosk with the unconscious speed of one who fears being excluded from something.

An old woman with a cart approached the newsstand. A vagrant, with those dirty bags, those ragged sacks stuffed full of things. But there was something that set her apart—a strange dignity, perhaps—from the desperate, the destitute who wandered like melancholy phantoms through the station and around the idle trains. She wore a thick sweater and a man's jacket; underneath was a long bright-colored skirt, cheerful; her hair was gathered under a carefully knotted kerchief. She began to attentively examine the magazines that the newspaper seller had not yet put away. She delicately leafed through one, as if she were looking for an article, or something.

Then she turned to the proprietor. She had a thousand lire in her hand.

"*L'Unità*," she said.

The newspaper seller looked up and hesitated a moment before answering.

"*L'Unità* costs two thousand lire today. It's Sunday, it has the supplement." He seemed to be apologizing.

The old woman withdrew the money hand with the banknote but remained in front of the newsstand. She was still there, unmoving, when Bovio's large hand reached out of his dark overcoat and placed a thousand lire in hers.

She looked up slowly, up to the marshal's face. "What a kind person." Her voice was thin but firm. "I hope that you may be granted everything you wish for."

Then she turned, passed the two thousand lire to the newspaper seller, took her paper with the supplement, and moved along with her cart.

He stood looking at her. He was slightly ashamed of that blessing, so disproportionate with respect to his own instinctive gesture, which now seemed to him petty. He watched her move into the distance, into a remote corner of the immense concourse.

He took ten thousand lire from his wallet, clutched it in his hand, and slipped the hand in his pocket. He would catch up with the old woman, give her that money, and then hurry away, before anyone could see him.

So he began walking, feeling strangely embarrassed.

The old woman, meanwhile, had taken out a small broom and had begun to sweep her corner. All around, against the walls, under a scaffolding in front of the billboards that displayed the timetables, the homeless were preparing for Christmas.

Some were already asleep, rolled up in newspaper sheets, sheltered in cardboard huts, having closed their eyes knowing nothing of tomorrow. Others, awake, scanned the void or tended to themselves like tired old cats. One had his pants rolled up; his calves were covered with scabs that he picked at conscientiously, one by one, concentrating, his eyes, like a stray dog's, red with some awful disease.

Now the marshal was just a few meters from the old woman. She had her back to him and continued to sweep. Serene, with the air of one who is placidly seeing to her own domestic affairs. Bovio was about to call out to her, when he felt a pang of nostalgia and the blurred memory of some distant Christmas. Corridors, lights, and lost rooms. Voices of excited children, yearnings from the vortex of the past.

Absurdly, he realized that it was not his memory.

Just as absurdly, he thought that he must return it to the old woman.

He took a few more steps, almost staggering, with a buzzing in his head and the hand in his pocket contracted around the ten thousand lire.

"Marshal."

The voice of the young police officer was like a rock smashing a window. The marshal turned suddenly, with a guilty expression, it seemed to him. He quickly pulled his hand out of his pocket as if hiding evidence; he began walking away in a hurry.

"What is it?" The voice sounded too high, and fake.

He didn't turn back.

BERET

BY CARLO LUCARELLI

Vicolo del Bologna

Translated by Kathrine Jason

There's a radio's playing. It's coming from one of the upstairs apartments, and it's got to be turned way up because we can hear it clearly, low but clearly. So much the better. It helps drown out the noise we're making.

Moretti gives me a look and nods, as if he's read my mind. This has been happening more and more often recently. He looks at me, nods his head, and says what I was going to say. Either we've become telepathic or he can read my face like a book.

"Hurry up, move it!" Moretti says, and Agello pushes the key further into the keyhole. It makes a loud, metallic squeak, but it's muffled by the music. The click of the lock is even louder, but now it's a question of moments, split seconds.

Moretti raises the pistol, holding it near his face, the back of his hand against the wool fabric of the beret covering his forehead. He gives the door a kick, straight-on, with the sole of his shoe, and it opens. In split seconds, one split second, we're all inside, me with the MP5 raised, selector set to rapid fire. Albertino, ready with the twelve-caliber SPAS, Moretti aiming the Beretta with two hands, thumb on thumb, and

Agello, with another Beretta and his arm raised to hurl a grenade, the pin already out.

But hurl it where? The apartment is just this, this room
behind the door—table, chairs, kitchenette, a fake brick arch-
way from which a transparent curtain hangs, and beyond it a
bed. The apartments in Trastevere are usually tiny, but this is
extreme.

A split second. Being the closest, I take a step, brush the
curtain aside with my arm, turn the barrel of the gun, but I
can see right away that there's nobody here.

No, actually, there is somebody: There's a sound like a
sigh behind a small door in the wall, next to the kitchenette.
It's barely louder than a murmur and it's muffled in the music
that floats down the stairwell to where we stand.

A split second. Moretti kicks the door and the lock in
the small door rips away from the jamb. Moretti and Albertino and I step in, weapons raised, and Moretti yells, "Police,
stop!" hollering so loudly that the music from upstairs suddenly stops.

The girl sitting on the toilet clearly has no intention of
moving. In fact, if not for her lips, which are trembling, she
could be dead. She's sitting paralyzed, a roll of toilet paper in
her hand and her underpants at her ankles, eyes fixed on us,
in our black body suits and ski masks, crammed together in a
bathroom of a few square feet, shower and all.

Moretti raises his fist and we all lower our weapons.

"Shit," he mutters.

There's a radio playing. It's from an apartment across the hall, at
the end of the landing. I know that because the last time the girl
brought me food, I asked her and she told me it was coming from
over there. She says she listened at the door and heard it. MTV,

she said. It's on practically all day, and it reaches all the way to my apartment, through two closed doors, not loud enough to be annoying but loud enough that I can hear it, as if the TV is on low in another room.

I've gotten used to it. That must be why I realized the second it stopped. Or maybe because first I heard a door slam, and then that shout I couldn't understand. Rude assholes, I thought, but then the music stopped and that made me suspicious. So I got up from bed, grabbed the 356 from the bedside table, and went to the door.

"He's not here," Moretti yells down the stairwell, and moments later everyone comes up: agents in uniform, top brass, the chief of the mobile squad, and even the judge. They rush up the stairs to the landing. "Stay back, please. Police!" shouts an official as doors open. Nobody comes out, except one woman in a bathrobe and slippers on an upstairs landing who won't back off from the railing, so we have to send an agent up.

"Bad tip," says Moretti to the judge. "Marcos isn't here and the girl's got nothing to do with it, she's shoots video for television. She went back into the bathroom, but I'll bet she raises hell when she comes out."

"Vicolo del Bologna," the judge says. "Number 5B. The informant was sure."

"The informant was wrong. This is number 5 and Marcos isn't here."

"What if he only got the side of the building wrong?"

I hear them knocking at the door. Police, open up! And they don't rush right in. They're cautious. They're right to be.

We go in with our weapons ready, shoo away the people on the landing, take a quick look around, then the agents follow and we move on to other apartments. We begin on the third-floor landing. A huge dog leaps out from one apartment and Agello nearly shoots him. Next door there's a journalist who wants to come along, and we have to shut him inside. Outside, the vicolo is blockaded and nobody can pass.

On the lam you can spend your dough well or badly. I spent it badly. I'm not saying on chicks and champagne—even though this one does bring food and she'd be willing. But at least I should have planned on having somewhere to run. That, yes. A skylight, the possibility of jumping down to another street. Here there's no way out, just a clothesline suspended across a closed courtyard.

So I'm thinking there are only three possibilities. I surrender, open the door, slide the gun down the stairs, say, I'm alone and unarmed. Or I don't surrender, grab the grenades on the dresser, throw them down the stairs, and then make a run for it with the submachine gun I keep next to the bed, and either I make it or I'm fucked. Or else, I stand ready with the pistol, the door open a crack, and decide what to do when the first mug appears.

The door of that last apartment is slightly open. Maybe they left it like that by accident and nobody's home, or maybe some cooperative citizen opened it and is waiting for us to arrive. I'm the nearest to it—clutching my MP5 like a pistol, my hand ready to give the door a shove—in my black combat fatigues and waterproof boots that keep sticking to the tile floor. Then, suddenly, something that hasn't happened to me in a long time happens. I can't stand the beret, and the wool ski mask is itching the hell out of my sweaty skin. My wet breath is slimy on my lips and I feel like I'm go-

REMEMBER ME WITH KINDNESS

BY MAXIM JAKUBOWSKI

Calcata

His budget flight landed in Fiumicino. It was a hot, humid summer day.

Even though he held a CEE passport, the uniformed border officer at immigration control looked up and actually asked him whether he was visiting Rome for business or pleasure. As inquisitive as an American airport official.

"Sentimental reasons," he answered, and was then allowed through with no further comment.

Maybe the border guard had been bored or something, as he had never been asked any such question on the occasion of his previous, numerous visits.

He had only hand luggage so went straight through into the main terminal's arrivals hall and made a beeline for the car rental desks. He had no need for anything fast or fancy in the way of transport, but he still had to convince the rental clerk that he actually prefered a car with a manual gear shift rather than an automatic. Habits die hard. After filling in the forms and signing on all the dotted lines, he was handed the keys to a dark blue Fiat and given the directions to the parking lot where it was kept.

He walked out into the midday sun and looked around. On his last time here, she'd been waiting, with her usual both wanton and joyfully innocent smile, wearing a white skirt and carrying a huge canvas bag embroidered with sunflowers, an ing to barf. It's broiling today, though I'm used to the heat. Still, this time I can't seem to go on. So I pull off the beret with one hand, then let out a sigh of relief, but fuck, the TV's off now. I reach out again with the ski mask clenched between my fingers and push the door open.

I'm thinking I already have three life sentences. I'm thinking I'll be better off if they kill me. I'm thinking: Now these asshole Rambos have me really fucked.

So I raise the barrel of the 356, and when the door opens, some guy's big red face appears right there in the viewfinder. His eyes are bugging in surprise, his mouth's hanging open, and a clump of sweaty hair is sticking straight up on one side of his head; it looks like he couldn't even brush it back down if he wanted.

Split seconds. Three. One, to mentally superimpose the mug shot onto that face: It *is* Marcos. Two, to realize I'm a goner. Three, to take the first shot. But then there's no need because he raises his arm, aiming the pistol at the ceiling, and keeps it like that until I grab it. Then the other guys rush in.

He keeps on staring at my head, even when we pull his hands behind his back to cuff him. He seems to be laughing. I put a hand up to my head and feel a stiff shank of hair that the beret pressed up at a weird angle. It sometimes looks like that in the morning if I've slept funny on the pillow. When I was little, my brother and I called it the arrow. I push it down with my hand but it springs back up.

"Hey, cop," Marcos says as I grab him by the arm to escort him out. "That hair of yours there, it looks like it needs a cut."

And he laughs, the jerk.

accessory she'd bought six months earlier in Barcelona and which made her look like a schoolgirl rather than a full-grown woman.

He settled into the driver's seat, keeping the door open for a few minutes to allow the heat to escape from the car's interior before the air-conditioning kicked in, while his feet found the measure of the pedals, getting himself accustomed again to driving a car on the opposite side of the road and having the steering wheel on the left-hand side. It always took a little acclimation, however many times he had to rent cars abroad.

And finally, he drove off toward the city. Considering it was the main road connecting Rome to one of its major airports, there was something old-fashioned and narrow about this street which made him think of all the legions of Caesar and past emperors and despots who'd in all likelihood marched down these avenues upon returning from or departing for battle many years before. No modern highway this, more of a cobblestone alley in places, with twin ramparts of trees on either side and occasional low stone walls pouring with ivy, possibly erected long before even Mussolini.

It was as if the twenty-first century hadn't yet broken here, despite the gleaming modern cars racing up and down the road, all splendidly oblivious to any speed limit. He was in no real hurry and, irritated by his leisurely pace, some of the other drivers honked at him repeatedly.

He'd found a room on the Internet in a small residential hotel close to Piazza Vittorio Emanuele II. It was a quiet side street and easy to park, even though he wasn't sure if the parking space he had chosen was illegal or not. At any rate, he couldn't be bothered about parking tickets and was confident the Fiat wouldn't be towed away since it wasn't blocking anyone, and many other local vehicles were lined up on the same side of the street. The hotel was situated on the fourth floor of a massive apartment building and suited him fine: a clean, spacious, if somewhat Spartan place, just a reception desk manned by a young student busy revising her journalism and publishing exams, she informed him, and a small breakfast salon at the other end of the corridor from his room. He didn't require anything more. There were bars all across the city, and anyway he didn't drink. Never had. More taste than principle, even if he found that it led to some people gossiping behind his back back in London, and he was often suspected of being an ex-alcoholic. Print the legend, he thought; it's miles more glamorous than the truth.

He changed into a clean shirt and walked toward Via Cavour and Stazione Termini. Here, the package he had ordered was left, as promised, in the luggage locker he had been sent a key for the week before. The transaction had not proven cheap, but then again, money was now the least of his worries. The gun had been left at the bottom of a plastic Rinascente bag in which the seller had buried it, with no sense of irony, under a crumpled mess of seemingly used women's silk lingerie. This was not the ideal place to check the weapon out, but it appeared in good shape, and should contain six bullets. He would not require more. He treated himself to an espresso at one of the station's cafeterias and watched with melancholy how the two spoons of sugar drifted slowly toward the bottom of the small cup. Just the way espresso coffee should behave, he recalled her teaching him when they were still together. He sketched a wry smile for any curious onlookers. The coffee and sugar boost gave him a fresh sense of purpose, renewed his determination to see this all through.

He walked away from the bar and the busy train station and took the direction of the Campo dei Fiori, past the
unescapable ancient monuments surrounded by wide-eyed
tourists. Shortly after crossing the Piazza Vidoni, the Roman
streets became quieter again, as if foreigners no longer ventured this far, beyond their self-circumscribed tourist enclave,
and he made his way down Corso Vittorio Emanuele II until
he reached the Feltrinelli bookshop. He walked upstairs and
ordered his second espresso of the day and a panini and sat at
the edge of the store's balcony watching the customers mill
below as they picked up random books and shopped at their
leisure. She had once written to him, a long time ago, before
they had even slept together and were still enjoying a mildly
flirtatious stream of e-mail communications, that this was her
favorite spot in all of Rome to waste time, meditate, observe
others, casually do her homework. On his fateful initial visit
here, this was also the first place she'd taken him and they
had spent an hour here, nervously silent most of the time,
knowing that a few hours later they would be in bed together
for the first time. He remembered every single moment—the
perfume she had worn, the heat radiating from her white skin
as their knees brushed against each other and she contrived
to make her cappuccino last forever as if scared to move on to
the next, concrete and physical stage in their affair.

He didn't expect to find her here today. She was now
studying in a different area, but still he had to come visit the
place again. Just in case. To commune with the past. To reopen
old wounds. To feel the hurt inside. It was foolish, he knew,
but if he had to march down this calvary road of his own making, the Feltrinelli bookshop could not be avoided. The latest
novel by Walter Veltroni and the Italian edition of the final
Harry Potter book were piled high by the cash registers and

staff kept on replenishing the displays on a steady basis. He'd
sent her the English-language edition of the Rowling when it
had appeared, but by then they were no longer on speaking
terms and she had not even thanked him or acknowledged
the gift, one of many over the months they had known each
other. The first book she had sent him as a gift was a collection of stories by Italo Calvino. Strange how he remembered
every single, irrelevant detail.

Finally, his stomach reminded him he hadn't had a real
meal since a dim sum in London's Chinatown the day before,
so he left the bookshop and headed across the Corso Vittorio
Emanuele II toward the Campo dei Fiori and the Pollarolla
restaurant where he had a pleasant memory of *fragole di bosco*
with a fine dusting of sugar. Of course, he had also taken her
there, once upon a time. Because of a stomach condition,
she was not allowed to eat any spicy food, which he'd always
considered something of a tragedy. But the meal today, *insalata
verde* and *risotto ai funghi,* could not feed the pain inside, and
later, as he walked back to his hotel, he made a detour by
Stazione Termini and under cover of darkness surrounded by
rushing commuters and loitering teenagers he slipped his left
hand deep into the plastic bag he had now been carrying for
half of the day and felt the hard grip of the gun down there. It
felt real. By Stazione Termini he sat down and wept.

He woke up early. Escaping the inevitable dreams of her, of
them. The sheer epiphany of her body, the ever so subtle and
patently unique color of her nipples, the broadness of her
smile, the terrible harshness of her words on the phone the
last time he had called her, the luscious sound of her sigh every time he had penetrated her. The places they'd been, the
things they'd said.

He always woke up early these days, maybe as an automatic reaction to the sleeping memories of her and the abominable pain they invariably inflicted on his soul.

He adjusted his eyes, wiped the night away, and moved his right leg.

Yes, he was in Rome.

Alone.

He passed on breakfast, picked up a map of the city from an older woman now manning the hotel's reception desk, and, avoiding the elevator and its ornate metal grille, walked down the stairs to the street and found the rental car. He hadn't been ticketed, after all. Small mercies.

He pulled the gun from the depths of the Rinascente plastic bag and moved it to the glove compartment. Not an ideal place to keep it, but there were few good hiding places in the hotel room. He would just have to drive carefully and not attract police attention. The busy Roman traffic would help.

Before driving off, he phoned Alessandra, Giorgio, and Marina and made appointments to see them separately throughout the day. They were all surprised to find out he was in Rome, but sounded happy enough to meet up with him.

With the festival organizers he talked about books and movies and cultural politics. As they always did when they met at events. It was amazing how buoyant they remained every single year in the face of mounting difficulties in obtaining funding, grants, and sponsorships. Of course, they asked him why he was in Rome. "Just passing through," he would answer with a fake smile, and this seemed to satisfy them. They embraced and made a vow to see each other again at the next festival and went their separate ways.

Alessandra knew a small trattoria in the Trastevere, concealed within a labyrinth of cobbled streets and small churches only a local could navigate with impunity and find a way out of again. He meekly followed her. Night was falling. Inside, he felt ever so empty. Following the break-up with Desi, he had almost fallen into bed with Alessandra since both had been on the rebound from heart shattering affairs. But it hadn't happened. They knew each other professionally, and she had also been aware of his relationship with Desi, as they both free-lanced for the same magazines. Maybe it was because neither of them were sufficiently head over heels about the other, or maybe they both lacked the energy for purely recreational sex. Sometimes you want the tenderness and the feelings, and the physicality wasn't enough to conquer the inner thirst. At any rate, after a failed attempt at meeting up in Paris for a tryst, they'd drifted apart, either to other adventures or, in his case, a desert of loneliness. He expected nothing of tonight either. It was just a way of saying goodbye to a friendship. No less, no more.

The cuisine was Sicilian and for the first time ever he tried pasta with sardines, followed by great bowls of steamed shell-fish, with a succulent sauce they both soaked up with freshly baked local bread. The small piazza outside the restaurant was shrouded in darkness as he looked out of the windows of the restaurant, somehow expecting Desi to walk by at any moment, like a ghost from the past.

"Still thinking about her?" Alessandra asked.

"Yes," he answered. "It's a sickness. I know. Don't tell me."

"There's a character in Marquez's *Love in the Time of Cholera* who tries to cure himself of a case of unrequited love by bedding 622 women," she remarked, as if proposing a cure.

"It would feel too much like revenge," he pointed out. "Anyway, it wasn't unrequited. I have pages and pages of e-mails, text messages, and letters to prove it. And I know every square inch of her body at rest and play, every obscene crease and every single silky surface."

"You always had a wonderful way with words . . ." Alessandra sighed.

"But words are insufficient now," he answered. "Powerless. She no longer answers my messages, listens to me. She probably thinks I've gone mad. And she's probably right."

"Did you come to Rome to try and see her?" Alessandra asked.

"No," he said. "I don't know. Maybe I just came for myself . . ."

He offered to drive her back to her apartment on the other side of the river.

The car moved along the Tiber on the Lungotevere heading north. Even at this time of night, the traffic was thick. Alessandra insisted on smoking a cigarette. He opened his window and looked out. Across the river was an old-fashioned building, white and functional under the light of a three-quarter moon: the San Filippo Neri Hospital. A knot twisted inside his stomach—wasn't this where she had been born or where her father, the surgeon, worked? Or both?

Alessandra invited him up for a final coffee, but he declined.

"I have to get up early in the morning," he said. It would have been pointless.

Back on the hotel bed, he prayed for sleep. When it finally came, hours later—the sounds of the Roman night punctuated by sirens and the odd boisterous laugh of passersby in the street outside—it was an ocean of despair and memories that he just couldn't banish. It was a warm night and he kept wiping away the sweat between his legs and under his chin, as he thrashed around feverishly between the crisp white sheets.

Even sleep was no longer a refuge.

She lived in the hills behind the Olympic Stadium.

He painfully managed to find his way there, maneuvering the car with difficulty with an unfolded map on his knees and dodging cars that sped past him. She had pointed out the area to him when they had driven nearby on the way to secret places where they could fuck, but he had a hell of a time today finding his way past the Olympic Stadium. Once in the hills, it was no better and he arrived at the top by mistake, enjoying a view of both central Rome and all the neighboring hills he remembered from his history and Latin lessons all those years past. Oh, there was the Vatican. And there was the road that led out of town to the lake and Calcata, past the neglected area whose name he couldn't recall where, she had told him, prostitutes and low-life came out at night, then further down the road the RAI buildings. She had confessed to an unholy fascination with the whores there when she had been a teenager and how she had always imagined what they were doing and how she would act if she were one.

He studied the map carefully and found her street. He drove off downwards in its direction.

Via Luigi Credaro was a cul-de-sac and a small supermarket occupied the ground floor of the apartment building where she still lived with her parents. He managed to park a hundred meters away on the opposite side of the road.

Though he had never been here, he seemed to remember her saying that the apartment occupied the top two floors of the building. Did her bedroom overlook the street, or was it on another side of the building facing the hills or a different part of the city?

So, this was where she had mostly grown up, apart from those years in the country when she had commuted to school in the city by train. It felt strange being here. He kept his eye on the door to the building; the supermarket was open and customers trickled in and out.

He opened the glove compartment and took out the gun and placed it between his thighs on the car seat. He'd never fired a gun in his life, let alone owned one. But he had read enough books and articles and knew the basics—the safety, the caliber, the damage it could invariably cause.

I'm crazy, totally crazy, he thought. He'd been in love before, of course, but never had he been so obsessed with a woman, a girl, or missed her so much. Without her, he had sadly realized, he was nothing.

However much he knew that things could never have worked out between them after the initial year-long honeymoon of covert meetings and fiery fucks in forbidden places, he still couldn't give up on her totally, admit defeat, let her, and him, get on with their respective lives. She was younger. She still had a life—*adventures*, as she'd put it—ahead of her. He didn't. Not without her.

It was a few weeks before when he had been doing some Internet research for a story that he had stumbled across a pornographic website replete with photos submitted by non-professionals; openly voyeuristic images of nudity, both simple and extreme, and of couples having intercourse. He had distractedly spent a quarter of an hour surfing through the images and noting the monotonous repetition of positions and angles, when he had come across a series of eight shots in which the woman's face was out of the frame but her opulent white ass stood front and center, her wet, pink gash circled by unruly black curls, fully exposed along with the puckered, darker areola of her back door. The young woman was on her knees, her rear right in the camera's face. From image to image the ass came nearer and nearer to the fore, and in the final three photographs a resplendently thick and hard penis took aim at the woman's cunt and was then seen entering it and finally deeply embedded up to the ball sack.

He had of course seen a thousand photographs of this kind before, but this time the shape, the color, the details of the woman's ass recalled hers in indelible resemblance. He'd been violently sick, rushing to the bathroom and spewing out all the contents of his stomach over the carpet long before reaching the safety of the ceramic bowl. It had been like a knife to his heart. Naturally, he knew that he could not expect her to keep on being faithful to him in the whole year since their break-up, and since when do women in their twenties have to act as nuns? But somehow the images on his laptop had brought it all home, the idea of another man fucking her, owning her, playing with her, and, worse, getting her to allow him to broadcast photographs of their terrible intimacy across the web.

A few hours later, he had hesitantly peered at the photographs again and realized it wasn't her, couldn't be her. A few meshes of the woman's hair were in the frame of one of the images and the color was not hers; also, there was a distinctive mole absent in a familiar area of her lunar landscape, he discovered, to his relief. But the scar was still there. Inside him. Who was she with now? Who did she love now, she who had once loved him?

The door to the building opened and a woman walked out, plump, dark-haired, almost a vision of what Desi might look like twenty years later. Her mother?

The heat of the day hammered against the parked car,

but he couldn't switch the air-conditioning on or the battery would go flat.

Was she now alone in her room in the large two-floor apartment?

Or maybe she was now in a small hotel room by Lake Bracciano, being ploughed by another man. It had been, after all, she who had discovered that hideaway.

Enough. Enough.

I am sick. I am sick.

Sick enough to climb the stairs to the apartment, ring the bell, confront her when she opened the door, and brandish the gun? *If you can't be mine, you can't be anyone else's . . . ?* The pitiful stuff of tabloid journalism. Come on!

He could sit here all day and not see her, he realized. And even if she did emerge, what would he do then? Follow her? Stalk her? He'd lose her in traffic most likely.

In her anger, when he would refuse to let her go and beg for a last meeting, a final embrace, a penultimate conversation, she would always fire back that he had no respect for her and could not accept what she felt. She had these crazy ideas about respect, but he did understand what she meant.

In a letter, one of so many, too many, he had written that loving her was also knowing when to let her go, but it was a precept he had proven incapable of adhering to.

What the fuck was he doing in Rome? What the hell was he doing with a gun?

There's no way he could kill her.

Damn.

He drove off, found the highway that led out of town, past the desolate and empty marketplace where the whores were said to congregate at night like in a Fellini film, sped past the RAI buildings and into the countryside.

The sky was blue.

Maybe he could find peace after all.

There was a junction with a road that led to Lake Bracciano and Trevignano. He sighed and drove past it, his mind assaulted by more memories of nearby hotel rooms where they had made love and had once been unbearably happy. Watching her emerge from the shower, her wet, unfurled hair hanging all the way down her back. Putting that cheap necklace around her throat.

The next turn-off was for the medieval town of Calcata. He was just over forty kilometers from the city, in the Parco Treja Tuscia. Here, behind the high, fortified ramparts in a small stone house, where the February cold had chilled their bones to the marrow and forced them to spend almost two whole days in bed—talking nonstop between the tender fucking, learning about each other, getting accustomed to the taste of each other, growing bolder with mind and body and plunging headfirst into transgression—he had moved inside her for the first time and fallen in love with her. Forever.

Calcata looked the same. In all likelihood it had not changed in a few hundred years. Once abandoned, the small town had been repopulated several decades ago by hippies and was now turning into a historical arts center, with medieval summer houses for rich Romans, artists, or visiting lovers, art galleries, and a handful of tiny country restaurants. The whole town, whose population still didn't number more than nine hundred people normally, was built on a hilltop of volcanic rock.

He parked the rented blue Fiat outside the ramparts and walked up the stone street into the town, past the arches and fortifications.

The small cottage where they had frozen and spent thirty-six hours all that time ago was still there. He wondered what sort of couple was now inside in that unforgettable bedroom you could only access through a shaky wooden ladder (aaahhhh, the vision of her climbing those stairs, stark naked, his eyes looking straight at the voluptuous and bouncing flesh of her ass as he ascended behind her, his cock hard and ready, his mind aglow with tenderness and desire . . .).

He walked by the steep stone steps to his forgotten paradise and ventured past narrow alleys, closed craft shops, and clothes hanging loose from windows until he reached the narrow promontory that dominated the valley below.

The view was quite beautiful, rugged, untamed. In the distance, forests dominated the landscape, but below the damaged stone walls protecting this side of Calcata was a giant lunar expanse of rocks.

He sighed.

Best remember the good times.

When she smiled at him and her eyes expressed a million things unsaid.

He pulled that silly gun from the plastic bag and hurled it into the void. It fell in a large arc and it felt like almost a minute before he saw it actually hit the ground some five hundred meters below. It didn't go off. He had left the safety catch on. No need to draw attention to himself, even though there didn't appear to be a soul for a mile around.

He closed his eyes.

My *sweetie*, she would call him.

He took a deep breath.

My *wild gypsy*, he would often say to her.

He pulled his left leg over the wall, raised himself energetically so that he now stood on the edge of the precipice.

Looked down a final time.

Those fierce and distant rocks should do the job, he reckoned.

And jumped.

EATEN ALIVE

BY EVELINA SANTANGELO

Via Ascoli Piceno

Translated by Anne Milano Appel

S pringtime in Rome, a dawn populated with chatter-
ing birds. An impalpable veil of smog that slowly dis-
sipates, as though steadily absorbed by the great sponge
of the sun in its methodical climb toward the vault of the sky.
White wisps of clouds scattered here and there in the blue
that watches over the peaceful city and its outlying areas, still
sunk in a stubborn Sunday morning slumber, broken by the
din of garbage trucks, the rumble of a bus. "The 105 or the
81," Quirino murmurs, rinsing the coffee cup under the fau-
cet and placing it on the drain board. He fills a glass, takes
some big sips. "Ah, the taste of Rome's cool waters!" With
a mechanical gesture he tightens the tie of his light woolen
blue-and-white striped robe and gazes at the beautiful, mutilated structure of the Colosseum, licked by the first rays of the
sun: the "big windows," as he calls them, that run along the
circular walls. "Solid," he murmurs, satisfied, the tip of his index finger following the play of depressions and reliefs carved
out of the fake marble with industrial precision, imitating with
the touch of a master the irregularities of the stone worn away
by time. "Centuries," Quirino murmurs, drawing himself up
and resting the palm of his hand on the edge of the credenza.

He slips his bare feet into his slippers, and goes over to the window that looks out on the street, a modest strip closed to cars and flanked by low houses: The cables of television antennae hang down along the façades from the rooftops like improbable, permanent festoons, working their way somehow or other into window frames or cracks in the walls below the sills. "Television . . . everyone has a television . . ." He lowers his eyes to the street littered with beer bottles and small shapeless piles of trash. A cat emerges silently from an empty dumpster still sunk in shadow, and quietly licks a paw.

The stillness is broken only by the monotonous swishing of a street sweeper's broom. The cat turns to watch the almost phosphorescent green plastic bristles, then resumes licking, indifferent to the other paw. It starts suddenly when it sees the broom rise—"Drunken kids!"—and angrily thump the dumpster's grimy metal, barely missing its tail. "Drunken kids," the street sweeper mutters again, wiping his forehead with his arm, his hands stuffed into enormous work gloves.

Quirino leans out, nods to him. "Got a bee up your butt tonight?" he says, relishing those first words of conversation. "Nice morning," he adds, throwing his arms wide in a gesture that embraces heaven and earth.

"Nice morning, nice morning . . ." the other man repeats, shaking his head and crouching down on the sidewalk to retrieve a bottle stuck between the wheels of the dumpster. He raises it toward the window, dangling it between the black fingers of his bulky gloves. "They've trashed the neighborhood, those sons of bitches," he says, waving the bottle in the air and tossing it in the bag. "You should see the garbage in front of that shitty store, where those deadbeat godless immigrants make money selling beer to young kids until 3 in the morning . . . A bottle factory? A *piss* factory!" he adds. He shrugs helplessly, looks around. "Filth everywhere . . . on the ground, on the walls . . ." He points to the layers of mimeographed posters pasted on the façades. "A person has his own problems, no place to live . . . rents here being what they are now . . . and there, they go and put stuff all over the walls . . . *What a life it would be without rent . . . What a life it would be without rent . . .*" he reads, stressing each word. "On all the walls . . . Some like it hot, some like it cold. And they think they're fascists . . . *social fascists* . . . and there, they go and print these and stick them on the walls! And they still have revolution in their heads . . . And they go printing that crap about their *laboratories for revolution* . . . and there . . . they go and stick their *proletarian solidarity* on the walls. Those spoiled brats! To them, going to live in Pigneto seems revolutionary . . . with money, of course! Not to mention those other . . . beauties . . . Chinese, Bengalis, Pakistanis, Indians, Senegalese. Only they know what the hell they are . . . They come to our country to bust our balls . . . with their posters . . . because, what do I know, they have their holidays and they want to celebrate them however and wherever they say. They have houses like this . . . and they want them like that . . . Do we have houses like that? Oh, do we? Eight hundred euros a month, yours truly, in Torpignattara . . ." He holds three black fingers up against the sky. "Eight hundred!" he repeats. "So much for rent control . . ."

Quirino, with a sudden feeling of embarrassment, puts on a contrite expression. "That's how it is," he says, "with these new euros . . ."

"That's how it is? The hell it is! Yesterday . . . yesterday, at the corner of Tor Pignattara, right next to my house . . . flyers everywhere. And why? Because these kids, immigrant sons of bitches, want to play cricket on Sunday . . . at Villa de Santis, in the park . . . and our kids follow right along, now they, too, want to play crick-e-crock . . . And what does it mean, huh, do you know what *We want to play crick-e-crock* means?"

Quirino shrugs.

"Not soccer," the street sweeper continues, carried away by the heat of his words, "everybody knows what *soccer* is . . . No! And where do they want to play that crazy game? In Pigneto! In *our* neighborhood!" He shakes his head again, ripping some shredded paper off a wall. He looks around gloomily. "They can all go to hell, a person has his own problems . . ."

"His own problems," Quirino echoes him, watching the man drag the garbage bag and the broom toward the end of the street. Then he sighs. He stays there a few moments longer to watch Sor Pietro come back up the pedestrian strip, dragged along by his mastiff, a coal-gray hulk that devours the street in great strides. He watches the man dig in his heels, tug on the leash—"Tito, heel!"— take off a loafer with a threatening gesture. The man argues with the animal, his small body shaking, his eyeglasses crooked on his nose. The mastiff lowers its head and, docile now, lets itself be pet; it slows its gait, now and then turns to its master, who adjusts his eyeglasses and nods blissfully.

"To each his own problems . . ." Quirino murmurs with a half-smile, closing the shutters and moving toward the little cage. "Good morning, Cesarì." He takes out the drinking tray. "Some fresh water, hmm, Cesarì?" He goes to the sink. "A little lettuce . . . a slice of apple . . ." He sticks his hand in the cage, arranges everything on the tray. Then he holds out a finger. "Like a ray of sunshine, my little canary!" He begins petting the soft yellow feathers, feels the beak delicately nip his finger. "Hmm, Cesarì . . ." He slides his hand out slowly, watches the bird cock his head and look back at him. "Good boy, Cesarì!" he exclaims, observing the white cage with the small trapeze hanging in the center. "Go and play, Cesarì, Papa has things to do now."

He looks up over his reading glasses when he hears a knock at the door. He lays the pen down on the notebook. He glances at the wristwatch that his father gave him more than fifty years ago. "So early . . ." he murmurs, surprised, pressing his hands down on the tabletop and rising. "Is that you, Massimì?" he says, standing on tiptoe and squinting at the landing through the peephole. He sees the curly, grayish fuzz that crowns the small, turtle-like head of Signora Lavinia. "What's happened?" He opens the door, peers down at the woman's pinched face.

"May I come in?" she stammers, through lips that are even paler and thinner than usual, her pupils glistening beneath her long, dark lashes.

Quirino pulls the edges of his robe tightly together. For a moment he remains motionless, half-framed by the partly open door.

"Something has happened," Signora Lavinia whispers, her voice almost hoarse from sobbing. "Something . . . terrible," she says.

Quirino runs a hand through the steely gray hair that gives him a fierce, youthful look that he has been proud of since he passed the "critical threshold," as he says, alluding to his accumulation of years. "Come in then." He shoves his hands into his wide, roomy pockets. "Shall I make some coffee?"

Signora Lavinia brings a hand to her chest, struggling against the tremors that shake her body. "No, thank you. My heart . . ."

Quirino takes off his glasses, presses two fingers against his eyelids. "Ah, the heart . . . the heart . . . When it goes, there's trouble . . ." Then: "Well, Signora Lavinia?" He gestures for her to sit down. He settles himself in his place, on the other side of the table, facing her, his hands on the notebook.

Signora Lavinia's eyes, now even brighter, look at him imploringly.

"We'll talk about this later, when the time is right," Quirino reassures her, closing the notebook.

Signora Lavinia lowers her head, presses her palm against her forehead. "What happened is that . . . my Valentina . . ." She bursts out in a deep sob that cuts off her breath.

"She was old, poor thing . . ." Quirino says.

Signora Lavinia shakes her head forcefully. "They killed her, Sor Quirì," she says, gulping a mouthful of air and then getting swept up in a vortex of words. "This morning I woke up and she wasn't there. *She must have gone to take her usual little walk,* I told myself. Still . . . I had a kind of premonition . . . a foreboding, Sor Quirì . . . I don't know. So then I went down and started calling her. Here, there. And . . . do you know, I found her under the little bridge, in the gravel on the railroad tracks."

"She was hit by a train?" Quirino asks with a sorrowful expression. "If you knew how many cats I saw end up like that when I worked for the railroad . . . Poor things . . ." He reaches a hand out to Signora Lavinia, who shakes her head again, holding back her sobs as best she can. "Killed, Sor Quirì. Killed by someone. Her head bashed in by a rock, or a club . . . I don't know . . . With all these terrible people running around . . . I don't know, Sor Quirì . . . Now what am I going to do?" She twists her handkerchief into a knot around her fingers. "Ten years . . . we ate together, slept together . . . everything, Sor Quirì. Now what will I do without those beautiful eyes of hers . . . a companion, Sor Quirì."

Quirino swallows a sour globule of saliva, glances toward

the cage. He brightens when he sees Cesarì swinging slowly on the trapeze. "What can you do, Signora Lavinia . . . ?" he murmurs. "Get yourself another one, another cat. What can we do against the blows of fate . . . ?" He shrugs.

"Fate . . ." Signora Lavinia repeats bitterly. "So *those people* can kill another one."

"Those people who, Signora Lavinia?"

"Those people, *them* . . . One of those newcomers in the neighborhood, I'm sure of it, they have no respect. What do they care about my little cat, about an old woman . . . There's no respect for anything anymore, Sor Quirì."

"What do you mean, Signora Lavinia? It was an accident. Surely. An unfortunate accident . . . Now go downstairs, go home, make yourself a nice hot cup of chamomile . . . And later, when you feel up to it . . . when you feel up to it"—he taps two fingers on the cover of the notebook, looks at his manicured nails—"we'll talk. All right?" he says, composing his face in a stern, paternal expression.

Signora Lavinia starts. She nods. "Yes, I know that the outstanding amount is considerable . . . but my pension check still hasn't come and so . . . I don't have the money, Sor Quirì . . ." She holds out the palms of her bare hands.

Quirino puts his index finger to his lips, as if to say, *Hush*. "Some other time, some other time," he whispers, getting up and walking her slowly to the door. "Tomorrow . . ."

Signora Lavinia looks at him despondently. "Tomorrow?" she stammers.

"Or the day after . . ." Quirino says obligingly. "That way we'll deal with the rent issue and the loan issue in a single stroke, otherwise the interest . . ." He slowly raises his hand, levels it in front of her eyes in midair. "The day after tomorrow," he repeats, meeting Signora Lavinia's forlorn gaze.

"The day after tomorrow, all right," she murmurs. Then she plunges back into her own thoughts: "They killed her," she begins to mumble, holding onto the banister and slowly moving down the stairs.

In the sunlight filtering through the skylight, the down on her head shines like an evanescent halo, as Quirino says: "Animals . . . there's no doubt about it, they're better than people."

"What's the deal with arriving here at this hour? So late!" Quirino says, looking his son straight in the eye.

"A problem."

"On a Sunday? The Lord's day and . . . your father's?"

"On a Sunday, on a Sunday . . ." Massimiliano says, irritated. "A problem on a Sunday. That can happen, can't it?"

"All the time, Massimì? Every Sunday?" Quirino says, putting on his glasses.

"The kid threw up all night, his mother wanted to take him to the hospital this morning . . . a lot of talk . . . *Let's go, let's not go . . . let's see if he gets better . . .*"

Quirino sits down at the table, opens the notebook. "And how is he now?" he asks, running a hand over the rough stubble on his chin, as if to say: *More of your usual nonsense.*

"He's better," his son says abruptly, sitting down in front of him and crossing his hands.

"And the new notebook? Did you get it?" Quirino asks, taking the key out of the pocket of his robe and inserting it in the lock of the drawer beneath the tabletop.

"I bought it, I bought it . . ." Massimiliano opens a plastic folder, pulls out an ordinary gray account book.

"What's that? Quirino asks, startled.

"What we need," Massimiliano says, adopting a professional tone.

"Me, I don't need that thing! For me . . . this one here . . . is all I need." He bangs the notebook down in front of his son's eyes, points to the gilded face of Botticelli's *Venus* printed on the cover. "I have my *method*, do you understand? My own way!"

Massimiliano gives him a dirty look, puts the account book back in the folder, and closes it angrily, with an abrupt snap. "A fine way . . ." he hisses between his teeth. Then: "Let's see, come on, it's getting late." He leans across the table.

"All right then, let's begin with the two small buildings. This one here should be nearly in order." He takes a stack of bills from the drawer. He counts them, moistening his fingertips with saliva from time to time. "Punctual, these 'out of town students,'" he says, stressing the words.

Massimiliano runs the bills through his hands, quickly glancing at them. He confirms. He watches his father record the figures carefully in the notebook. "And the ones from the catacombs?"

"Those. . . they asked me for a little more time," Quirino says, concealing his annoyance.

"A little more time . . . after being a week late?" Massimiliano exclaims, fidgeting in his chair. "So, even with ten of them, those deadbeat immigrants can't manage to scrape together the pittance that they owe! And if they can't even pay for that rathole . . . why are they complaining, huh? Now they've even started kicking up a fuss at the Local Rights Department because *There's mold on the walls*, they say! Because the electrical system is not *up to code*! What do they expect, those deadbeats!"

Quirino looks at him bewildered. "And what does this Rights Department do?"

"What does it do, what does it do . . . ? It's a pain in the ass! But they can stuff it, those jerks, because it's not like they have proof that they're paying us! It's not like anyone sees the money they hand over, right? Who's ever seen that money? Are there checks? Money orders? No!"

"So then?"

"So then, if they continue to give us a hard time, we'll evict them for arrears, and they're gone! Problem solved." He slaps down the palm of his hand as if crushing an insect. "What shit . . ."

Quirino runs his fingers through his hair. "A person does all he can to try to please them . . . turning a blind eye . . . putting ten people in a house . . . ten . . . and just look at what they do—"

"Case closed, I told you," Massimiliano cuts him off. "Let's continue."

"Fine, let's continue . . . So then"—he clears his throat. "So then, the other small building . . . in order, let's say."

"And the girl? The 'artist'?" Massimiliano urges him on with sarcasm.

"The girl on the top floor . . . she'll pay in a few days, she says. Because it's a little expensive for her . . ."

"And we have a painter in our building who wants to be an *alternative* artist!" Massimiliano retorts. "And the Chinese?"

Quirino takes the money out of the drawer. "On time." He puts the bills on the table. "Decent people, who work . . . and pay the rent."

"Decent people, fine people," Massimiliano mimics his father, shaking his head. "Do you know how many clothing stores they supply, those people? Do you know?"

Quirino shrugs.

"Of course they pay . . . that pathetic amount we charge."

"A storeroom, Massimì. How much should we make them pay for a storeroom?"

"And how much do you think they pay those poor devils who work for them day and night like chickens? Nothing! So let's take it out of their hide, why not?"

Quirino doesn't answer, he counts the hundred-euro bills, enters the amount in the notebook. "There, done," he murmurs. "And then," he adds quickly, almost taking the words out of his son's mouth, "and then . . . there's the whole thorny matter of this building here." He taps his finger on the tabletop.

Massimiliano twists his lips into a grimace that distorts his handsome, carefully shaved face. He suppresses a sudden fit of anger.

"Where sometimes they pay, sometimes they don't pay . . ." Quirino continues. "Their pensions aren't enough . . . *Sor Quirì, another day or two* . . . And a little loan here, a little loan there . . . and the interest is too high . . . What can I do about it, Massimì, if the bank doesn't want to lend them money?"

"What can you do? Throw them out, once and for all, that's what you should do!" his son snarls.

"What, I should start throwing people out on the street now? All these old people whom I've known a lifetime, Massimì? I have to keep duplicate keys to their apartments, in case they leave theirs inside, they're so forgetful . . . What can I do? I raise the interest on the loans . . . What more can I do? . . . And then they come crying to me over a dead cat and whatnot . . . and what am I supposed to do? *We'll talk about it later,* I tell them."

"I'll tell you what to do!" Massimiliano barks. "Sell, that's what you should do." He bangs his palm on the tabletop an inch from his father.

Quirino looks at him stubbornly. "Sell . . ." he says ironically.

"Sell, that's right. To my real estate friend, who tells me every day, *Whatever you want, Massimo, for that building there*

194 // ROME NOIR

on the pedestrian strip. Name your price and I'll pay it on the spot."

Quirino throws up his arm. "Your *friend* the real estate agent . . ." He gives his son a scornful glance that makes him draw his head back between his shoulder blades. Then he points a finger right between his eyes. "Get it through your head." He shakes his finger. "Quirino buys, he doesn't sell. A little at a time . . . A loan here, a loan there . . . That's how you get ahead: a little at a time." He lowers his hand, begins stroking the open page of the notebook with his fingertip. "Was Rome built in a day? A little at a time, that's how the *urbs* was built! Was it those real estate agents of yours who think they're God—did they build Rome?"

Massimiliano offers a doglike expression. "What does Rome have to do with it?" Then he raises his voice. "Everything's changing fast," he exclaims, snapping his fingers. "The people, the money that's circulating . . . And if we don't jump at the chance we'll lose our ass, get it, with all these whining beggars. We have to be shrewd, Dad! *Shrewd!*" he repeats, almost shouting. "And then"—his eyes travel over the room—"if you, too, were to go, to—"

"*To* . . ." Quirino interrupts, flaying him with his eyes. "Where is it that your father should go?"

"Away from here . . . if you were to leave here," Massimiliano says hastily, changing his tone, "to a nice apartment, I mean . . . You can afford it."

Quirino drops the pen on the notebook. He sets his eyeglasses on the table. "Render unto Caesar that which is Caesar's, and unto God the things that are God's," he says, pronouncing the words one by one. Massimiliano frowns, not understanding. "And I," Quirino continues, "*we* . . . are not God, who can create the world in seven days. We have to take our time . . . without biting off more than we can chew . . . in our own way . . . in our own house," he adds.

Massimiliano shoves his chair back abruptly. "Then go on . . . go on letting these good-for-nothings take you for a ride."

He sneers as he heads for the door, followed by Quirino's voice: "The notebook, don't forget!" Quirino then puts everything back in the drawer, turns the key in the lock, slips it carefully into his pocket. He gets up. He goes over to Cesarino's little white cage. He watches for a while. He removes a golden feather stuck between the bars, blows it away. "Beauty is important, Cesarì," he says, as if to justify himself. "Money and beauty . . . and some manners, as well . . ." He lets the bird peck his finger. "With good manners, everything is possible." He smiles faintly.

"Killed!"

Signora Iolanda spreads her arms wide as she wanders desperately around the small courtyard that opens up beyond the entrance to the building. "They've killed them . . ." she whispers, turning her eyes toward her husband, who watches helplessly as she bends down, her breasts hanging like swollen pouches on her belly, brings her fingers to her mouth, then places them on the small bodies lying on the ground. "They've killed them," she repeats, racing around like a madwoman in the courtyard's faint light. She turns suddenly, frightened, when she hears a key fumbling in the door. She clings to her husband, who presses her head to his chest.

"It's probably one of the tenants coming home," he stammers, also turning toward the entrance in a rigid, unnatural movement.

Sor Quirino closes the door behind him. He leans the umbrella against the wall. He straightens his light overcoat that has been pulled to one side. "Some spring," he mutters. "Who can figure out this crazy weather anymore . . ." Then he falls silent. He squints in an attempt to bring into focus the two shadows framed in the space beside the open glass door leading to the courtyard. He picks up the umbrella and takes a few steps. "Who's there?" he calls out to bolster his courage, then breathes a sigh of relief. "Signora Iolanda . . ." he says, as the woman comes toward him, unspeaking, gesturing for him to follow.

He walks the few meters that separate him from the courtyard and turns a questioning glance toward Sor Antonio, the greengrocer, who mutters, "An atrocity," pointing mechanically at the ground.

Quirino apprehensively lowers his eyes. "Poor things . . ." he whispers. He gets down on his knees with some difficulty, reaches a hand out toward the bloodied neck of a tiny kitten, curled up in the doorway, then spots another ragged heap behind the cistern, then another, and another . . . He turns his head, incredulous. He gives a start when he sees the red *drip, drip, drip* slowly staining the ground behind the cleaning bucket, where the body of the mother cat hangs, upside down and gutted. "Poor thing . . ."

"And there were two more," Signora Iolanda whispers, "that . . . I can't find anywhere." She starts searching again, desperate.

Quirino pulls himself back up, holding onto the handle of his umbrella. "Who was it?" he asks, just to say something.

Sor Antonio widens his arms. "Who could it have been? Someone—"

"The person who . . . who also stoned Signora Lavinia's cat, who scalded Sor Giacomo's dog with hot water in the middle of the street the other morning," Signora Iolanda breaks in, still wandering around the courtyard. "That poor dog, he was just going around doing his business, not bothering anybody. Who would Sor Giacomo's dog bother, right, Sor Quirino? Who could he bother . . . ? The drunks who live it up until the early-morning hours? Who? Who were these kittens bothering? So clean, their mother licked them every morning . . . and how they meowed in their tiny voices when I came down to give them their food. And someone . . . someone . . . without a heart . . . Who knows where the other two have ended up . . . They must have eaten the other two . . . I'll bet you anything, they ate them . . . those Chinese people!" Signora Iolanda finally bursts out. "Those . . . those . . ." She covers her face with her hands.

"What do you mean, Signora Iolanda?" Quirino exclaims, looking for some sign of agreement on the stony face of Sor Antonio, who, lowering his eyes, mutters, "They must have eaten them."

"What do you mean, *eaten* them?" Quirino asks, pointing to the mangled bodies of the cats in the courtyard. "What about these? Did someone eat these?" His hand moves to his neck, he opens the top button of his shirt, takes a deep breath. "Those sons of bitches," he cries out suddenly, starting up the stairs, climbing faster and faster as a thought begins gnawing at his brain; he stumbles, and his hand trembles as he fumbles with the lock, and "Cesarì!" comes out in a stifled scream that dies in his throat when he sees the little bird curled up quietly on his perch, his head tucked under the beautiful feathers that slowly rise, swelling in rhythm with his breath.

There is a dazed silence in the lobby. "Like during the war, when we were all quiet, mute, so we wouldn't get bombed," Sor Giacomo whispers, wringing his hands.

"Under siege," Signora Iolanda echoes him, following Quirino's restless steps, as he paces up and down in silence, waiting for everyone to sit down on the chairs, which have been arranged in a circle.

Signora Iolanda looks up at the ceiling, stares at the naked bulb of the lamp hanging overhead. She shudders. She twists in her seat. "Who could have told Tito, poor thing, that it would end like this?" Sor Pietro looks at her, beside himself. "In his sleep," he adds. "In his own house . . . in *our* house . . ." His head sags, he cleans his glasses and places them on his sweaty nose. "A good dog, a decent soul . . . big . . . I taught him everything . . . hanged by the neck from the television cable, with his teeth out . . . such a decent dog." His eyes hidden behind the glasses turn toward Quirino, who continues to pace, trying to come up with an idea, something appropriate to say, fingering the drawer key in his pocket as if it were an amulet. He clutches it in his fingers. He hears an agitated whispering in the corner. "Let's begin the meeting," he says uncertainly, but giving his voice an authoritative pitch. All the residents start, as if those were the first words of God on earth. They instinctively turn their heads toward the front door, to make sure that it is firmly shut.

Quirino watches the two Zorzi brothers, who are huddled together. "Do you have something to say?" he asks, trying to maintain his tone.

The two exchange a few nervous glances. Then: "Yes," says Sor Paolo, raising his hand to ask for the floor. "I do." But he is silent when he sees all those eyes turn toward him expectantly.

"The fact is," Sor Geno intervenes, with a nod of agreement toward his brother, "the fact is that we two . . . we don't have animals at home and . . . who are they going to take it out on, those people, if they get it into their heads to break a window, a door, whatever . . . in our house . . ."

"*We're* the only ones they can take it out on," Sor Paolo concludes, his bald cranium sinking between his shoulders, while Sor Antonio says, "Because the point is, Sor Quirino, that now they're even entering our homes, you see? *Entering our homes . . .*"

"To terrorize us," Signora Iolanda chimes in.

"When we're asleep, when a person . . . How does one defend oneself, Sor Quirì? How can a person defend herself alone," Signora Lavinia wails.

"By talking to the district committee," Sor Antonio speaks up. "That's how we defend ourselves!"

Quirino gives him a dubious look. "And since when has there been such a committee?"

"The *district committee*," Sor Geno says sarcastically. "That bunch, all they do is make up questionnaires 'to survey people's needs,' they say . . . And what are the people's needs, according to them?" He spreads his fingers and starts to count: "Bike and pedestrian paths, maintaining the green spaces, urban quality of life, chemical toilets . . . chemical toilets, for God's sake! How much do you think people like us are worth in their eyes, huh? A bunch of penniless old people . . ." He feels his brother nudge him in the ribs and turns. "Am I wrong, Paole?" he mutters, his face livid.

"So what do they want, then? For us to go away? Is that what they want? To throw us out?" Sor Pietro says in a low voice. "To hang us all?"

"They want to eat our hearts," Signora Lavinia breaks in, pressing her hands to her chest.

"All those drunken kids, those filthy immigrants, those Chinese, those junkies, those spoiled daddy's boys, those building speculators who buy and sell and buy . . . and open new businesses . . . and we don't have the slightest idea what they're planning to do with this neighborhood of ours . . ." Signora Iolanda rants, to a murmur of agreement. She fidgets in her chair while her husband grabs her by the arm and casts a furtive look at the door.

"Calm down," he says quietly. Then he turns firmly toward Quirino. "Let's get back to the point. Who's the one who has keys to our houses?" he hisses. "Who's the one who can come and go as he pleases? Who's the one who takes the bread out of our mouths . . ." He breaks off, stifling his rage and continuing to stare at Quirino, who turns pale.

"What are you trying to say, Sor Antonio?" Quirino murmurs, sneaking a glance at his watch and cursing his son, who still hasn't shown up. Finally, trying to compose himself, he says: "If you want the keys, we can give them to you," as if to evoke, with his words at least, the son who should already be there, at his side.

"Keys, what keys?" snaps Sor Pietro. "I . . . I'm going," he says, leaving them all dumbfounded.

"Where are you going? To Stazione Termini?" Sor Geno asks with a flare of sarcasm.

"To join the beggars?" Sor Paolo is more precise, helping his brother out.

Signora Lavinia, looking around as if lost, moans: "Now what will we do? After forty years . . ."

"We'll occupy a building," Sor Antonio interjects. "We'll certainly be better off than here, with all this moisture—"

"It's eating us alive," Signora Iolanda interrupts. "It's eating us alive," she repeats, glancing at Quirino, who leans against the wall.

"I'm eating you alive," Quirino mumbles in bewilderment,

clinging to the key to the drawer jammed in the bottom of his pocket. Then he bends down and opens the leather folder on his chair. Feeling the breath of all those angry dogs hot on his neck, he begins rummaging, dumps everything out, then lifts his head, his hair falling over his forehead. "They're not here," he whispers with a groan, "the keys . . . they're not here." A voice insinuates itself furtively amid the confusion of his thoughts, rivets him there in the middle of the lobby. *Well? What do you think, Sòr Quirì?* Then the voice impels him up the stairs. *He's getting away now, Sòr Quirì!* One floor, then another. *He's going down, he's going down . . .* and he finally reaches his door.

Ready to drop, he rushes to the drawer and searches it frantically. "They're not here," he repeats, sunk in evening shadow, while the voice has now become a phrase stuck in the exact center of his brain: *We have to be shrewd . . .*

"That son of a bitch!" he hisses in a flash of lucidity, slamming his fist on the table. "He thinks he can throw people out just like that!"

He feels a sharp pain start along his arm and spread throughout his body, now trembling with rage. He takes a deep breath. He tries to calm down. "Cesarì, see what he did, that son of mine?" he groans, holding onto the credenza and making his way with unsteady steps toward the cage—"Cesarì . . . Cesarino . . . Cesa . . ."— which hangs there, shattered.

PART IV

La Dolce Vita

FOR A FEW MORE GOLD TOKENS

BY ANTONIO PASCALE

Quartiere Pigneto

Translated by Ann Goldstein

The Architect

On May 20, 2006, a hot sunny afternoon, the young architect-in-training Riccardo Tramonti, thirty-one, was completing an exploratory tour of the Pigneto neighborhood. In a few minutes—at 4:10, according to the police report—and just a few steps away (around two hundred meters) from the café where he had stopped (he had felt himself becoming weak, and dizzy, and he wanted something cold), the crime would take place. Of what happened next, which he would witness as the involuntary protagonist, Riccardo knew nothing. At 5 in the afternoon the next day, which is when he woke up, after nearly twenty-four hours in a coma, the first thing the nurse said to him was: You're in all the papers.

It was, in truth, the only sentence that impressed itself in his memory, at least until, finally, after seventy-two hours in intensive care, he was taken to a rehabilitation ward, where he could have visitors. The first people to cross the threshold of his room (his mother and father; his girlfriend came that evening, just before visiting hours were over) said to him, taking for granted that he was fine, You're in all the papers. There are even television cameras outside.

Riccardo was supposed to draft a report on "structural changes in the Pigneto neighborhood." The job had been commissioned by the City of Rome and was part of a larger project of assessing the redevelopment of outlying neighborhoods. The firm (quite a well-known one) where Riccardo had been working for three years now (without anyone having recognized his ideas, Riccardo claimed) had won the contract; as a first step, it was supposed to review "the anthropology of the neighborhood," and the young architect-in-training had been sent there on this exploratory mission.

Riccardo's first sensation, as soon as he set foot in the neighborhood, was that of belonging: His appearance was not at all out of place among the inhabitants. Riccardo was tall and thin. He always knew what to wear, how to dress, in order to emphasize the idea that he was an architect—that is, someone who could devote himself to the spaces of others because he was able to devote himself to (taking care of) himself. Although he had undergone a notable loss of hair while preparing for an exam (which covered engineering concepts through difficult and obscure applications of mathematics and physics), he had pretended not to be very concerned about this change in his physical appearance. The reaction to this unpleasant development had occurred in three stages: He had shaved his head, grown a beard, and bought some stylish nonprescription glasses with thin gold frames. He could see perfectly well but thought that the look he had created for himself more closely resembled what people expected to see when they shook the hand of an architect.

The neighborhood was in the process of transformation, this was the first thing he would have written in his report. What had at one time been a neighborhood on the outskirts, in every sense, was on the verge of becoming fashionable.

There were fewer and fewer old men playing cards, cursing some saint because luck wasn't on their side. Fewer and fewer old ladies sitting outside doorways on straw chairs, while hens pecked in the dirt nearby. And more and more young people like Riccardo.

Even if all of them hadn't lost their hair (although a percentage that Riccardo estimated at between twenty-five and thirty-five resembled him in a striking manner), they could be defined in every respect as young people who were heading toward a rosy future. Young people with ideas, a little like Riccardo, who maybe struggled to express them completely, perhaps because (a little like Riccardo) they worked in cold and coercive structures (even if the furnishings of those structures conveyed the contrary). And yet these young people wanted to react to all this, to create an image of themselves that would nurture optimism. Therefore, the young people seemed truly young, and those who were forty or older did their utmost to seem like young people.

The neighborhood was in the process of transformation, so Riccardo would have written. The houses, built of mortar and stucco, without solid foundations, and once inhabited by poor people who got by as best they could, were gaining value in the real-estate market. Those poor people, since they had reached the age limit (approximately seventy) beyond which it is no longer possible to pretend that everything is all right, were selling (en masse) the houses they owned. With the money obtained they had (almost en masse) decided to move out of that neighborhood (or die in exotic places). The young people who bought (using in part the family inheritance) spent more than the value of the apartments (thus contributing to the distortion of the market) and proceeded to renovate them. Wealth was arriving and the pace of life was changing; the young seemed younger, hence with more future before them.

The neighborhood was in the process of transformation, so Riccardo would have liked to begin and end his report. It was, in fact, the last thought that his mind formed before he came out of the bar in a pitiful state, with his blood pressure falling rapidly and his legs trembling in a truly suspicious manner.

Francesco

The only thing Francesco, now nearly eighteen years old and a longtime resident of the Pigneto neighborhood, had understood in his life was: My father is a moron. This discovery had become a source of pride and power. His father was a moron because he didn't understand anything, he wasn't aware of anything, he didn't look at anything: a moron, that was all.

Awhile back, Francesco had stolen a motorbike (Honda SH). Not that he needed it; he just wanted to go to the stadium. Since his motorcycle was broken, and since there are always people (Francesco said) who leave their bikes unlocked, hoping, therefore (not just unconsciously), that they will be stolen, Francesco, after seeing all the fans setting off for the stadium with their folded banners, was not overcome by fear (which a first theft generally involves) and, instead, inserted a screwdriver in the starter of the Honda SH, turned on the engine, and headed for the stadium on the stolen bike.

The motorcycle had to do with his father's moronicness. It was really a perfect example.

His father was a moron, Francesco thought, on the way to the stadium, mounted on the stolen bike. Especially as Francesco considered him responsible for everything, even his own passion for the Rome team that he had transmitted at a tender age but then hadn't known how to cultivate. Something that morons do in general—they open a pathway and are unable to follow it. Precisely because they are morons.

His father had in recent years suffered a financial collapse. It wasn't that he had attempted to scale a significant height and, just before the peak, had fallen. In that case one might have appreciated his courage. No, he, the father, had had a financial collapse because he had fallen in love with someone else and had left the family: Francesco, his mother, and his sister. Not to say that the father had ever made a lot of money. Occasionally he wrote for television. They had come to live in Pigneto when it was not yet fashionable and prices were low. Francesco's mother had repeated every other day that it was time to buy a house in this neighborhood, where houses were cheap. But he, the father, like the idiot he was, kept putting off the purchase: These houses are going to fall in on themselves soon, they'll implode, they're old, decaying. Let's wait, when we have more money we'll move to another neighborhood. Typical moron's rationale. They continued to rent. Then he, the father, had the clever idea of falling in love with someone else. Another moron, worse than him. Of course, morons seek each other out, so to speak, they pair up. So the mother thought she'd better kick him out on his ass, and now he has to work double to pay two rents, for the house in Pigneto and for his own, practically a hovel, on the Prenestina. And this he does, the moron, a little to his woman and a little to the family. A little money here, a little there. Both women kick him in the ass, and he goes along like that, like the moron he is.

Now, Francesco thought, the day he went to the stadium on the motorbike, is it possible that a person never learns from his mistakes? Because his father was like that, someone who never learns. Even when Francesco was caught with the stolen motorbike and all hell broke loose, and he was taken to the police station in handcuffs, even then, when his father came to get him, the first thing he did was hug him, tight. In front of the cops, who looked on in embarrassment. They all expected his father to slug him, kick him in the ass or whatever, whereas he, on the contrary, in front of the cops, had hugged his son. Then, as if that were not enough, he said to the police captain: When your son steals something, it's the time to give him a present. Like a moron, no? A father who quotes an old Zen saying, a saying that among other things he was using in a TV script. He says it in front of everyone. To explain that a son who steals is only asking for attention and affection, that's why it's a good time to give him a present. The captain had run his hands through his hair and said under his breath, How will we go on like this . . .

The Father . . . and His Lover

One morning, early, Mario Cirillo, motorman on the Metro, found a person locked in a car. There's another one, he thought. He didn't expect that there would be any further surprises. It can happen that a passenger doesn't get out at the last stop. And then gets stuck. The train, at the end of its run, is taken to the local yards. The doors are closed, the electricity is turned off, and the train is abandoned. And then generally the locked-in passenger begins to yell like a madman and the motorman, hearing these shouts, thinks: There's another one. Every year, at least one passenger, for one reason or another, forgets to get out at the last stop and finds himself alone, on the point of tears, on the edge of a panic attack, stuck in the car.

That morning, it happened that Mario Cirillo had found not one but two people locked in the train. A sign, said the motorman, that those two not only hadn't realized that they were at the last stop; they hadn't even noticed that the train was heading for the yards. They hadn't realized anything, they hadn't shouted, or begged, or stamped their feet. Nothing. Or maybe they had, but it was too late, the train had already been sitting for a while.

Francesco's father, Carlo Chirico, was one of the two locked in the car. There's another one, thought the motorman, not suspecting that there was a second person with him. A woman, Marta della Rosa. Two morons, the motorman had remarked to his friends while they were having coffee. Today I found not one but two morons.

At the beginning of that adventure, Carlo was in the next-to-last car, Marta in the last. Both were reading books: Carlo *Asylum*, and Marta *Ocean Sea*. In the grip of literature they hadn't been aware of anything. Then, trying to get out, they had come face to face. Both were frightened, and screamed as if they'd seen a ghost.

What morons, Carlo said to Marta later, how could they not have noticed anything? For Carlo it was his first experience, so to speak, of being possessed by reading. In Marta's case, on the other hand, it often happened that she didn't get off at her stop. Now they were both locked in the metro. They couldn't even inform the emergency services, there was no way. They spent the night together somewhat fearfully, they talked to each other about many things, and when, early in the morning, the motorman got them out, they began to laugh. The sort of laughter that covers embarrassment: at having been a bit foolish but, at the same time, at having said some important things. At having bared themselves, so to speak, in front of one another. An inversion: They had been underground together, and had been so comfortable that when the morning light illuminated them they were pained, as if they had been hurled out of the earthly paradise, which this time, however, was down below.

What a moron, Liliana, Carlo's wife, said to him, when she saw him again. I'm here in this place working all night and you're in a train reading *Asylum*. Practically the same thing that Liliana said again when, a few months later, she discovered that her husband not only was fucking Marta but was in love with her. Really, his wife said to him. In love? What a moron . . . I'm here in this . . .

Francesco and Cinzia

The boy had noticed awhile ago that there was something odd. If there was any value in what he did—that is, almost nothing, from morning to night—it was that he could look around. And looking around, Francesco had noticed the storefront. He had his girlfriend look, too, saying to her, There's something odd. To this observation his girl, Cinzia, had replied: Right. A word that she repeated often, especially when Francesco commented on something he saw: Right.

Cinzia adored Francesco. She saw in him everything she didn't see in her other contemporaries and schoolmates. Francesco was someone who got respect. He used his fists. That was how he resolved things, with his fists. And he was successful. He wasn't like her classmates, all very polite and very fake, according to Cinzia. Francesco and Cinzia went to the French school, a private school. They were in the same class. What am I supposed to do? My father is a moron, he enrolled me in this school, so in his view I'm learning important things and hanging out with fancy people. But what can I learn from some filthy rich morons?

Right, Cinzia answered. She found herself in the same situation. Her father and mother had a lot of money and could afford to have all sorts of luxuries. And they had them. And in having them, according to Cinzia, they contributed to the devastation of the world. Cinzia detested people who were devastating the world. They got on her nerves. She bought clothes from street vendors without worrying about the label or the quality. She didn't even worry when her mother borrowed her clothes. Cinzia's mother, in fact, considered her daughter a born style-maker. Someone who wherever she shopped would buy the right thing. In fact, Cinzia created trends. So her mother said. Right, Cinzia commented, my mother doesn't understand shit about anything. You should see my father, Francesco added. As a matter of fact, the two had become acquainted talking about their fathers and mothers. Then they had gotten together when, during a discussion about pacifism, the girl had seemed to go crazy because her interlocutor, according to her, not only underestimated the problem of imperialism but also made some out-of-place remarks, partly to undercut Cinzia, the style-maker, and partly to tease her. The discussion ended when Francesco got involved and started punching the boy. Every time he hit him he said: What's the matter? You're not laughing anymore.

Right, said Cinzia, some time later, when they kissed for the first time. From then on no one wanted to have a discussion with Cinzia the pacifist or her warrior companion, Francesco. And the two formed a close, intimate couple. But isolated.

Now, this storefront which had something odd about it was actually a warehouse: Twice a week a van arrived and unloaded refrigerators, dishwashers, washing machines. And on an almost daily basis, these household appliances, one by one, left the place. The operations occurred in a regular, straightforward fashion. Matteo Cosentino, the owner, waited in the doorway of the store for the arrival of the van and helped unload it. His wife, Daniela Lo Prete, came out and handed over the receipt. The business was repeated in the opposite direction immediately afterward, in the sense that Matteo loaded into his minivan, a Fiat Ducato, a television, a refrigerator, but also a chair, a lamp. His wife gave him a packing list, and then every other time, according to her mood, she said goodbye to her husband, who, every other time, according to his mood, departed saying goodbye to his wife with a wave of his left hand.

These were all simple operations that went on without any interference. The neighborhood was in the process of changing, it's true; for much of the day someone with a truck was loading or unloading goods, but there were no traffic jams or parked cars that got in the way of movement. Matteo loaded up and left.

There was something odd, however.

Matteo and Daniela (and Little Giulia)

Once a week, Matteo and his wife, Daniela, lowered the metal shutter halfway. This happened when the gold tokens arrived. Matteo and Daniela had the job of counting them and delivering them to the winner. There was no danger as long as the whole operation unfolded in low profile, so to speak. It shouldn't attract attention. To keep the operation's profile low, the gold tokens, placed in a canvas sack decorated with a red ribbon, were put in a gym bag and loaded into the back or, sometimes, left on the rear seat. What in the world could there be of importance in a gym bag? Not to mention the fact that the gold tokens were not a very desirable haul; even people who received them as a prize had to exchange the gold for money. In this exchange the tokens lost twenty percent of their value—imagine if you'd stolen them.

For two years Matteo and Daniela had managed the franchise for third-party delivery of prizes won on television.

It was a modern business, certain to expand. Television will give away more and more prizes (of all varieties), and there will have to be agencies to handle the delivery, at least one in every major city, to reduce the costs of transportation. Anyway, if you won a television, it did not reach the winner directly, by courier. From the factory it went to the agency and the agency took care of delivering it to the home.

Matteo and Daniela, who had been married for three years, had decided to take this job. They had also decided something else: to have a child. The truth is, Daniela had made (and imposed) the decision. Matteo temporized. Now that the business was about to get going, a child could slow its progress. You had to take care of a child, Matteo always said; we can't leave it to grandparents or babysitters. Let's wait. We're just getting going and then we bring a child into the world. If we wait for the right moment, Daniela answered, it will never arrive. There are no right moments. Since Daniela believed in what she said, one fine day she simply informed her husband that the right moment had arrived: in the sense that she was pregnant. Nine months later Giulia was born. Adorable, happy, healthy, good-natured. If only she had slept at night, it would have been perfect—the right moment, so to speak. But she was a child who liked to be up, maybe she was already immersed in the sweet nightlife of the Pigneto neighborhood. Matteo rocked her whenever he could. In brief, the matter stood like this: Matteo no longer slept. And the work suffered from it. I told you so, he said to Daniela. She put up with it; she had to devote herself to the child, she couldn't worry about her husband's sleep. It will pass, calm down, that way you'll calm Giulia as well.

So Matteo also had to take on the guilt of the child's insomnia. It was a vicious circle: He was sleepy, in the morning he was irritable, and because he had to do all that unloading, his irritability was passed on to the child, who wouldn't go to sleep at night, etc., etc. The fact is that Matteo simply kept repeating to Daniela: I told you so. He got more irritable, because Daniela didn't listen to him or even offer a nod of comprehension. Indeed, some time ago Daniela had even stopped saying: It will pass, calm down. She limited herself to accusing her husband directly of being a weakling. Of giving way for so little: Is there time to sleep or not? All this tension had dug into Matteo's face and his constitution. One day, after a sleepless night, he left a refrigerator on the sidewalk. He forgot to load it into his van and just drove off. Luckily, Mario, the bartender, immediately informed him on his cell phone. When Matteo returned, Mario offered him a coffee. He needed it. And as long as he was there, Matteo vented a little: himself, Daniela, the child, the job. He also said: I'm glad it was a refrigerator, imagine if I'd left the gold tokens on the sidewalk. Francesco, since he did nothing from morning to night, heard (and understood) everything, and a thought flashed in his mind: That's what's odd about that place. Right, Cinzia had responded when Francesco told her about it. When, however, he confided to her what he wanted to do, that is steal, without spilling any blood, a bag of gold tokens and move to a tropical island, far from that moron his father and all the rest of the disgusting world—when Francesco confided all this to Cinzia, she didn't say, Right. She said nothing.

Peppe

For three weeks Peppe had said nothing to anyone. He withdrew into himself. Things were not going well, a brain tumor had been diagnosed. How long did he have left to live—a month, three months? Peppe was spending all his savings, spending it on crazy things. A month, three months of life. Peppe no longer had a family. His wife was dead. His son didn't want anything to do with him. He had gone away. He had even sold his house in Pigneto, bought by his father with many sacrifices. Once he had the money in his pocket, he had flown to England. To be a baker, an honest job with a good income. Unlike his: Peppe, for his whole life, had been a pusher, drugs and other such substances. He had even smuggled Viagra. Now that he was about to die, a single thought tormented him: not to be able to hand over his knowledge to someone. All that criminal experience would be lost like tears in the rain. If only he had had a different son, more inclined to humbly learn the job, rather than be a baker. In England, worse. Knock himself out from morning till night. Why? A life of sacrifices for what? The two-family house, the family, the lousy pay? Was this the life his son wanted? Come on. His work required skill. Now the contacts, the friendships, the relations he had built, had managed, and had been able to exploit would no longer have meaning. That thought tormented him more than the brain tumor.

Peppe, Francesco, and Cinzia

It was in the grip of this obsession that Peppe began to look around. And he found Francesco and Cinzia. Almost as if someone on high or down below had heard his prayers. What more could one ask? Two aimless kids hanging around the neighborhood, with an obvious desire (especially the boy) to learn. When Peppe got in touch with him to arrange a quick sale of amphetamines, Francesco let him know immediately how he saw things: It's better to sell drugs than to use them. Morons use them. If it wasn't for the morons, there wouldn't be so much money around. Once the three agreed about the inexorable presence of morons in the world, they became conspiratorial and exchanged confidences. Peppe said that he was about to die, Francesco that he wanted a life different from the one he had lived up to now. Rather than continue like this, he preferred to be like the old residents of the neighborhood—get some money in his pocket and go to a tropical island. They would open a bar, far away from the morons. At least from the ones he knew. And here came Francesco's bright idea: the gold tokens. An easy job. After listening to Francesco, Peppe agreed. The problem was not so much that of taking the tokens as of converting them to money. Of finding a fence. Peppe knew someone who might be just what they needed: Tonino. Right, said Cinzia.

Tonino

Tonino had a problem: He spent everything he had on high-class whores. On Saturdays, on one pretext or another, he headed toward the Marche. He knew certain Ukrainians who worked in private brothels. Fabulous. He took care of everything, even the cocaine. Three hours of luxury. Of unrestrained vice. Then the return home, without a euro in his pocket. Too many gifts, handouts, tips, and little somethings for everyone, whores and friends of the whores. Tonino was old and when he turned sixty he had been seized by this mania: to fuck without limits. For a man like him, shut up in a shop for almost fifty years, there was only one thing to do: spend, throw away money. What use was it to him? His children already had money. They, too, were jewelers. Besides, his children were morons.

It can be done, Tonino said to Peppe. I know where to sell them; you bring them to me and I'll pay you half the value. How many can you bring?

Carlo and Marta

Although Carlo occasionally worked in television, he didn't know that the gold tokens awarded as prizes had different values: thirty, fifty, a hundred and fifty, two hundred and fifty, five hundred thousand euros. He discovered it by chance on May 18, 2006, because the mother of Marta (his new girlfriend) had won gold tokens as a prize. A hundred and fifty thousand euros. A twofold fortune. Marta's mother was up there in years and so, apart from using some of the money to pay her caretaker, she wouldn't have known what to do with that sum. She had decided to give it to her daughter, and the daughter wanted to divide it equally with Carlo. The two had shared a night on the train, they were in love, and after that night they had to share any fortune that might come to them. Carlo inquired about collecting the prize and found out it was the agency in Pigneto that would deliver the money. So, since Carlo knew the owner by sight, one day he went to see him. When Carlo came in, Matteo was sleeping in a chair (in fact, a prize to be delivered). It was Daniela who shook his hand first and asked him not to make any noise, her husband slept whenever he could, because the child mistook night for day. When Carlo left the agency he knew more about his life: (a) the gold tokens would arrive on May 20 at Matteo and Daniela's agency, and would be delivered to his house directly; (b) Carlo was so fascinated by the business of the gold tokens that he asked the couple if he could see how the job was carried out, and sooner or later he would find a way to tell their story; and (c) with his portion he would give his children a present, especially his son Francesco. The boy needed a gesture of affection. Maybe a motorcycle.

Peppe, Francesco, Cinzia, and a Mysterious Man

Peppe had taken care of all the details of the heist. His brain still functioned, and as long as it functioned (time was running out, another month), he wanted to use it to make the kids happy. For himself he asked nothing—no money, no benefits, no percentages . . . nothing. What would be the use? To pay for more treatments and live a few more days? All pointless. Better to do something useful for the kids, his two godchildren.

There would be no bloodshed, no gun or other weapons. The mysterious man would come with them. Actually, his name was Ugo. A stout clerical worker who had two hobbies: he was a practitioner of judo and a fan of bondage. He liked to tie people up and watch their contortions. Some time ago, Ugo had entered the world of clandestine films; in particular, he produced films in which acts of violence were simulated or reenacted. Ugo wouldn't know anything about the gold tokens; besides, all he cared about was tying people up and filming the scene. The plan, then, was simple. Peppe had persuaded Ugo to set up a real snuff movie, to sell later on the clandestine market. Peppe and Ugo would go into the agency, and tie up Matteo and Daniela. The whole thing would be filmed by a small camera. After that, while Ugo was preparing to film the two of them, bound and gagged, Peppe would hit him on the head, tie him up, grab the gold tokens, and deliver them to the kids. Francesco agreed to everything except one small detail: He wanted to take part in the robbery. Peppe insisted that he shouldn't. Why take that risk? Francesco was ready for a risk. Francesco trusted Peppe only up to a certain point; he liked him but felt that basically Peppe would always be a piece of shit. Yet Francesco didn't consider him a moron. Peppe, on the other hand, had understood Francesco's doubt. More than legitimate. Good sign, Francesco was right not to trust him. Smart, that kid. He would let him come. The robbery couldn't be fully set up in advance, they would have to act on the moment. When the storefront's metal shutter had been lowered halfway. There, that was the signal. Ugo would be ready, he lived just across from the place. They would wait at his house for the right moment. There were plenty of films for diversion. Right, said Cinzia.

Peppe

On the morning of May 20, shortly before going to Ugo's house as he had for the previous three days, to check on the activity at the agency, Peppe received a phone call. A kind, solicitous voice told him that he had better sit down. At the end of the call, Peppe said to himself: What do I do now, I don't have a cent.

Ugo

Ugo had all the equipment ready.

Francesco

Around 11 in the morning, through a window at Ugo's house, he thought he saw his father walking around the neighborhood. Odd, he said to himself, this isn't his day to visit.

The Agency

Matteo lowered the shutter halfway down around 3. About a

minute earlier two private guards had delivered several bags. Matteo seemed to be asleep on his feet.

The Architect

At 3 he had arrived in the neighborhood to begin his exploratory tour.

Peppe, Francesco, etc., and the Final Unfolding of Events, According to the Police Report

The three of them, Peppe, Francesco, and Ugo, entered the agency. The plan had been organized this way: Right after the robbery, Peppe and Francesco, on the motorcycle, would head for Tonino's. The important thing was to deliver the gold tokens, get them to a safe place right away. Peppe and Francesco had discussed who should drive. Francesco wanted to drive, because, as he reminded Peppe, his brain, unfortunately, played nasty tricks. Peppe himself had told Francesco about the time he thought he was braking and accelerated instead. The first terrible symptom of the brain tumor. Peppe, however, insisted on driving: With him driving, they would seem a pair, father and son, and would attract less attention. And after that one day, it had never happened again. When he had to brake he braked, and when he had to accelerate he accelerated. That type of symptom had disappeared. In the end, the older man's wish was respected.

Wearing ski masks, the three entered the agency at 3:50 p.m., and the first person they came across was, unexpectedly, Carlo, Francesco's father. He was trying to take notes, in a notebook. Carlo, seeing the three in their ski masks, and imagining that they were there to grab the gold tokens, did something that he had never in his life done before and would never repeat: He violently struck the first man he came to—his son Francesco. Who, after the blow, stood absolutely motionless, as if he had received an order to stand at attention. Carlo stopped, in turn, because the blow seemed to have paralyzed his hand. At this point Ugo intervened and, with a handkerchief soaked in chloroform, immobilized Carlo, then knocked him out, while Peppe flung himself on Matteo, using the same approach. It didn't take much; Matteo was already asleep on his feet and expected it. The only problem was Daniela, who started screaming, but she was immediately restrained. Once this was done, Peppe—while Ugo, already excited, began to tie up the three and film them—glanced at Francesco. The boy was staggering about the room, as if stunned. Peppe immediately grabbed the bags. They were very heavy. He put them in a gym bag, then made a sign to Ugo, who immobilized Francesco too. Francesco put up some weak resistance before the chloroform knocked him out. When he came to, he found himself in an embarrassing position: He was in his underwear, and his legs were tied together with his arms—like a salami. His father was next to him, bound in the same position. For all practical purposes, they were two morons. In front of them was Ugo, tied to a table. The camera was shooting him, half-asleep. Peppe went up to Francesco and said: I'm sorry. I didn't mean for it to go like this. I found out a little while ago about a miracle—they made the wrong diagnosis. I'm not going to die, and that is good news; the bad news is that I didn't have a cent—I've spent everything, and I'm desperate. I need money. I'm taking it all and getting out. When they find you, you'll be able to say you were the victim of a robbery. Or confess everything, including my name. But don't do that. First of all, because it will be too late, I'll already be gone. Second, because if you become known at your young age, then you're finished in this line of work. And you have the stuff. Don't waste your talent.

After which Peppe got on the motorcycle and sped off in great excitement, the wind cooling his sweat.

It Was an Instant

The first symptom hinting at a brain tumor had been difficulty walking. Peppe had wanted to accelerate and instead he braked. It was an instant, then he retook control of the situation. When, shortly before the robbery, the doctor, a woman, in tears, apologizing over and over again, explained about the mistake—a simple, stupid, imbecilic mixup of X-rays—Peppe felt as if he had been reborn. And as a result of that sensation, he was like a child who has not yet learned to walk. For long minutes, in fact, he couldn't remember how to walk. Now, on the motorcycle, with the gold tokens, he felt that he had regained full control of his faculties. He was happy. The horizon was clear.

He certainly didn't expect a drunk to cross the street like that. Obviously Peppe tried to brake, but because of a sort of strange, unexpected symptom, he accelerated and hit the man.

The Architect

Riccardo came out of the bar and realized that he was about to faint. A classic drop in blood sugar. Riccardo often watched the TV show *Paperissima*, which featured people caught at embarrassing moments, and laughed heartily when he saw couples passing out at the altar from emotion. He couldn't understand how it was possible to lose your strength like that, so that you seemed like a sack of potatoes left to itself, or someone who, given a push, staggers slightly, then, taking a dozen steps forward, falls flat on his face, powerless, like a dead man. He had the thought that the neighborhood was in the process of being renovated, before his sight darkened; and in spite of the blackness into which he was plunged, he took five steps, like a drunk, right into the middle of the street, and was violently struck by a motorcycle proceeding at high speed. When, after seventy-two hours, Riccardo finally regained consciousness, he realized, reading the newspaper, that he had been an involuntary hero, one who brings about the arrest of the foolish old protagonist of a comic heist of gold tokens, because, having fainted, he ends up under the motorcycle and flies forward a few meters. Every article he read emphasized the fact that the gold tokens, scattered all over the street, had been set upon by the neighborhood residents. Of every age, old and young, new arrivals and longtime inhabitants.

SILENCE IS GOLDEN

BY BOOSTA

Tangenziale

Translated by Ann Goldstein

The sports car speeds along the asphalt ribbon. The last mechanic who worked on it said that a car that low brings bad luck; the mechanic is a Jehovah's Witness and he's convinced that the closer you are to the ground the farther you are from the grace of God.

He drives looking straight ahead, she tilts her head slightly to the right; her forehead, hidden by blond bangs, hits the window at every bump. An almost constant noise, monotonous, grating.

Jolt.

Thump.

Jolt.

Thump.

He would like to tell her to move, to pay attention, but all he manages to do is grunt. He opens his mouth as if to speak but remains suspended between the last thought and the first word, in apnea. She won't help; she watches the unbroken stripe that marks the emergency lane and remains silent. At the interchange for the Castelli Romani he takes the ring road; the car points south.

Signal, a glance in the rearview mirror, the engine grinds as he slows down and lets himself be swallowed up in the darkness by the broad asphalt ribbon filled with tires and metal plates.

He's trying for the fourth time—he's begun to count the number of times he tries.

He does it partly to occupy his mind and partly to make sure that everything is really happening and that it's not the fault of some nausea-inducing systemic bug in the universe that spits us out by the billions onto earth.

How are you? he manages to say.

Then, again, there's that pale forehead knocking against the glass, and the silence.

For one, three, ten interminable seconds.

She opens her mouth, parts her crimson-painted lips, and says, in a very distant singsong, Look out, you should be in the right-hand lane.

Suddenly he feels a crash beneath his breastbone, the collision between a raging and unsustainable irritation and the knowledge that you need patience if you want to be the superman of a woman like this.

For an instant he hates her.

For an instant it seems to him that two yellow eyes are approaching in the rearview mirror and he feels like laughing and shouting in fear.

He doesn't need a reason to hate her.

He doesn't need a motive to kill her.

He would give an arm to have her again the way she was at the beginning.

He brings a hand to his heart and feels nothing.

He lowers the volume on the radio with the index finger of his right hand and sighs loudly.

Again he tries to say something, I . . . but she interrupts him.

Shut up. Shut up. I've never seen anyone act as ridiculous as you so many times in a single evening. Why can't you leave me alone, let me live and breathe? Why are you so incredibly insecure?

Tonight? he asks as if he hadn't been aware of a thing.

Yes, tonight. Always trying to find my hand, hand, hand. As if you were a five-year-old child looking for his mother . . . Will you get it through your skull that I'm not your mother? I need a man, a real man, who gives me security but doesn't suffocate me. You suffocate me, you're like a murderer strangling his victim. I can't breathe anymore . . .

He watches the knuckles of his fingers turn white, he feels the grip of his hands crushing the leather steering wheel. He accelerates, now the car is pressed tight to the road, aggressive and fast.

She continues, Always whining, demanding. First you don't want me to talk at all and you're insulted by everything I say, then I mingle at the party and your eyes are following me like radar. I don't recognize you anymore . . .

She knows that to end the sentence properly she has to take a long pause and say . . .

I don't know.

He brakes in order to avoid hitting a truck that's traveling as slowly as an elephant.

He sees himself reflected in the sloping windshield of his car.

Thin, tan, curly hair mussed, white shirt at least as tired as he is.

Why do you talk to me like that? he asks, defenseless.

But he knows perfectly well why she talks like that.

Because he's been transformed into a coward.

Because together they've completely destroyed the monument of their story and he can't bear it.

For months he's been crying at night, secretly, drowning his sobs in the pillow and getting up every five minutes.

He signals right, he needs gas.

The station is deserted, the self-service pumps work twenty-four hours a day. On the automatic cash register there's a flyer, the face of a smiling young man in an IP cap. He reads the caption while he inserts twenty euros in the slot. It's a newspaper clipping.

The boy was a gas-station attendant.

He worked at that station.

He was killed three weeks ago in a robbery, by thieves after the cash.

Two hundred and forty euros.

And so?

And so? she asks.

Let's get going, I'm tired and my contact lenses are getting dry . . .

He finishes reading quickly, chooses a pump, and thinks that the kid didn't deserve it.

Maybe no, maybe yes, but not like that, and anyway he feels bad for him.

He feels bad.

He thinks that she, lustful and fierce as a mantis, would have deserved it much more.

For what she's doing to him, to them, to the monument of the two of them.

To die a terrible death, the death of a woman who leaves her man instead of caring for him through hard times.

A few drops on the side of the car, if he had a match it would all be easy.

He gets in and drives off, now she's staring at him.

I don't know . . . I think we should talk about it.

He thinks that with a little luck he could make the car crash against the guardrail in just the right place so that the window would shatter and the corner of the trailer would pass right through her without leaving even a scratch. A couple of spins and he'd come to a stop there, straddling the lanes, in a state of confusion. Ready to start again.

He doesn't want to listen and raises the volume on the radio, she turns and looks silently at the dark outline of the hills, the fires burning on the smaller parallel roads, the shadows of the whores running along and jumping in cars like theirs.

He passes the truck without signaling, locks his jaw, one step away from cramping his facial muscles.

The radio is playing The Police.

This is the song you need. Learn to leave me alone, learn, she says, happy and exasperated at the same time.

Don't stand, don't stand so close to me.

He shakes his head. He'd like to have cascades of words ready to pour out of his wounded mouth, legions of truth endowed with conviction, like Christians in the middle of a crowded arena. But not a thing, he can't say a thing because grief strangles him, and to have imagined her dead has upset him even more.

Weak, he feels weak, and the light of the dashboard projects an orange stigmata on his shirt.

Finally he manages to mutter, Then why are you still with me?

His eyes are shining.

Again she pauses for a long time while she pretends to hum. She knows it, the why, but she says, I don't know.

He accelerates.

He thinks about jerking to a sudden stop while she's unbuckling her seat belt: She would hit her head and with a little luck some interesting scenarios might open up.

But he repents.

There is no revenge, there is no redemption, only tears.

You're driving worse than a blind man, watch out.

She is so beautiful that looking at her makes him feel terribly immoral, like someone spying through the chinks of a confessional.

She shouldn't exist.

That old adage that the higher you go the harder you fall sounds more and more real.

He thinks of his friends, all absent spectators at this farce. They, too, are ready to stab him, because basically it couldn't last.

Life is a serious business—if you start thinking about how much pain, you risk swerving off the road. If he weren't crying silently he would have thought he'd fallen asleep at the wheel.

Five hundred meters to the Autogrill on the ring road.

He downshifts and with his left ring finger engages the right turn signal. He goes into neutral for a moment in the emergency lane because he's always liked hearing the wheels spin freely, out of control, for a few seconds, it lets him breathe.

He steps on the clutch and puts the car in gear, takes his foot off, and the engine screeches while the revolutions get slower and the wall approaches a little too quickly.

It could end like this. She's right, everything is unfolding badly, tiredly, for the worse.

He heard her say to a friend, Do something for him, he's gotten heavy and boring.

He saw her smile several times at another friend.

Friends, how many infiltrated in the ranks of the good . . .

An abrupt turn of the wheel, and he is calmly controlling the approach to the brightly lit bar.

They get out of the car and separate.

He leans on the hood, which is hot, and peers at the sky; she heads, hips swaying, in the direction of the rest room.

She walks the way princesses of ancient Egypt must have walked.

Slow, sinuous, she glides over the asphalt without touching it, without hurrying. You need nobility of soul or an extreme lack of control to walk like that.

The same voice from before tells him that now, right now she can't see him, he could take off and leave her there.

Or he could set fire to everything, run away, and let her burn. It would be the bonfire of vanity, the fire of catharsis.

Would a fabulous cunt like her be transformed into a phoenix as she runs maddened into the night, he wonders.

Would the gas station explode?

Would he die too?

Would the poor attendant survive or join his former colleague of a few kilometers and a few minutes earlier?

Would there be a big bang?

And what if he were saved but disfigured for life?

He doesn't have the stuff of a pyromaniac, not him.

He turns on the engine while she touches up her makeup in the passenger-side mirror.

He puts it in first, drives off with a little jerk, and brakes suddenly after a dozen meters.

She screams.

A deafening, terrifying sound, like a trumpet. A noise not human stops his heart while a divine light floods the car's interior.

The biggest truck in the world passes by with its horn blasting a few centimeters from his door.

Then it grows distant in the night.

Her makeup is all smeared and she is weeping hysterically, out of fear.

Sometimes it simply happens that the whole universe plots against you.

He is silent, dazed, the car stops along the edge of the road, clouds of gnats in the headlight beams and brave crickets singing of lovely death.

The silence hurts more than death's scythe.

It's toxic and humiliating, terminal.

Sorry, sweetheart, he stammers.

Shut up and take me home, she says.

The words bounce first against the window on the passenger side, reaching him only on the rebound.

But they are faraway words, he is alive and this for now is enough. Fear, the sudden terror has distanced him from her. Now it's as if he has grasped the good and the bad, the drama and the farce. His love finished, and his love with makeup smeared like a clown or a whore at the end of the night.

He scratches his nose.

He starts off again.

He turns up the music a little and, out of the corner of his eye, lets himself glance at the cheap imitation of the woman he's in love with. He hums, he tries to stay in tune to show that he can do something well.

You lousy shit, you practically got me killed. I can't deal with you anymore, I'm not happy.

She says she's not happy and he somehow understands.

To be in love does not imply being completely stupid.

In his new privileged position he manages to feel opposing

feelings at the same time, the joy of survival and the torture of abandonment.

He struggles to swallow the knot that rises in his throat, he would like to be able to tell her that everything's fine, that they'll be happy, that there won't be any room for sadness between them.

But again nothing comes out.

He would like to tell her that he's been struggling for a lifetime, that he's felt bad for a lifetime, that the only time he feels good is when he sleeps with her, tightly embraced.

If he took the key out of the ignition while they're hurtling toward the curve they could talk about it in the afterlife.

Now he has so much darkness in his head, so much that she wouldn't be able to find his face to hit him.

Sweetheart, I'm doing everything and the opposite of everything to make you happy, but it's so complicated, it's incredibly painful to never see you happy, I don't know what to do, he says all in one breath.

She laughs in his face.

Now he stops talking.

Homicide can also be an evolved feeling of mercy, even if he's not thinking about it anymore.

He downshifts, puts on the turn signal without listening to the music anymore, and musters courage.

Why are we stopping?

She might have said it, he doesn't know with certainty because he's not listening.

The place is completely deserted.

He pulls up to the most invisible point and turns the key. The engine sighs and then is silent, only the fan whirs loudly.

What the fuck are we doing here? Now she's definitely said it.

You know that I love you? he says, staring at her.

Now she's worried, she gets out of the car, dark and aggressive, so that she seems as never before a dangerous animal, well camouflaged.

Why don't you accept this very simple, very beautiful thing? I love you and I don't want to be forced to pursue, to suffer, to always ask . . .

Now she looks behind him, as if hoping for the arrival of someone, something.

Please, let's go, she says.

He puts a hand in his pocket and she starts to back up.

I could never treat someone the way you do, I could never humiliate you the way you humiliate me, I couldn't hate you . . .

Suddenly the wind rises, strong, violent.

His shirt, open to the second button, swells. She backs up some more and in spite of that his eyes seem to approach, burning.

All I ask is to be able to love you.

She continues to look at his right hand in the wide pocket of his pants.

All right, but you scared the hell out of me and . . .

He brings his left index finger to his lips, making a sign for her to be silent.

They go on this way a little longer, one step after the other, she retreating and he advancing slowly.

She glances back and notices that she's getting close to a billboard, the ad pasted to it promoting the wine of the Castelli, a wine that's good for your blood.

He sees it too.

Blood.

The highway, in the distance, begins to grow light.

On the slight incline the headlights of a truck appear, bright and powerful.

I've done everything for you, forever, I can't understand what I could have done wrong this time. Every time! he shouts.

She stumbles and ends up on the ground, her hands reaching forward, her voice strangled by fear.

Listen, I can't do it, I didn't think you would . . .

The lights are getting closer, and he stops.

This is the scene of the moment when it's all over.

She is sitting.

He is standing.

The car is far away.

The car is low.

God is distracted because the car is low.

The truck is arriving swiftly.

The truck proceeds toward them, facing him. He takes a step forward.

She cries out desperately.

He takes a step sideways.

The truck hits him directly.

He knows he has always loved her.

She didn't know that another *she* hadn't loved him.

To the police, while the emergency workers scoop up the last shreds of white shirt off the asphalt, she says absently that it was the first time.

That he had paid in advance.

That she had never seen him before.

That he had told her what to do, how and when.

That he had told her what to say.

A policeman gives her his wallet.

Inside is a photograph, there she is.

Another she.
A she who didn't love him.

CAPUT MUNDI

BY GIUSEPPE GENNA

Montecitorio

Translated by Anne Milano Appel

Rome, early, brisk May morning. The sky is clear and the air surprisingly chilly. Tension converges in the frigid sunshine, an unperceived tension. Humans, tourists and natives, walk along Via del Corso in dense throngs, their clothing vivid, smiling, thinking about what they have to do, where they have to go, the office, monuments to visit: everyday banalities. What is commonly called happiness. What others more warily call serenity—or indifference. Everyday life: banal, feverish, cheerful, Roman . . .

Police cars are packed tighter than usual around Montecitorio. Palazzo Montecitorio, seat of the Chamber of Deputies: the political heart of the nation. The old, yellowish Baroque building, which the genius Bernini distilled from an incubus of the imagination, twisting and bending the forms in dizzying abysses, complicating the internal labyrinths, widening the staircases, violating the door of the guarded entrance that faces the hunchbacked piazza. Here there are soldiers everywhere. And near the hotel to the left of the Chamber's façade as well. This is the hotel where uniforms of American pilots were stolen in 2001, along with their badges: the access source for the terrorists who brought about September 11. It came out in subsequent investigations: a robbery in Rome for the attack in New York.

A butterfly flapping its wings in Beijing can become a tornado in New York, according to fractal theory. A banal theory, a serene butterfly. Don't trust butterflies, or serene banality.

Montecitorio surrounded by soldiers: Inside, there's no one. The sessions are adjourned.

Evidently, not all of the sessions are adjourned. The Premier, pale, rushes out of the smaller side door, not intended for television cameras, which for that matter are absent. What is he leaving behind on a chilly, luminous day of adjournment like this one? A rare chat with some listless deputies in the Transatlantico, the excessively Baroque hallway called "dei passi perduti," the corridor of "lost footsteps," where the Republic's intrigues, both transparent and obscure, are hatched.

Outside, the chill does not seem to ease up. The Italian flag, limp in the cold air, hangs over the main door of Montecitorio along with the blue European one: bright in a cloudless sky.

In the narrow streets around Montecitorio: centuries-old dampness, the reek of cat piss, of animal piss. Gaps in the bricks, irregularly set. Some pigeons hunker in the cracks of the wall to protect themselves against the cold: They coo. Cats cross paths with one another. People walk along, some toward the Pantheon.

Via Sant'Andrea delle Fratte. Two hundred meters from Montecitorio as the crow flies.

The surreal atmosphere of this cold spell. An imperceptible tension glances off the walls encrusted with nineteenth-century plaster, the old niches of the masters, the rust-brown paint of the closely set buildings. Via Sant'Andrea delle Fratte:

its strange, not-quite-right opening. Abnormal, narrow, difficult, yet expansive, forcing all eyes to the church, which dominates the street and the opening. The church's façade is a flat barrier, peculiar, it seems to bear down on the back of the skull. It is naked, pure masonry, the color of tufa almost. A further work of the architect Bernini, a bell tower that impresses tourists, though Romans have grown accustomed to the sight of that anomaly. The bell tower is indescribable: It is a small temple, joined to the ground by an unreal masonry volute. The main entry of the church is a door: a plain door. There is no rose window; there is just a window.

In front of the entrance: armored cars and a doubled guard. The Italian Premier is very Catholic and prays here every day.

Now he is inside.

Inside the Church of Sant'Andrea delle Fratte there is an explosion of gold. Periodically, the Santissimo, the consecrated Host of the body of Christ, is exposed, and for this reason one must kneel upon entering. It is a scene that is enthralling for tourists, customary for Romans. Only a few faithful come here. Right now there are four of them. They are praying to the monstrosity of the Santissimo, the walled altar, the worked gold. The small shrine in which the body of Christ is exposed to view: a masterpiece of the goldsmith's art and faith. Wherever you are, inside the church, you see the Santissimo, you look at Christ. The church is very small, with one nave. There are four rows of benches for the faithful, very close together.

The Premier is kneeling down in his dark overcoat, his oversized glasses smudged with fingerprints and dust, his head bent, his eyes shut tight, his hands joined at his breast.

This is the part that makes your head spin.

A small gold almond appears.

The Madonna appeared here in Rome in 1820, and two Jewish bankers of the Ratisbonne family were instantly converted.

The small gold almond quivers and expands.

It appears to stream forth from the altar, it instantly inflames the altar's gold like an ultra-body, a blazing spirit.

It is the void exploding.

The void explodes and grows larger, the flame is hungry for air, it mushrooms.

The Premier of Italy only has time to be astounded, to raise his bent head.

The church collapses in a roar.

The bodyguards are killed in the blast.

When the attaché, former FEMA, of the United States third intelligence service in Rome, the real secret agency, arrives at the scene of the devastation, the disaster has not been reconstructed: Italians, those clever people, spaghetti-eaters good for patting him on the head or endlessly running around behind the bench of the Court of New York, in perpetual trials against the Mafia. Clever guys good for Scorsese. The attaché who arrives at the "scene of the slaughter" (the dirge, repeated over and over, audible above the dense ring of reporters droning on like automatons in front of their cameramen) has the advantage of language: He is a fourth-generation macaronic and knows how to listen, knows how to speak Italian, and knows what the Italians are hiding under this language that is the oldest and most ambiguous modern tongue in the world, intact for eight hundred years, from Dante's *Inferno* through to today.

What Joe Spiazzi sees, zipping his jacket up to his neck, occasionally flashing an embassy badge, is an inferno of concrete and centuries-old beams of moth-eaten wood, the remains of an unseemly bell tower, a few meters from the political heart of the nation that generated, digested, and excreted its great-grandfathers to the New World. The church is no longer there. The bodies have been extracted from the rubble. The cars are ulcerated scrap iron.

A sublime country, Italy, for those who adore ruins: These are new ones. It's a nice place to visit: The food is good. But right now the scene is nauseating. The beauty of Italy, not understood by those who come from outside, lies in its complex, esoteric mysteries, in its architectural heights that radiate age-old struggles: stone gargoyles and demons directed toward Saint Peter's, the perennial clashing ground between one Spirit and another: The first speaks Latin, the second English.

Joe Spiazzi has the nerve to smile. He shakes his head. His cream-colored jacket matches the extreme hue of his wrecked incisors, his salt-and-pepper hair, his almost jaundiced skin, despite his excessive body bulk: He adores suckling pigs . . .

He despises Rome. He is fifty-two years old and his family is miles and miles away, an astronomical distance away, in a city with a name that eternally recalls Italy, Assisi, where Saint Francis spoke to and tamed the wolf: Ciudad de la Iglesia de Nuestra Señora de Los Angeles sobra la Porziuncola de Asìs—otherwise known as Los Angeles. Or better yet, to teach a lesson to the Spirit who speaks convoluted Latin: L.A. Where his wife, on the West Coast, at this hour, 1 in the morning, having put the two kids to bed, is studying the sparkle in Jim Morrison's eyes in the mural in front of their house, in the neighborhood of Venice—built to imitate the network of Venetian canals, Italian hydraulic and urban engineering exported to the world: *Made in Italy*. A little like Joe Spiazzi's family bunch: wacky in Italy, reborn in the American dream.

Just a short time left now before he returns home. He's served two years in this Muslim crossroads, central to the geopolitics of U.S. intelligence only because the Polish Pope was suffering from Parkinson's and the next Pope would be a German to be controlled and tamed as Saint Francis did with the wolf. This country is shaped like a boot and, as everyone knows, boots sink into mud. This peripheral mud that for years now has been outside any borders that matter. This city that calls itself eternal and proclaims itself to be the second Jerusalem, with its bell towers that are better suited to postcards than the heart of a dying faith.

Checks on the Muslims: routine. In actuality: to ascertain destination routes. Those shits from al Qaeda don't plan anything in Italy: Italy doesn't exist, it's just a channel to move through—an empty boot. There is nothing critical here. Joe wasted his time on satellite surveillance, the monitoring of subjects by SIGINT, SIGnals INTelligence, even old-fashioned tailing. He hates the black terrorist bombers, the young guys in Iraq should do what nobody has the guts to say: drop the Bomb and so long to everyone—Sunnis, Shiites, Kurds, imams. He voted for Bush Jr. in the embassy ballot box. He hates the Democrats: ticks who feed on blood indiscriminately, who don't even know what and where Rome is, sucking Joe Spiazzi's blood and that of his family.

It's almost over, not even a month left until his return to L.A., and this mess erupts. The Italian Premier killed and dismembered by an exceptional explosion, in the very heart of Rome. Fuck. There's now a chance his boss might keep him here. All of a sudden, Italy becomes a boiling point—and not because it's sunny here.

He looks around: It's a shambles. Italian police, colleagues of Joe dressed as Italian policemen: This is, after all, the fifty-third state. Firemen. Scientific teams. Dogs. Tape to cordon off the area.

It's pointless to stay here. Better to return to headquarters. Behind Palazzo San Macuto, a building of gray ashlar where the Italians form their governmental commissions, endlessly discuss attacks and massacres, and struggle like ants to bring home a crumb of power that comes from above—never reaching any conclusion. The Palazzo that should solve Italy's mysteries: All they'd have to do is call him, Joe Spiazzi, he would teach a class to the commission members for a couple of hours, and they would go home with three-quarters of the solutions that they stopped seeking years ago.

Time to go. Leave the "scene of the slaughter." He crosses Via del Corso, obviously closed to traffic. He sees two bums passing a bottle of liquor back and forth, laughing obscenely.

Obscene. He swerves away from them. And suddenly he hears . . . in the immense din of the excavation, in the jumble of acute siren wails, he hears . . . one of the two tramps. Who shouts: "Hey, Joe!"

Joe Spiazzi turns, he doesn't know where that call is coming from, whether it's even directed at him. A 360-degree scan in a few fractions of a second and he intercepts one of the two bums who raises the bottle to him and shouts again: "Hey, Joe!" Nobody pays any attention to those two bums, nobody notices the anomaly, and with his hands in his pockets he clutches the two Beretta Px4 Storms, feels the technopolymer grip of the two semiautomatics. Thirty shots available. And the bum approaches swaying, smiling . . .

"Joe . . ." he murmurs, smiling, bottle in hand.

Joe smiles back, twisting his neck to the right, and in his slow Italian, devoid of inflection, he says: "Move and you're dead."

"You too," and the bum keeps smiling. "My companion shoots if you shoot. We don't want to shoot. You don't want to shoot."

Joe smiles.

The bum is motionless, bottle raised in the air. "It's just to talk. We won't move. There's nothing we're supposed to do to you, just something we have to tell you. If you call your colleagues disguised as Italian cops, we'll shoot. We'll shoot everywhere. We just want to talk. Briefly . . ."

Joe smiles and has time to think about the sparkle in his wife's pupils; his wife, who is now, in the Los Angeles night, staring at the sparkle in the pupils of that two-dimensional, faded Jim Morrison on the wall at 17th Place.

"In less than fifteen minutes you'll get a call on your cell phone. It's your boss at the Third Service. He will inform you that the perpetrators of the massacre, four Arabs belonging to al Qaeda, have been caught. Within an hour the TV networks will go crazy. Your president will go crazy. All this is fake. The church blew up, and you don't know a thing."

Joe stops smiling and asks: "What should I know?"

"You, nothing. That's why we're using you as a contact. We know and we want those who know to know that we know."

"And who knows?"

"Nothing will happen to you. It's just a short time before you go back to where you came from. Venice is a very nice area, you have a very nice family . . ."

Joe's index fingers squeeze the triggers, the triggers are at the halfway point of their short arc. "What do you want?"

"For you, who don't know anything, to know. That you make it known. And to give you some advice. Take your family and move them. Not because we have any intention to do anything to you. You understand. The important thing is *now*,

Joe. Joe Spiazzi, when he receives the telephone call from his boss, won't be here: He'll be a few hundred meters away from here. Piazza Minerva. The Minerva Obelisk. The one in front of the Dominican church. Designed by Bernini. The one with the elephant whose ass faces the entrance to the church, as an affront to the Pope. You know the one?"

Joe knows it. A hundred meters as the crow flies. "And why should I go there?"

"Because the tapes will be handed over to you. You'll take in as much as you want to take in, but it's important that you see them and then report to your boss. Your boss knows, but he doesn't have the tapes. He knows what they were up to, but he isn't clear on how and why."

"What *who* was up to?"

The bum falls silent, takes a slug, moving the bottle cautiously.

Joe: "And if I don't do it?"

"No big deal. We'll find other channels. You, however, will stay in Rome. For sure: How could four shitty Arabs who blew up the Italian Premier in a centrally located church have escaped you? It's your problem. And your family's. I think it's essential that you move them. To understand what I mean, you have to see the tapes." *Ipse dixit.* Another slug of liquor. "Only twelve minutes until your boss calls. You should go. You can turn your back on us, there's nothing more we have to do, we won't do anything to you."

Joe Spiazzi is motionless: human granite compressed at the moment of decision.

He turns his back on the bums.

He trusts them.

He goes to Piazza Minerva.

* * *

He photographed the two men. What service are they agents of? As soon as he gets back, digital images of their features: They'll be entered in multiple databases. Joe will know who the players are. And what the game is.

There it is. The elephant designed by Bernini supports a pointed obelisk, dazzling in the chilly morning. The dust of the blown-up church covers everything. He has left traceable footsteps on his way here.

Six meters of monument—faded red granite. An obelisk erected by a pharaoh. Joe remembers when he dealt with sculpture and esotericism in Rome, when there wasn't a thing to do all day except locate Arabs and blacks in *bubu* outfits; it was interesting. The elephant, exotic and adorned with hallucinogenic fabric, has a significance: It supports the obelisk.

. . . *a robust mind is necessary to support solid wisdom* . . .

A time when stones radiated, spoke. Even now those stones radiate—the late Italian Premier knows something about it.

The cell phone rings. Fourteen minutes have passed since the bum called out to him.

"Yeah?"

"It's Robert. Come back to headquarters, it's urgent. We've been hit by an earthquake. You fucked up. Our men have intercepted and captured the four guys who committed the massacre. They say they belong to al Qaeda. Saudis or something like that. We have to plug the leaks. You should have stayed on top of them. They've confessed. In less than an hour the news will be given to the press."

Joe swallows a filament of gastric acid. "I'm coming. I need some time. It's chaos here."

Robert cuts off the call.

What's going on? Joe leans against the elephant: the resistant granite eaten away by weather which erodes everything, which turns everything into excrement. Metabolism: this superhuman, temporal force. Ashes to ashes, dust to dust: even that of a church blown sky high.

"Stay there. Leaning like that. It's perfect." The voice, Italian, is deep and penetrating. From under the elephant's belly, Joe glimpses only an abdomen and the crotch of the man's Prada pants. The man who is speaking, his voice calm, not commanding. "With your hand propped like that, I can see that you're holding only one of the Berettas in your pocket. Fifteen shots. There's no reason to use it. You should know, however, that you are in someone's sights. The building to your left, third window on the right, on the second floor."

Joe moves his head with infinitesimal caution. He sees the glitter, guesses that it's an altered AK-47. He cannot guess who is behind the weapon.

Joe returns to his position. "What do you want?"

"They already told you. Watch the DVD before going back to Third Service headquarters. Turn everything over to Robert McIntire, the section head. You will be given an immediate transfer. Home. They will know that we know. We want one more thing: for you to say that it is now too late. It has begun. It's already done. Think about your family, Spiazzi. Stay where you are, in that position, for another two minutes, and don't take your eyes off the DVD that I will now place on top of the monument, here, under the elephant's belly."

The hand sets down a small unlabeled DVD case.

The man goes away.

Joe continues leaning against the elephant designed by Bernini: a strong mind, supporting wisdom.

He turns cautiously to the window on the second floor: Nothing glitters anymore, the room is empty.

Two minutes. He grabs the DVD case, opens it: an unlabeled disk.

He looks for an Internet café.

It is not a wise choice, but since it isn't, it is: an Arabic Internet café. Outside the walls of San Giovanni. Appia Nuova. The opposite direction from his agency's headquarters. There would be a saturation check on all Arabs. In a few minutes the Italians would be able to raid and inspect. If the DVD was risky for him, the Italian police would nonetheless provide a delay to plot his next moves.

He is the most out-of-the-way customer. No one can see the screen of the computer he's using. He has the headphones half on, so he can hear what's happening in the place and at the same time listen to the audio of the DVD.

Twelve files. Twelve film clips. He double-clicks on the first.

Images shot from a video camera outside Palazzo Montecitorio. There is a date and time: an evening twelve weeks earlier. The view shifts, scanning the way to the service exit. A car. Political figures get out. Here is the slain Premier. Leaders and representatives of the opposition. Last: a cardinal. The one most cited for the next Consistory, after the brief parenthesis of the German Pope who won't last long: He has already had two strokes.

A cardinal at Montecitorio?

The number of guests: eleven.

Change of scene. An interior. Joe recognizes it. The main room of the President of the Chamber. There he is, the President. Bugs everywhere in that place. Joe himself had been there, to replace someone who didn't show up, passing himself off as one of the Italian Services. The image is blurry, the lighting dim. The President. The Premier. The Cardinal. They are all seated at a large, round table: twelve of them. A table of the Basile school, the Masonic architect who designed Montecitorio's interiors. Esoteric symbols on the table's Baroque legs.

They begin. Is it a séance?

The audio jumbled: "*. . . so then let us concentrate, and together, through the visualization taught to us by the Masters, take action on the weak point, which will not give way unless we intervene . . . Let us invoke the Great One . . .*"

Obsessively they invoke the Great One. It is the Masonic god, the Great Architect of the Universe . . . Joe wonders what it means. What does it have to do with the massacre on Via Sant'Andrea delle Fratte? They continue invoking the Great One, hands linked to form a chain.

The image shifts. The group emerges from Montecitorio. First to go, the Cardinal with his retinue.

Joe Spiazzi doesn't understand. He clicks on the remaining eleven clips. The same scenes, few variations, the same participants.

The last one: the date and time: today, an hour before the explosion. The President releases the chain ahead of time, prompted by the Cardinal, who says: "*Done. The process is irreversible. Rome is triumphant once again. I must thank all of you. The head of the world will be beheaded.* Caput Mundi *for eternity: It comes back to right here, it is we . . .*"

Joes sees the Premier stand up.

A gap. The Premier leaves by the side door of Montecitorio. The escort speeds up, passes through the piazza, the camera follows the guard up to the church, visible on Via Sant'Andrea delle Fratte.

The blast.

Fade.

Joe Spiazzi is baffled. There is still a snippet of video file left. The same camera. It's night. The time in liquid display, the time when his wife gets bored at the desk of the advertising agency in Santa Monica. Here come some men. A van. Joe knows that van perfectly well. Four men get out. Joe knows those agents personally: They are his agents. They unhinge the door without making a sound. They come back out after a few minutes without a case they had taken in. Joe knows exactly what it contained.

They did it. Not the four from al Qaeda. Them. The Third Service.

Why? Joe checks the urge to vomit, his stomach shaken by a seismic shock.

The trip on a subway: slow, everything is blocked because of the massacre. He comes out of the metro's dark hole, looks for a taxi, it's hopeless.

He's at the gate of San Giovanni. He looks around, ponders whether to call someone out from the agency. The agency . . . The agency perpetrated the massacre, he was not informed—has he been cut out of the loop?

A car, a Fiat, slows down, stops alongside Joe. A tourist leans out, seems to ask him something. Joe grips the Beretta in his right pocket. His left hand is in a nervous contraction, clutching the DVD case. He approaches the Fiat. And from the rear window, which is slowly lowered, the face of Robert, head of the Third Service in Rome, leans out.

Joe's jaw drops.

"Joe—the DVD."

"You did it, Robert, the massacre . . ."

"It's something that doesn't concern you, yet you've already seen the files."

"But . . ."

"You have no way of knowing. The stakes are high. You aren't aware of everything. It's as if they launched ten atomic bombs on American soil. You don't realize what they've done . . ."

"Pray for the Great One?"

"Yes. Not God. The Big One. There are techniques for remote viewing, and there are techniques for moving objects from a distance. They moved the fault . . . mentally. Let's hope we intervened in time, before they were able to finish the job. We don't have tapes."

The Big One. The San Andreas fault. Not Sant'Andrea delle Fratte, another San Andreas. The Big One: the greatest earthquake the human race will ever experience in the technological era. California destroyed, seismic waves reaching as far as Canada. The San Andreas fault runs in a north-south direction along almost all of western California, passing through two major cities, San Francisco and Los Angeles, to then merge with another one farther south, the San Jacinto fault. The crustal plate that lies west of the fault moves northward, while that which lies to the east moves south, a phenomenon that gave rise to the term "transcurrent" or "strike-slip" fault. The friction between the two giant plates of rock builds up large amounts of energy which, when released, produces violent earthquakes.

Venice reduced to a Pleistocene landscape.

A tsunami that returns from the Pacific, while the West Coast is in flames.

The Americans, from what is gathered from the movies they export all over the planet, value the family a great deal.

Joe leans close to his boss and whispers: "It's already too late. They did it. They moved the fault."

"Get in the car, we'll see what we can do."

They begin shooting, thirty shots from the Beretta Px4 Storms riddle the car and the car is bulletproof. It's all over in an instant, in a few seconds the Third Service Italian ambulance is on the scene: It was ready and waiting a hundred meters back. There's a street accident to be cleaned up, an Italian-American tourist killed by Roman bandits.

In Venice, as the widowed Mrs. Spiazzi finally conquers her insomnia, a slight chink makes the pupils of the mural appear walleyed: Jim Morrison's gaze slips, but keeps staring long after he's gone.

1988

BY NICOLA LAGIOIA

Via Appia Antica

Translated by Ann Goldstein

Saverio Candito, Giancarlo Colasanti, Danilo Giovinazzo. My best friends. We grew up together in the flamboyant prosperity of the last economic miracle. Out of an absurd desire for revenge, or maybe because we were imbeciles, we decided at a certain point to vex our parents by devoting ourselves to an activity that at the time, 1988 more or less, around Rome and all over Italy, still represented a real scandal. And this is our epilogue.

The police cars arrived, sirens off, around 4 in the afternoon. They circled in vain a few times, cleaving the banks of hot air in which the neighborhood languished. Then, by dint of trial and error, they turned onto the right street. The roadway narrowed, forcing them to go single file. They downshifted to second gear near a villa surrounded by plaster discus throwers and other travesties of good taste that even the ignorance of our professors of design would have called "an obscenity." They slowed further and turned off their engines. Now they were stopped behind a Testarossa, each of whose wheel rims was worth the annual salary of the ten men in uniform who, with the excuse of cutting short a crime, did the same thing to my adolescence.

The Ferrari Testarossa was not the only plow tracing the furrow that separated the lovers of excess from the rest of the world: those without significant desires, high-school teachers, family men who month after month put away the leftovers of other people's revelries in the furnace of health insurance. Driving along the main avenue, the five white-trimmed blue Alfettas of the cops had already come up against similar metaphors. For example, the other villas. They were almost all illegal. They rose two or three stories, taking their cues from the fake lawns littered with mountain bikes, yellow and red T-shirts signed with felt-tip pens by Bruno Conti or Falcao, half-empty champagne bottles. Every villa culminated in a terrace overflowing with ornamental plants, and two out of three had a pool. They were what's called a slap in the face of poverty, but they stood out in the splendor of the summer light—the blinding white of the stucco against the blue of the sky—so as to make you think that a pardon had already been granted in the parliamentary wings of the Almighty.

The first to notice the arrival of the law were the Saggese twins. But it's also likely that the men in uniform, just getting out of their cars, managed to extract from the background music of the cicadas the unmistakable signs of a tennis match. *Dunlop ball against synthetic string—squeak of sole on Mateco concrete—rubber against racket accompanied by the typical "huh!" with which athletes emphasize the heave of their chests—silence—net—curse.* The tennis courts were confined to the southern part of the residential area, well hidden by the pines near the Appia Nuova, and on one of the two rectangles Cristiano and Stefano Saggese lived in voluntary exile. They shared thirty-two years, perfectly divided between them, in addition to a low forehead and a particular mixture of prudence and lack of imagination that, if I had been able at the time to play with words, I would certainly have called homozygous idiocy.

Michele Saggese, the boys' father, was the only one in the neighborhood who in his youth had frequented the halls of the university, the only one who used an accountant to pay his taxes, the only one who was seriously tormented by the thought that his children might hang out with those of the neighbors. That is, us. He lost sleep at night over it. Cristiano and Stefano, in turn, believed that a journey through the urethra of an individual convinced that government securities and the separation of garbage for recycling were the basis of civilization deserved to be repaid in the coin of obedience. As a result, they stayed clear of us. And, given that the southernmost reaches of the neighborhood gave us a sense of melancholy (we couldn't bear the sober schematicism of the courts), the Saggese twins made tennis the St. Helena of those who have never passed through Waterloo. How many matches did they play thanks to us? Hours and hours of perfecting their technique, entire afternoons of following the ball. Every so often their father showed up too. He watched them with satisfaction, nursing the impossible dream of a Davis Cup win in doubles. But in general the only difficult finish line that losers manage to cross has to do with logic: They are capable of reaching excellent levels of mediocrity. In fact, at the time there was talk everywhere of Serena and Venus Williams. But of the Saggese twins at Wimbledon, only the intimation of a study vacation.

Thus, when Stefano Saggese went to retrieve a ball that had ended up outside the fence, the scoreboard with which he mentally covered the distance that separated him from match point shattered in the face of a different sort of calculation. One, two, three, four, *five* police cars . . . He raised his head and shared with his clone the same conclusion that receivers of stolen goods come to before vanishing silently through one of the many service doors available to those who—in an immense kingdom of speculators, small-town whores, and drug addicts such as Rome was in the '80s—appreciate a certain discretion along with the flow of cash.

"Something is happening . . ." Stefano Saggese said.

Since at a certain point the number of kids with no police record was not sufficient even for a bridge tournament, I never really understood the procedure. Ten cops surround a neoclassical-style villa full of expensive junk. While two or three approach the gate, two more take down the license number of the Ferrari, one maybe communicates with headquarters, but who is authorized to talk to the passersby? Whoever this nameless man is, his job is even more monotonous than that of the person playing the role of the herald in a Shakespearian tragedy. Two lines and exit: Usually passersby haven't seen anything, and the cop has to let them go.

But this time the script was twisted. The cop who was assigned to interview the passersby, and whose gaze up to that point had been drifting among high-cylinder still lifes, saw the sunny desert of the street disintegrate because of two figures in movement. Spontaneously they advanced toward him. Neither was more than five-six: red Lacoste shirt, blue shorts, each holding a Maxima Corrado Barazzutti racket. If you looked closely—the herald in uniform was tempted to squint—it was the same person.

"Need help?" asked the optical illusion.

It wasn't curiosity that impelled the Saggese twins toward the police cars. They were not fans of adventure, and they would not have approached the Canditos' house even if they had found out that a UFO had landed on it. Another force was pushing them, an impalpable feeling of rancor nursed for years, serve after serve after volley after serve, a grudge fueled by the hypnotic monotony of white stripes on a red background, a revenge that the cowardly little twins could satisfy only with the weapons of an informer.

"Yes," the policeman smiled. "Does the Candito family live here?"

"This is their house," one of the boys confirmed, coming dangerously close to the first orgasm of his life.

Then love of pedantry overcame love of betrayal. Stefano Saggese felt compelled to add: "But Mr. and Mrs. Candito aren't home. They're on vacation in the Canaries."

"We aren't looking for Mr. and Mrs. Candito," the policeman explained. "We're looking for Saverio, one of the kids. Do you know him?"

Stefano Saggese turned pale, and from that moment he was unable to distinguish the explosion of joy from an abortive experience. His twin lowered his eyes and assumed the thoughtful expression of one who can never enjoy a victory. If it had been Pippo Candito, Saverio's father, who in a few minutes was to come down the steps of the villa with handcuffs on his wrists, his face swollen with shame, the Saggese twins would have received living proof of that maxim which their father would never tire of repeating with stylized gravity, even if it had concerned a Pilgrim just off the Mayflower: the same maxim that the fruit of those loins believed to be confirmed when, shut in their room, they read comics whose every detail—including the name of whoever did the lettering—they grasped, except for the subtle ironic streak ("Crime doesn't pay," Dulls reflected, behind bars at the end of an episode of *Alan Ford*, only to be found, a few issues later, safe, relaxed and smiling, in a presidential suite surrounded by women in leopard-skin jackets). But the police wanted Saverio. Which, logically, should have made the Saggese twins even happier: Up to a certain age a sense of competitiveness emerges only between contemporaries. But the thought that someone their age, in fact someone who, along with five or six others, had been able to win for himself a disproportionate amount of chaos and diversion, had now used that same mysterious magnet to attract to the driveway of his own house five police cars—well, that was a very complicated thought to come to terms with: The Saggese twins felt the dizzy sensation of envying even the downfall of their bitterest enemy.

"We know him," Cristiano Saggese confirmed. "What do you want him for?" he added, his cheeks completely red.

"Pushing heroin. Is this him?" The policeman showed them a small salmon-colored rectangle.

The twins nodded. The cop asked if they had seen him in the past hour, hour and a half, and the two boys shook their heads no. At that point they were dismissed, and they vanished obediently into the haze, just as, probably rightly, they exit from this memoir as well. I don't know what happened to them. Usually, small concentrations of rancor and servility condemned to burning defeat on the playing field of youth re-ascend the slope, with the passing of time, to discover a tenacity, a sense of struggle . . . they find themselves with the entire armamentarium needed for nursing what the MBAs call "ambition." So I can imagine them in the role of financial consultants, as, in their office in Prati watched over by images of the Pope and fake Campbell's soup can silk screens, they inundate a potential client with patter. Neither debilitating tumors nor fifteen months in jail for price-fixing: My only wish for them is that at some point during one of these informal encounters—in order to hook the wallet of their prey, the postgraduates cunningly offer some sort of anecdote—the potential client feels free to depart from the subject long enough to ask: "And how was your adolescence?"

"Good, thanks," one of the Saggeses would answer.

Then he would go out to dinner at the Cavalieri Hilton, return home, and wake up in the middle of the night covered with sweat, believing that he still has in his ears the sounds of a hundred thousand tennis balls that won't stop rebounding off the walls of an empty room.

The plaster discus throwers were nothing. After having made vain use of the intercom and then the doorbell, the police went over the gate, slid a thin object very much like a credit card along the front door lock, and faced the semidarkness of a hall tiled in pink marble. One of them loosened the cord of a curtain. The spectacle that met their eyes outdid the murkiest fantasies of a prop man with an unlimited budget.

The shutters let in thin streams of light that would be transformed into clouds of multicolored dust when they touched the peacock feathers that, grouped in bunches of ten, greeted the visitor, peeking out from the mouths of amphoras as tall as a standing greyhound. Not that real dogs were lacking: Ten examples of an eccentric dog lover's passion in white porcelain, five on one side of the room, five on the other, exchanged aquamarine glances, thanks to large turquoise gems embedded at nose level. First Communions at the church of San Giovanni in Laterano and other sacraments were guaranteed remembrance in massive silver frames, just as an unintentional colonial tribute was given life on the ceiling (white tiger skin) and on one of the carpets (stuffed crocodile). It was as if two irreconcilable images had found a point of contact: The humor of a Barberini tormented by vice and bombast matched the happiness, the innocent exultation of joy, the expressive apex of one who, stuck until the day before among anonymous ragpickers, could say to himself, *Now I am a rich man.*

The police looked around and split up. One to check the garden, one in the kitchen, four upstairs, the others to the basement.

I spent a lot of time in that villa over the years. And its layout is still vivid to my eyes: I can remember perfectly the tables, the brocades, the big jukebox with Claudio Villa always in pole position. I can visualize every inch of those rooms and, wonder after wonder, despite all the time that has passed, I can, in lucky moments, touch the jugular, recalling, with great precision, the cardiac tumult of a pusher on the run. But I cannot enter into the minds of the enforcers of order. So, really, I couldn't answer the following questions:

What did policeman number 1 think when he turned his back on the veranda—two large palms arching over his head, gaze driven beyond the slides, the bushes, the swing, and onward, as far as the gladiolus that beautified a stone wall crowned by the opaque sparkle of shards of glass?

How did policeman number 2 kill time, left alone in the kitchen among unknown appliances (many imported from America) for the entire duration of the search?

What was the reaction of numbers 3, 4, 5, and 6, who, moving up to the second floor, found themselves facing a ten-million-lire Steinway whose only purpose was to be stroked by a dust cloth? Above all, what did numbers 5 and 6 feel—not those who searched the bedroom of the Candito spouses but the other two, the ones who entered a room with peach-colored wallpaper, a space saturated with the fruit-flavored oiliness of lip gloss and populated by life-size stuffed animals, necklaces, posters of Jennifer Beals in *Flashdance* in track suit and leg warmers? What did numbers 5 and 6 feel: the reproof that certain adults reserve for spoiled girls or, on the contrary, the hot, suffocating sensation of vice imprisoned in a cotton camisole, the violent ambiguity of bitter fruits and little girls that lead men to ask forgiveness for crimes that we might all be driven to commit? Silvia Candito, sixteen years old in 1987, now married with two children: one of the few to be saved.

What was to be found was found by policemen numbers 7, 8, 9, and 10. They signaled quickly to one another and took the stairs that led to the basement. It was one big space, without dividing walls, set up as a game room: billiard table, jukebox, strobe light, a long stone bench that stretched around the entire perimeter of the room. Two boys were squatting under the billiard table. Their calves had been straining for who knows how long, their bottoms a few inches from the floor. Both with arms around their knees.

"Saverio Candito," said one of the policemen.

The boy hugged his knees tighter behind the reddish down of his forearms and gave his notorious look of surrender. If he had stood up it would have been immediately obvious that he was extremely short for a seventeen-year-old. He had a stocky body, muscular arms and shoulders, a small belt of blubber around his hips, that copper-colored hair, curly, very short. When he was in trouble he fixed his adversaries with a harsh look of capitulation, the sort of look that a boxer might be facing who has dominated the entire match and who now, in the last round, wants to satisfy his desire for a knockout: a look that didn't say, simply, *I'm yours*. It said: *I'm in deep shit, and if you want me you'll have to come in and get me*.

But the cop couldn't be intimidated by this boy's code,

whose nuances he barely grasped. He reformulated the question.

"Saverio Candito. That's you, right?"

"No," said Saverio.

They were used to more complex situations. This type of emergency was kids' stuff, you could handle it by following the rules in the manual, step by step. Lately, they had been dealing with men who cursed saints and madonnas while with one hand they grabbed another man by the hair and with the free hand shoved a gun in the guy's mouth. Thus, a second policeman decided that he could make a little scene. He raised a hand toward his colleagues, as if to say, *Leave it to me, now let's have some fun.* So he took a salmon-colored, plastic-covered rectangle and threw it in the boy's face without saying a word.

Saverio caught it. There he found his name and surname and date of birth and all the rest, and a photo from two years earlier in which he was smiling with half-closed eyes. He wondered how the police could possibly have his ID. For an instant he entertained the completely absurd hypothesis of a forgery. Then he realized that he had simply lost it in the wrong place. He emerged from under the billiard table, giving himself up to the cops.

At that point the second boy also came out. He was wearing jeans, sneakers, a T-shirt with blue writing in swirling rodeo-type letters: *Country by the Grace of God.*

"Don't tell my parents," Danilo said with a sad smile.

"The third one's missing" was policeman number 7 or 8's sole response.

The two boys, who were now standing with their heads down, and practically on the point of holding each other by the hand, said nothing.

"There were three of you," the man explained. "We know, they saw you. Come on, where's the other boy?"

Maybe at this point the two kids felt challenged. Something was rekindled in their eyes. They were coming from two years of confrontations that were like jumping into rings of fire, and that invitation to betrayal was like an injection of hope. They continued to say nothing, but suddenly, in their looks, things seemed okay in this world.

"Listen," said the man, and from his tone it sounded like the standard speech in which one says how you should and shouldn't behave to avoid compromising an already very delicate situation. But one of his colleagues didn't let him get started.

"Shh . . . quiet . . . wait."

On the opposite side of the basement, to the left of the big window that looked onto the garden, there was a door lacquered in white, one of those coffer doors that never close perfectly. It was water. When, growing silent, they tried to focus their hearing in that direction, they realized that strange but indisputable aquatic noises were coming from beyond the door, a *choof-choof* of bodies forcefully moving in a pool, a regular sound that had, however, nothing mechanical about it—it wasn't a mill or a washing machine, it was someone playing with water, a dimension like rocks thrown in a pond, like water polo, shipwreck and premeditation at the same time.

"That's me," said the man, placing the glass with the Bellini on the parapet of the balcony. An umbrella with a rice-paper shade was sticking up out of the mixture of champagne and peach juice. He covered the convex surface of the receiver with the palm of his right hand and threw his left back: "And goddamn it, be quiet!"

His daughter snickered without taking her eyes off the small mountain of summer dresses thrown on the bed. His wife peered heavenward. She rose lazily from the wicker chair, slipped her enameled toes one after another into her sandals, and closed the sliding glass door that divided the hotel room from the balcony.

He took the receiver and put it back to his ear. Now he was alone before the ocean. What in the offices of police headquarters might be perceived as interference was, to the eyes of Pippo Candito, the watery wake raised by two motorboats challenging each other a few yards from the shore.

"Fucking hell, go to hell!" he said.

He was silent for a few seconds. Maybe someone was suggesting that he calm down. But at some point his daughter stopped playing with the summer dresses bought in the market in Las Palmas: The shouts had penetrated the barrier of glass. His wife again left the wicker chair, and she, too, headed for the balcony.

The policemen slid open the door through which the noises could still be heard. They found themselves looking at a small horseshoe-shaped room from which a stairway led down, curving to the right. Meanwhile, the men who had searched the bedrooms without finding a soul had also descended to the basement. Four to keep an eye on Saverio and Danilo. The others ventured over to the stairs that led down another level. The stairwell was a sort of narrow tube with white walls, onto which at a certain point a luminescent wave was projected, a pale-blue spot waving like a flag, giving a slap in the face to anyone who thinks that certain kinds of ambience can be experienced only in movies.

At this point the Heavenly Father was called in. Or rather a silent widening of the eyes, hands groping for support. I wasn't there with the police but I was familiar with the reactions of people arriving for the first time in the underground part of the villa. In the shouts of boys there was astonishment; adults, on the other hand, wondered how much money it must have taken to set up something like that. With their eyes they measured the ceiling, then gazed along the surface of the water for more than twenty-five meters.

It wasn't an Olympic-sized pool. An Olympic pool would have been twice as long. It was a hymn to waste in four lanes separated by the typical floating ropes, with overflow grating and backstroke turn indicators. Along the right wall were the doors leading to the bathrooms and changing rooms. On the side opposite the diving board was a piano bar: a half-circle of concrete livened by tiny glass tiles, behind which an old mirror retrieved from some second-hand dealer gilded the reflection of the whiskey bottles. On either side of the diving board stood two monsters: enormous papier-mâché statues taken from the carnival in Ronciglione that were supposed to represent the grandeur of ocean divinities. Scattered around the PVC-vinyl floor was everything that could further subvert the cold sobriety of indoor sports into the no-holds-barred games of an opium smoker: leopard-covered sofas, old pendulum clocks, miniature galleons, and so on.

The underground pool was something new. They had seen Mercedes cars transformed into mobile discotheques, ox quarters filled with video recorders, but not this thing here. Yet there was no time to be amazed. The policemen surrounded the pool and stood staring, without saying a word, because what was happening in there surpassed in strangeness the entire scenic display.

A human figure. The body of a boy. He was swimming.

The small atoll of a back emerged, a portion of flesh illuminated by neon lights that ran in long tubes forty-five feet up, a burnished oval that broadened and then offered itself to the flow of the water. One arm after the other cut the blue field as a pin suspended above a dead swamp would have done, leaving behind a ripple that disappeared in a dawnlike silence.

They were used to men who, to avoid capture, threw themselves into the Tiber and then, undone by panic, floundered, begging for help amid the tracery of foam. This boy was something else. It was impossible that he could be unaware of their arrival, but he swam as if he would continue infinitely: His style didn't reveal the least disturbance the whole time they watched. They probably wondered if it was the expression of a particular form of fear, a panic that instead of exploding in every direction was compressed into a single obsessive gesture. (Once, they had raided the office of a city councilman who hadn't deigned to look up, but had remained bent over his desk, writing; when they got closer, they noticed in the registry he was holding a series of calculations that at a certain point came to an end in incomprehensible scribbles similar to the product of a seismograph.) Or maybe it was a strategy of desperation: As long as I keep swimming, no one will catch me.

They didn't know, they couldn't know, that Giancarlo Colasanti, that was the boy's name, had an infernal brother. Not a blood brother or, worse, a twin: something more intimate and at the same time more distant. They were in constant contact. They were aware of each other's presence, they talked to one another in their sleep. Every action undertaken by Giancarlo was a challenge, a mutiny, and a desperate attempt to gain the approval of this presence. He paid attention to no one else, nothing mattered to him that did not have to do with the pursuit of this relationship that we all knew about. They never made peace but they never separated. And in particularly difficult moments they entered the arena as adversaries and, fighting, became a single thing.

He reached the edge of the pool, executed the turn, and continued in the opposite direction. To swim so well, and so long, he must have had tremendous physical strength and perfect control of his breathing. But he couldn't stop, because someone else was doing the same thing in the waters of the Styx, surrounded by volcanic vapors and the sound of drums. He completed another length, and another, and still another. It was something more than a simple contest with himself. And at the same time, the sound of his passage, amplified by the resonance chamber of the enormous subterranean structure, was a distillation of rage and starlike solitude.

When the contest was over, the policemen saw a shockingly thin, sensual body climbing up the ladder. And, amid the streams of water descending from his curls, a smile that spoke of illness and contagion. They covered him with a bathrobe, as if it would serve more than anything else to protect him. They led him upstairs.

I arrived later, when it was all over. Simply, a girl had kept me all morning and so that day I hadn't gone with them to sell. One might say that in this way I was saved. But time is a master capable of destroying even its favorite students, and the slender profile of the '90s was ready to spring the trap. I didn't see them again for some years, my best friends. And when I did see them again we were no longer us.

ABOUT THE CONTRIBUTORS

BOOSTA is well-known in Italy as both a writer and a musician. His real name is Davide Dileo and he was born in Turin in 1974. He has released four albums and performed over five hundred concerts with his group Subsonica, which won MTV's Best Italian Act at their European Awards. He has also become a major producer and mixer for various artists. His first two books are *Dianablu* and *Un'ora e mezza*, which will soon be made into a film.

GIANRICO CAROFIGLIO is a former anti-Mafia prosecutor based in Bari. He is the author of the international best sellers *Involuntary Witness*, *A Walk in the Dark*, and *Reasonable Doubts*. *The Past Is a Foreign Country*, a darker and more personal novel, is currently being made into a film. He is the only Italian crime writer whose full catalog has been translated into English. While not writing, he works as a consultant to an Italian parliamentary commission investigating the Mafia.

DIEGO DE SILVA is a criminal lawyer whose first novel, *La donna di scorta*, was published in 1999. His follow-up, *Certi bambini*, about growing up in the south of Italy, was turned into a film by the Frazzi Bros. His novel *I Want to Watch* was translated into English and has been compared to Bret Easton Ellis's *American Psycho*. He has since written *Da un'altra carne* and *Non avevo capito niente*. He is a regular contributor to *Il Mattino*, an Italian newspaper.

MARCELLO FOIS is an award-winning Italian author, poet, and screenwriter, born in Nuoro in 1960. His first novel, *Ferro recente*, was published in 1992 and was followed by *Picta*, which won the Premio Calvino, and *Nulla*, winner of the Premio Dessi. He has written a crime trilogy—*Sempre caro, Sangue dal cielo*, and *L'altro mundo*—the first volume of which appeared in English as *The Advocate*. He has also written extensively for TV, radio, and film.

CRISTIANA DANILA FORMETTA is a young Salerno author who has never set foot outside Italy. Her books include the collection *Il nero che fa tendenza* and the novella *The Sex Lives of Chameleons*, which was translated into English by Maxim Jakubowski. A frequent contributor to leading Italian underground magazines, Formetta is known for her complex mix of erotica and noir. She is currently writing her first full-length novel, while also working as an editor for an independent Italian publisher.

ENRICO FRANCESCHINI is a well-known Italian journalist and broadcaster. Born in Bologna in 1956, he has worked for twenty years as a foreign correspondent for the newspaper *La Repubblica*, stationed in Moscow, New York, Washington, Jerusalem, and now London. He won the prestigious Europa Prize for his reporting of the 1994 popular uprising in Moscow. In addition to nonfiction, he has written novels, including *La donna della Piazza Rossa* and *Fuori stagione.*

GIUSEPPE GENNA was born in Milan in 1969. His novels include *Catrame, Assalto a un tempo devastato, In the Name of Ishmael* (which was translated into English), *Non toccare la pelle del drago, Grande Madre Rossa,* and *Dies Irae.* He is also a member of the notorious Luther Blissett writing collective.

MAXIM JAKUBOWSKI is a British editor and writer. Following a long career in book publishing, during which he was responsible for several major crime imprints, he opened London's mystery bookshop Murder One. He reviews crime fiction for the *Guardian*, runs London's Crime Scene Festival, and is an advisor to Italy's annual Courmayeur Noir in Festival. His latest crime novel is *Confessions of a Romantic Pornographer*, and he edits the annual Best British Mysteries series.

NICOLA LAGIOIA was born in Bari in 1973. He is one of the leading lights of a new generation of young Italian writers, having edited a number of anthologies, along with the Nichel imprint, for the publisher Minimum Fax. His first novel, *Tre sistemi per sbarazzarsi di Tolstoj*, was published in 2001, and was followed by a collection of essays, *Occidente per principianti,* and a nonfiction book, *Babbo Natale.*

CARLO LUCARELLI is one of Italy's national treasures: author, screenwriter, television personality, academic. He has written over thirty books, including the Bologna-set Grazia Negro series, *Lupo mannaro, Almost Blue* (winner of the British Crime Writers' Association Silver Dagger Award), and *Day After Day.* His Inspector De Luca series, set during the time of the Salo Republic, has also been translated into English.

FRANCESCA MAZZUCATO splits her time between the Ligurian coast and Bologna. A prolific and controversial writer, she is also an active presence on the web, with two important web sites: *Books and Other Sorrows* and *Erotica*. Her books include *La sottomissione di Ludovica*, *Relazioni scandalosamente pure*, *Transgender Generation*, *Amore a Marsiglia*, *Hot Line*, *Web Cam*, *Diario di una blogger*, *Enigma Veneziano*, *L'anarchiste*, and the recent collection *Magnificat marsigliese*.

ANTONIO PASCALE was born in Naples in 1966 and now lives and works in Rome. His first book, *La città distratta*, a nonfiction story set in Caserta, won the Elsa Morante Award. He is also the author of the story collection *La manutenzione degli affetti*, and his controversial first novel, *Passa la bellezza*, was published in 2005. This was followed by *S'è fatta ora* and a travel book, *Non è per cattiveria*. He writes regularly for the newspaper *La Repubblica*.

TOMMASO PINCIO'S first book, *M.*, a literary reinterpretation of *Blade Runner*, was published in 1999. Later novels include *Lo spazio sfinito* and the controversial *Love-Shaped Story*, which was translated into English, about the imaginary life of Nirvana singer Kurt Cobain. A fan of contemporary American writing, which he chronicles in the Italian edition of *Rolling Stone* and leading newspapers, Pincio lives in Rome. His writing pseudonym was inspired by Thomas Pynchon.

EVELINA SANTANGELO was born and raised in Palermo. She studied English and linguistics at Cornell University in Ithaca, New York, and worked as a journalist for *L'Ora*. She now works in book publishing in Turin, teaches creative writing at the Scuola Holden, and writes. She is the author of the novels *L'occhio cieco del mondo*, *La lucertola color smeraldo*, and *Il giorno degli orsi volanti*.

ANTONIO SCURATI was born in Naples in 1969 and is a writer and academic, which includes his role as the coordinator of Bergamo University's center for the language of war and violence. He has published several books of nonfiction, and his first novel, *Il sopravvissuto*, published in 2005, won the Premio Campiello. His major historical novels, *Il rumore sordo della battaglia* (2002) and *Una storia romantica* (2007), were best sellers in Italy.

CHIARA STANGALINO worked for many years for one of Italy's leading publishing houses. She is now a freelance festival organizer, including her work on the Courmayeur Noir in Festival literary events and Festarch, the Sardinian architecture festival. She has also directed a documentary film about American crime writer Joe R. Lansdale. She lives in Turin.

NICOLETTA VALLORANI began her prolific writing career as a science-fiction author. Born in the Marche region, she has a degree in foreign languages and American literature and currently teaches at the Statale University of Milan. She won the Premio Urania in 1992 and published her first crime novel, *Dentro la Notte, e Ciao* in 1995. She has since published ten more novels, including *Occhi di lupo, Come una balena, La fatona, Eva,* and *Cordelia,* as well as several children's books.

Also available from the Akashic Books Noir Series

PARIS NOIR
edited by Aurélien Masson
300 pages, trade paperback original, $15.95

All original stories from Paris' finest authors, all translated from French.

Brand new stories by: Didier Daeninckx, Jean-Bernard Pouy, Marc Villard, Chantal Pelletier, Patrick Pécherot, DOA, Hervé Prudon, Dominique Mainard, Salim Bachi, Jérôme Leroy, and others.

Paris Noir takes you on a ride through the old medieval center of town with its intertwined streets, its ghosts, and its secrets buried in history . . . But *Paris Noir* is not only an homage to the crime genre, to Melville and Godard, it's also an invitation to French fiction.

ISTANBUL NOIR
edited by Mustafa Ziyalan & Amy Spangler
300 pages, trade paperback original, $15.95

Brand new stories by: Müge İplikçi, Behçet Çelik, İsmail Güzelsoy, Lydia Lunch, Hikmet Hükümenoğlu, Rıza Kıraç, Sadık Yemni, Barış Müstecaplıoğlu, Yasemin Aydınoğlu, Feryal Tilmaç, and others.

Comprised of entirely new stories by some of Turkey's most exciting authors—some still up-and-coming, others well-established and critically acclaimed in their homeland, as well as by a couple of "outsiders" temporarily held hostage in the city's vice—*Istanbul Noir* introduces a whole new breed of talent.

HAVANA NOIR
edited by Achy Obejas
360 pages, trade paperback original, $15.95

Brand new stories by: Leonardo Padura, Pablo Medina, Carolina García-Aguilera, Ena Lucía Portela, Miguel Mejides, Arnaldo Correa, Alex Abella, Moisés Asís, Lea Aschkenas, and others.

"A remarkable collection . . . Throughout these 18 stories, current and former residents of Havana—some well-known, some previously undiscovered—deliver gritty tales of depravation, depravity, heroic perseverance, revolution, and longing in a city mythical and widely misunderstood." —*Miami Herald*

BROOKLYN NOIR
edited by Tim McLoughlin
350 pages, trade paperback original, $15.95
*Winner of Shamus Award, Anthony Award, Robert L. Fish Memorial Award; finalist for Edgar Award, Pushcart Prize.

Brand new stories by: Pete Hamill, Arthur Nersesian, Ellen Miller, Nelson George, Nicole Blackman, Sidney Offit, Ken Bruen, and others.

"*Brooklyn Noir* is such a stunningly perfect combination that you can't believe you haven't read an anthology like this before. But trust me—you haven't . . . The writing is flat-out superb, filled with lines that will sing in your head for a long time to come."
—Laura Lippman, winner of the Edgar, Agatha, and Shamus awards

LOS ANGELES NOIR
edited by Denise Hamilton
360 pages, trade paperback original, $15.95
*A *Los Angeles Times* best seller and winner of an Edgar Award.

Brand new stories by: Michael Connelly, Janet Fitch, Susan Straight, Héctor Tobar, Patt Morrison, Robert Ferrigno, Neal Pollack, Gary Phillips, Christopher Rice, Naomi Hirahara, Jim Pascoe, and others.

"Akashic is making an argument about the universality of noir; it's sort of flattering, really, and *Los Angeles Noir,* arriving at last, is a kaleidoscopic collection filled with the ethos of noir pioneers Raymond Chandler and James M. Cain." —*Los Angeles Times Book Review*

TRINIDAD NOIR
edited by Lisa Allen-Agostini & Jeanne Mason
340 pages, trade paperback original, $15.95

Brand new stories by: Robert Antoni, Elizabeth Nunez, Lawrence Scott, Oonya Kempadoo, Ramabai Espinet, Shani Mootoo, Kevin Baldeosingh, elisha efua bartels, Tiphanie Yanique, Willi Chen, and others.

"For sheer volume, few—anywhere—can beat [V.S.] Naipaul's prodigious output. But on style, the writers in the Trinidadian canon can meet him eye to eye . . . Trinidad is no one-trick pony, literarily speaking."
—Coeditor Lisa Allen-Agostini in the *New York Times*